The Mist Before Our Eyes

R.P.G. Colley

R.P.G. Colley

Fiction:

Love and War Series:
Song of Sorrow
The Lost Daughter
The Woman on the Train
The White Venus
The Black Maria
My Brother the Enemy
Anastasia
The Darkness We Leave Behind
The Mist Before Our Eyes

The Searight Saga:
This Time Tomorrow
The Unforgiving Sea
The Red Oak

Non-Fiction:

History In An Hour series

Other non-fiction:
The Savage Years: Tales From the 20th Century
The Hungarian Revolution, 1956
A History of the World Cup: An Introduction
The Battle of the Somme: World War One's Bloodiest Battle

The Mist Before Our Eyes

rupertcolley.com

Those who can make you believe absurdities, can make you commit atrocities.

Voltaire

PROLOGUE
Russia, October 1942

It is autumn, the day bright, but tinged with a cold breeze sweeping across a huge field of burnt wheat and furrows of stubble, some hundred kilometres south east of Smolensk. The field is dotted with landmines, planted by Russian partisans. A Waffen SS Sergeant and a number of privates point their rifles at Felix Stoltenberg and his doomed companions.

The sergeant makes it clear to them that they have no choice but to walk across this field, from this side to the other, some six hundred metres. They fan out, thirty men, thirty traitors of the Reich. They could simply skirt around it, advance through the adjoining forest. But no, this is a test for those, like Felix Stoltenberg, whose lives are worth nothing; men who, through their foul and traitorous deeds, have forfeited their right to life.

Dark plumes of smoke rise into the air on the horizon, a burning village, its inhabitants killed, every last one of them. A murder of crows fly by, heading for the trees, their raucous cawing mocking the condemned men beneath them. And so

1

they start, these traitors. The walk of death. One fearful foot in front of the other.

To Felix's left is a boy called Walter, a blond, handsome young lad of about twenty, with a dusting of a moustache, cadaverous cheeks. Perfect Aryan material until he'd done something so awful, so bad, that this, this walk of death, is the result. His face is filthy, streaked with dirt, his eyes rimmed red with fear and tears. The boy, like the others, can't stop shaking. Death is but a step away; it has reached out its hand for them.

A man with a bandage around his skull to Felix's far right has already found a mine. He is on one knee, hands shaking, gently removing the soil, muttering to himself – or is he praying? Felix walks on, one careful step after another. *Why bother praying*, he wonders. *God forsook them a long time ago*. He has never prayed; he will not start now. The field stretches ahead, skeletal trees on the horizon blurred in the mist, the far end light years away.

Why had he rescued her? Was it love? Was it pity for her daughter? Or atonement for the humiliation he'd heaped on the girl that day in the classroom? He could still visualise her, standing before him, looking straight ahead, trying so hard to be brave. It took him a long time to appreciate just how brave. So many years ago. Had he stopped and thought about it, considered the consequences, he may not have been so hasty. For now, he is to die a traitor's death. But he tries not to think, it's best not to; best to keep his memories sequestered in a dark corner of his mind.

A sharp explosion shatters the peace behind him, to his right. The earth shudders. He doesn't look back. He knows it's the man with the bandage. The sergeant and his men, watching from the sidelines, laugh and cheer, enjoying the diabolical spectacle.

Walter stops, his whole frame shaking. He has wet himself. The sergeant yells at him, tells him to move on.

Felix thinks of his father, arrested and 'shot while trying to escape,' another traitor's death. His father had been right after all. The difference was, his father had known from the start, had known the folly of dancing to Hitler's tune. Felix had been ashamed of him, ashamed of having a traitor as a father. He wants to apologise to him. He should have listened. He feels an arm around his shoulder, a gentle, reassuring touch. There is a warmth to it. But no one is there. It is his imagination.

Walter, to his left, stops short again. 'Fuck,' he says. 'Felix, help me.' His voice is shot through with terror. He is as still as a statue, his left foot clamped on the dry earth. Tears run down his face forming rivulets through the grime on his boyish cheeks. 'Help me, Felix.'

Felix shakes his head, mute with fear.

'Felix, no, please don't leave me,' he says, his voice splintered, his hand outstretched as if wanting Felix to take it.

Felix steps forward, knows he has to get some distance between them, knowing the next step could be his last, knowing there is nothing he can do for Walter. The boy cries, calls out for his mother, a pathetic sound. He must know death has come for him.

Felix glances back.

Walter is skewered with terror, his left leg shaking, his face in his hands, his filthy hands.

Felix turns round again, concentrates on what's in front of him, on the misty horizon far ahead. The explosion rips through the air. Felix feels the blast of air on his back.

The far side of the field is a blur; it seems to be receding further and further back. He moves on, step by fearful step, knowing full well he could be next.

3

PART ONE

Chapter 1

A month earlier: Berlin, September 1942

They'd locked Felix in a cell.

He tries to keep fit. Touches his toes, stretches left, right, up and down. He runs on the spot and imagines he's running through a woodland on a bright summery day, the sun slanting through the trees, the sound of birdsong filling the air, the smell of the leaves and forest flowers. Or he's running on a beach, or through the city park, anywhere but here, this tiny cell with its bench, a bunk bed with a threadbare blanket, a bucket in the corner stinking with excrement, and the cold that leaks from these thick, thick walls.

He's been here just a day or two but already he is losing weight. He could feel his ribcage now. Have they forgotten about him? If it wasn't for the daily ration of grub, he might think so. Strange, how a person's perception of food can change. When first confined to this tiny cell, he thought the food awful. And it was and it still is. Now, he is so accustomed to it, he almost enjoys it. He still doesn't know what it is, has no idea what he is putting in his stomach, but that doesn't keep him from enjoying it.

Footsteps sound in the corridor outside his cell. Not the usual shuffling steps of an orderly bringing him his food, but the sharper, purposeful steps of three, perhaps four men. Is this it? Have they come for him? He stands up from his bed, stiffens, breathes in and throws his head back, ready to face whatever and whoever is coming to see him.

The cell door swings open. A man stumbles in, pushed from behind. The door immediately closes. The man straightens. He stretches his neck, as if trying to regain his sense of decency. He looks at Felix fiercely. But the darkness in his eyes quickly dissipates and instead he offers his hand, saying, 'How do you do?' Such an incongruous gesture in a place like this. 'The name's Karstadt. You can call me Rudolph, if you like.'

He smiles and looks Felix kindly in the eye; such simple gestures but they tug at Felix's insides. No one has smiled at him for such a long time; no one has greeted him as a man, a human being. He catches his breath and swallows the emotion down; wouldn't do to get all tearful now.

'I'm Felix Stoltenberg. I used to be a lieutenant until…' He lets the sentence hang.

A ghost of a smile passes over Rudolph's thin, bloodless lips. He's not young, in his forties perhaps, fair hair, sharp cheekbones, a beard flecked with a dusky red. He shivers and looks around, as if trying to find where the cold is coming from. The man's tunic is filthy, unbuttoned, revealing his shirt, once white, now heavily stained. 'Do you mind if I lie down a minute?' He stretches himself out across the bench, his gangly legs hanging off the side.

He closes his eyes. Felix covers him with the blanket. Poor man. Felix notices the deep lines either side of his mouth, the mesh of crow's feet framing his eyes. They've removed the insignia from his tunic's collar and shoulders but the faint lines of stitching remain. Rudolph Karstadt had been a captain. Felix wonders what catastrophe has befallen him, what dreadful sin he committed against the Reich to have him stripped of rank and thrown into this dungeon.

After a while, Rudolph opens his eyes. 'Christ, I wish I had a fag,' he says, swinging his feet off the bench. 'And something to eat.' He stands and stretches. 'Do you think we'll ever get out of here? Alive, I mean.'

Doubtful, thinks Felix. But he says nothing; instead, shrugs his shoulders. It's best not to think of the future.

Rudolph starts pacing the cell, head down, hands in pockets.

'What brings you here?' asks Felix.

Rudolph hesitates. Felix knows what he's thinking, can he trust this man he's only just met? Perhaps he thinks Felix is a stooge.

'You don't have to tell me.'

'What does it matter? I'm as good as dead anyway.' He sits again. 'They found out about me. About...' He pauses. He fidgets with a thread hanging from his shirt cuff. 'You can judge me if you want, I'm past caring. I'm a man who made the mistake of falling in love with... with another man.'

Felix glances away; he can't look at the man. He pulls at his collar. 'That's enough to condemn you,' he says.

'Don't I know it. I'd rather not talk about it. I can't.'

'Fine.' *Good*, he thinks, he'd rather not know.

'And you? What about you?'

'Me?' Felix leans forward, scratches at the dirt beneath his fingernails. 'It's a long story.'

'Isn't it always? You can tell me if you want to; it's up to you. Some people find it helps to talk. I wanted to be a priest once.' He stops for a moment; his eyes gaze up at the ceiling. 'Instead, I became a soldier. Not your usual progression, I grant you. I was good at listening; people told me things. We all have a story though, don't we? A story that starts somewhere, that has a beginning. It's just that we don't always know the end yet. So, tell me, what sort of house did you live in? No, don't tell me; a boy like you, you look like you come from a solid, middle-class background.' He laughs. 'One of those fine three-storeyed townhouses on a wide street with flower pots on the front steps, that sort of thing? Am I right?'

'Maybe.' He's unerringly right, damn him.

'And you were an only child.'

'How do you know this?'

'So, former Lieutenant Stoltenberg, tell me all about yourself. I'm interested. Anyway, might as well kill some time.'

Felix thinks back. He doesn't want to, tries to resist. But there's something about this man with his pretensions to priesthood that is strangely reassuring. He tries to remember a beginning. And there was a beginning, an exact moment. His beginning lay in his brittle loneliness, a childhood plagued by uncertainties. He didn't see it as evil, didn't recognise the evil that seeped through their door and into their home so many years back. But, like a cancer beginning its destructive journey, there was a precise moment when it appeared and the only person to recognise it was his father. His poor father.

'I guess you were in the Hitler Youth,' says Rudolph. 'All boys were, I suppose. It was mandatory.'

'Not at first, it wasn't. I wanted to join. I knew if I could I wouldn't…'

'Go on. You can tell me. I'm hardly going to be telling anyone.'

'I was desperate to join but…'

Rudolph tilts his head to one side. 'Don't tell me. Your father.'

Felix smiles despite himself. 'Yes, my father.'

Rudolph brushes the surface dirt off his trouser leg, as if it would make any difference. 'You don't have to tell me any more. I'd understand.'

Felix realises that his boast is not an idle one – he is a good listener, something almost reassuring about him.

'In the end, even he wasn't able to stop me. And that, I suppose, was the beginning.'

'The beginning?'

Felix sighs. Why not tell him, he thinks. He has nothing else to do, and he knows he wants to now, to lay out the sequence of events, to chart the spread of the cancer that brought him here, to this cell, to this moment. 'It was a long time ago,' he says. 'But I can pinpoint it to the hour, the minute almost.'

'And that minute?'

'It was the moment that Klaus Beck knocked on the door.'

'Klaus Beck?' Rudolph leans forward. 'You serious? That bastard? *The* Klaus Beck?'

'Yes, the very same. *The* Klaus Beck.'

Chapter 2

Nine years earlier: Berlin, early February 1933

The day Felix Stoltenberg realised he wanted to be like Klaus Beck was the day he first saw him in his Hitler Youth uniform. Felix had always been a little bit frightened of Klaus. And at the same time desperate to be his friend. Klaus, a year older, lived down the street, and had a swagger about him. Felix had known him from a distance for as long as he could remember but never spoken to him. It had never bothered him until just before his fifteenth birthday when, quite suddenly, he became almost obsessed by him. He watched him from afar at school and knew Klaus was everything he was not. Klaus was confident, brash and strong and, with his jet-black hair, his high cheekbones and Roman nose, was attractive to girls. He possessed a certain elegance. Klaus Beck certainly didn't play chess by himself.

Everyone wanted Klaus as their friend, so what chance did he have? Unless, of course, he too joined the Hitler Youth.

Hitler was a constant topic of conversation in the house. Rare was the dinnertime when his name didn't crop up. Felix's grandfather, his mother's father, a headmaster in a mixed school, had come for another of his weekend visits. Father loathed the "Austrian corporal with the stupid moustache" while Granddad, Gottfried, saw him as the nation's saviour. Father would never allow Felix to join the Youth but if Felix could get his grandfather on his side...

One Sunday afternoon, Felix brought his grandfather a cup of tea and told him outright that he wanted to join the Hitler Youth. Gottfried was making a penny whistle, his sharp knife whittling away at a length of wood.

Gottfried furrowed his brow. 'Your father will never allow it. You know what he's like.'

'It's not fair. All the other boys on the street are members.'

Gottfried pulled on his beard. 'We'll work something out.'

As it was, he didn't have to. Klaus simply appeared at their door one wet February Sunday, the day of Felix's fifteenth birthday. His parents had given him a new chess set, his grandfather one of his penny whistles. Later, if he was lucky, there'd be birthday cake, light sponge with a nice thick layer of oozy jam in between, a candle or two. No friends though. There were never any friends. 'Invite some boys over,' his mother had said a couple days earlier. He didn't though. Better not ask than to hear the excuses, to see the mocking expressions.

Klaus Beck's unexpected appearance caused an uproar, the reverberations of which would be felt for years to come. It was almost dinnertime, time for birthday cake, the day fast fading away. Felix was in his bedroom setting up the chess pieces, ready to play against himself. He'd ask his father but Papa claimed he didn't know how to play. Then came the knock on the front door. Felix looked up, feeling a prick of apprehension. Was it a visitor for him, maybe? Someone come to help him celebrate his birthday, perhaps have a game of chess? His mother answered the door.

'Heil Hitler. Good evening, Frau Stoltenberg,' said the visitor.

'Why, hello there,' said Klara. 'Heil Hitler. It's... it's Klaus, isn't it?'

Felix's heart jumped on hearing the name.

'Have you come for Felix's birthday?'

Felix hated the desperate tone in his mother's voice. He crept out of his bedroom and onto the landing, kneeling and peering through the bannister. Klaus stood at the door, wearing his uniform, his Sam Browne belt criss-crossing his chest, his shiny boots reflecting the hallway light.

'Birthday?' said Klaus.

Felix spotted the flash of a smile; *what a ridiculous thought*, he was thinking. 'No, meine Frau, I have not. I wish to speak to your husband.' He removed his hat, exposing his greased-back hair.

'Yes, yes, of course, if you want. Do come in.' She ran her fingers over her hair, flattening it. 'But, later, if you have time, do stay for some cake.'

'Thank you, meine Frau.' Felix could see Klaus taking in the house – the grandfather clock, the flock wallpaper, the thick hall carpet, the large pot of dried flowers in the alcove. In a flash, he saw it anew, as Klaus saw it – and knew it to be shabby and old-fashioned and that word he often heard at school – bourgeois. Yes, distinctly bourgeois.

Felix's father appeared from the living room, his newspaper in his hand. 'What's this about?' he said, *rather too abruptly*, thought Felix.

'Heil Hitler. Good evening, *mein Herr*,' said Klaus. 'I've come to see you about your son.'

14

'Felix? What about him?'

Klaus hesitated. The moment stretched.

Felix's father, perhaps realising that this wasn't the sort of conversation to have standing in the hallway, invited Klaus through to the living room. Felix heard his grandfather say hello and a round of heil Hitlers as they all settled – Klaus, Felix's parents and his grandfather. Felix's father slammed the door shut. Felix skipped down the stairs and pressed his ear against the door. If this was about him, he was damned if he was going to miss out on what Klaus had to say.

'So, what is it you want?' he heard his father say.

'Mein Herr, I am recruiting on behalf of the Hitler Youth. Your son is of age now, and –'

'So what?' said Peter. 'I don't care how old he is, he's not becoming a foot soldier for Hitler.'

'Mein Herr, it is the duty of every German child to –'

'No, please, don't come into my house and spout this nonsense.'

Felix could hear Klaus almost spluttering with indignation. 'S-sir, it is not nonsense. We, the youth of Germany, are heading a revolution.'

'Oh, so you see yourself as a revolutionary? How quaint. How old are you?'

Felix groaned. Did he not realise you couldn't speak to the Hitler Youth like that, whatever their age.

'Sixteen, mein Herr. Almost.'

Gottfried cleared his throat. 'Most of the boys in my school are members and many of the girls too. It's harmless stuff, really. It's just another youth group, just bigger and more organised.'

'Oh really? You think so?'

'Felix's desperate to join,' said Gottfried. 'He's told me

15

himself.'

'Did he, indeed?' There was a pause while Peter absorbed this. 'Do you mind if we have this conversation in private.' He said it more as an instruction than a question.

'He… he d-doesn't want to b-be left out,' said Klara, hesitantly. 'You know what kids are like, Peter.'

'Oh, for goodness sake, he doesn't know what he's talking about.'

'Why don't we ask the boy?' asked Gottfried.

Felix ran back up the stairs, two steps at a time, reaching the top just as the living room door opened. His father called him down. Felix walked back down the stairs with as much dignity as he could muster while his father waited at the bottom. His father had turned red; Klaus had rattled him. He followed his father into the living room, conscious of his every move, aware that all eyes were on him.

Klaus was leaning against the mantelpiece, clearly enjoying the commotion his appearance had caused. His grandfather sat on the piano stool, his elbow on the piano lid.

Felix blushed as he said hello to Klaus. Klaus shot his hand out and bellowed his heil Hitler. Felix, rather weakly, returned the salutation. He never thought he'd see Klaus inside his house, looking like he belonged.

Peter picked up his pipe from the sideboard. He set about refilling it as he spoke to Felix. 'What's this rubbish about you wanting to join Hitler's boy army?'

Felix swallowed. The air chilled around him. Like most boys, he was frightened of his father but, even worse, he knew Klaus' eyes were fixed on him. Felix glanced at his grandfather hoping for an intervention, a word or two to help him out, but Gottfried simply winked at him. He was going to have to do this alone. 'Everyone's joining,' he said, his voice brittle.

'That doesn't tell me what *you* want to do, does it?'

'I want to join too,' he managed to say despite the constriction in his throat.

His father slumped a little. He lit his pipe, a huge cloud of blue smoke briefly obscuring him.

'And so he should,' said Gottfried.

'Maybe Felix could join on a trial basis,' said Klara. 'Would that be possible, Klaus?'

Klaus smiled a sickly smile. 'No, Frau Stoltenberg. The Führer expects and demands full commitment.'

'Fine by me,' said Felix, emboldened but still conscious of how small his voice sounded.

'Yes, Hitler would,' said Felix's father, smacking his lips against the stem of the pipe. 'He wants to brainwash a whole generation so that when the time comes, he can spill your blood on the battlefield.'

Klaus stiffened. 'It is our duty, sir –'

'Oh, I know all about duty. I fought in the war, young man. No doubt your father did too. I have an Iron Cross to prove it, and a wartime Luger. We served with honour and the one thing I learned is that I know where these things lead, and I don't want to see my son, or you, for that matter, forced into another war at the behest of a –'

'It's just a youth group,' said Klara. 'Please, Peter, calm yourself now.'

'Mein Herr,' said Klaus. 'I appreciate this is your home but –'

'Damn right it is. And it is time for you to leave it.'

Felix wondered how a boy, not much older than himself, could speak to an adult like that. It was that uniform; it gave him an authority of some sort. He couldn't bear it a moment longer. He had to say something, if only to save his father from saying anything else he might regret but more because he couldn't appear weak in front of Klaus. 'I want to join. And I'm going to.' Never had such simple words been so difficult to say. He resisted the urge to clamp his hand against his heart, to quell its frantic beating. His grandfather winked at him again.

Peter spun to face him. 'Now wait here, young man.'

'Your son is right, sir. You have no right to stop him. A boy's first priority is to the Führer. Felix belongs to us now, mein Herr.'

His words seemed to wind Peter. Klaus put his cap back on.

Klara rose. 'You sure you won't stay for a slice of birthday cake?'

Klaus looked at Felix, a look that diminished him somehow. 'I think not. Thank you, anyway. Goodbye. Heil Hitler.' He shot out his arm. And with that, he was gone.

Felix collapsed into an armchair. His father glared at him, his face flushed. He stormed out of the room.

Gottfried laughed nervously.

His mother, sitting next to him, patted Felix's arm. 'I know that was difficult for you, *Bärchen*.'

Bärchen. Little Bear. Her nickname for him. 'Please don't call me Bärchen.'

He knew his father had fought in the war, knew his father had that Iron Cross and had kept that Luger pistol from that time, but had never given it a moment's thought. He was, despite it all, rather proud of him but... that was then. This was now, and this time, History, surely, was on their side.

And thus, against all expectation, Klaus Beck had walked into his life, and Felix, by squaring up to his father, had taken his first step on the path to ruination.

Chapter 3

Felix blew into his hands. Klaus, standing next to him, stamped his feet. The sky hung heavily, a blanket of grey. The trees were still bare, their branches weighted down with noisy, cawing crows. A dozen boys huddled together on the path next to the lake, shivering in their T-shirts and shorts, their cold breaths rising in puffs. The lake loomed, foreboding in its icy stillness, covered with a shifting layer of mist, its tendrils obscuring the far side. A jetty that looked as if it might collapse any moment jutted out into the water.

Their leader, Heinrich Richter, consulted a map, looking warm, thought Felix, in his greatcoat and gloves and his woolly scarf. 'Yep, once round the lake. Five kilometres give or take,' he declared loudly, folding his map into four. 'Shouldn't take you long.' Heinrich was only three years older than the boys but three years was huge – Heinrich was a man, strong, confident and sure of his place in the party hierarchy. 'I want to see some proper running, right? No dilly-dallying. Imagine you're chasing after some bloody Jews, you have to catch them and teach them a lesson. Now, as an added incentive, the boy who comes last will walk the plank.' He laughed, pointing at the jetty.

Felix laughed too, thinking it was expected of him.

'What's so funny, Stoltenberg? You won't be laughing when it's your arse in the water.'

Felix considered his feet, his eyes watering with cold.

'Right, get ready,' said Heinrich. 'Line up, line up.' He glanced skywards while the boys shuffled into line. 'Looks like rain. All the better. Follow the path all way round. Towards the end, it'll veer off into the trees for a bit before bringing you back to the lake.' He scraped the point of his shoe across the gravelled earth to mark the finishing line. 'OK, on your marks…'

And they were off, clockwise around the lake. The boys darted off at speed, their running shoes crunching on the stony path. Felix hung back hoping they'd soon tire. Best to preserve energy. Klaus ran beside him.

Felix had been a member of the Hitler Youth some six weeks now. His father had resisted, of course. His anger had turned to concern: 'We can't allow ourselves to be governed over by a fanatic,' while Felix's mother and grandfather tried persuading him that he exaggerated and that his concerns were unfounded. In the end, he declared, 'What chance do I have if I can't even persuade my own wife of this man's madness?' And so, Klara took Felix to the next meeting, got him signed up. As they left, Felix caught sight of his father, sitting in his armchair, wistfully holding his Iron Cross.

Felix loved being a member, being part of something now, something important, vital even. The boys could be rough with each other but underneath it was a sense of camaraderie he'd never experienced before, a togetherness, a joining of the hearts and minds for the greater good. It gave him a sense of pride. He wore the uniform most of the time. People respected the uniform, some even feared it. You could see it in their eyes, that little sideways glance. The uniform gave him an authority that, as a fifteen-year-old kid, he had no right to expect. For so long, Felix saw himself as an outsider. Not any more. Finally, he had direction in his life, a sense of belonging. He had Klaus Beck to thank for that. Klaus and the Führer.

But despite that, he was still no closer to being friends with Klaus. He thought, assumed even, that by becoming a member, they'd have a connection, one forged by the uniform, one bound by their shared love of the Führer. It hadn't turned out that way. Klaus acknowledged him now, but nothing more. Felix guessed the one-year gap between them was too wide a gulf to allow friendship. Yet, this was his whole reason, to *belong*, to be friends with the boy at the centre of the axis.

Felix reckoned that they'd covered about four of the five kilometres. They were taking the gradual bend, soon heading for the final half kilometre, the home stretch. He was still behind the main pack of three boys but closing in on them with every step. He'd wait, benefit from their slipstream, before overtaking in the last couple hundred metres. This was textbook stuff, like Lauri Lehtinen of Finland winning the five-thousand-metre gold at the '32 Olympics. He imagined he was at Berlin's Olympic Stadium in three years' time, running in front of one hundred thousand spectators, their cheers ringing in his ears, urging him on, chanting his name, desperate for German gold. The Führer in his box, on his feet, clapping and admiring the German wonder boy heading for victory. The finishing line beckoned; glory would be his, his and all Germany's. How could his father not see and have tears of pride clouding his vision?

The path now veered away from the lake, just as Heinrich

said, taking the boys up a muddy track and into the woods, the air damp under the canvas of trees. A squirrel darted up the flaking trunk of an elm tree. Klaus maintained his place, just a few steps behind him, but Felix knew from previous experience that Klaus lacked his explosive finish. Neither of them would have to face the indignity of being thrown into the lake. He had the leading pack in sight now. Time to step up a gear, to start the final assault. But then, he heard a cry, a yelp almost. He turned to see Klaus skipping on one foot, his face creased in pain. 'You all right, Klaus?' he shouted back.

'Fucking twisted my ankle,' came the sharp response. A couple of boys passed him. Klaus waved his hand at them. 'Hold up, help me out here a minute, will you?' By the time he'd finished his sentence, the boys had already run on, leaving Klaus to hop and screech by himself.

Felix grimaced. He slowed down. The leading pack disappeared round the bend while the two boys passed Felix, their running shoes smacking against the earth, their heavy breathing breaking the silence of the woods. The race was lost, he knew that now, but he needn't come last, and that was the main thing.

'Felix, help me out a bit,' shouted Klaus. 'I can't walk.'

He couldn't decide what to do; he so wanted to win the race, to win Heinrich's praise and enhance his standing within the group. But here he had the chance to win Klaus' favour. He knew, other way round, Klaus would never have stopped. But Klaus wasn't new, like Felix; he had nothing to prove. Another set of boys appeared, passing Klaus, ignoring his cries for help. Passing Felix, one of them managing to flash a smile at him as he laboured past. Felix swore but he went back.

'Here,' he said, 'put your arm around me.'

Klaus did so. 'Thanks, comrade.'

'S'alright.' His heart beat that bit lighter. *Thanks, comrade.* Just a simple acknowledgement, but he'd said it. Winning the race was, in the scheme of things, immaterial. There'd be other races, other opportunities. His need to have Klaus as *his* friend trumped it all.

And so together, Felix completed the last half kilometre propping up Klaus as the final stragglers passed them by with their running shoes caked in mud, with a whoop and a cheer on realising that none of them would, after all, have to face the icy waters of the lake.

As they came into view of the finishing line, Heinrich led the slow handclap. Many of the boys were still doubled up, hands on knees, catching their breaths. 'So, who's gonna be last?' shouted Heinrich as they approached.

'I twisted my bloody ankle,' said Klaus through gritted teeth.

Yes, thought Felix, *and it was me, not any of you, who stopped to save him.*

Heinrich grinned, enjoying the spectacle. 'No matter. The rules still apply.'

The boys started cheering and shouting, egging Klaus on, clapping and laughing. Felix could see the finish line marked out by Heinrich's shoe. They approached it, one laboured step after another. The clapping intensified. And then, just as they were about to cross it together, Felix hung back a fraction.

The boys erupted into a round of cheers. Heinrich slapped Klaus on the back before turning to Felix. 'Silence,' he shouted. 'Silence.' He waited while the boys stifled their mirth. They lined up in a semicircle, eager to witness Felix's humiliation.

'Go on,' said Heinrich. 'You were last. It's time to walk the plank.'

'But it's not fair –'

Heinrich laughed. 'It's not fair,' he repeated in a singsong voice. 'If you're not on that jetty in five seconds, I'll show you not fair.' But Felix saw something in the leader's expression, a slight softening around his eyes. It was almost as if he regretted his threat, as if he was playing a part. The boys started chanting. *Walk the plank, walk the plank.*

Klaus sat down on the grass verge, his sock rolled down, massaging his mud-splattered ankle. The two of them looked at each other through the throng of gleeful, chanting boys. Klaus gave an almost imperceptible nod, as if to say 'You have to do it'. Something in his expression pierced him, something Felix had never seen before… an acceptance of sorts, an appreciation, a realisation. Felix had sacrificed himself for him, had proved worthy of his friendship, and Klaus knew it. They were more than simply comrades now; they were friends.

Felix turned to face the water, brown, murky, sinister, the swirling mist mocking him, the chanting drowning out his thoughts. *Walk the plank, walk the plank.*

He placed a foot on the jetty.

Chapter 4

One Saturday afternoon, Felix returned home from a shopping errand. Having deposited everything with his mother, he went into the living room and stopped short. Ingrid Walther was there, perched on the edge of a settee with a penny whistle in her hand. His grandfather sat at the piano that no one ever played. He turned to leave, having no desire to speak to the girl. Gottfried stopped him. 'Hey, not so fast, Felix. Come in, come in, don't be shy.'

'Hello, Granddad.'

'You know Ingrid, don't you?'

'Yeah.' He nodded a dismissive hello at her. The Walthers lived nearby. Felix's parents liked them; they were a 'good family', respectable, educated. He knew his father viewed Ingrid as a potential suitor for Felix, but Felix had no idea how to speak to girls, had no desire to. Herr Walther was an architect and actually owned a car, a shiny Opel. Peter suspected Herr Walther was 'one of us', someone else not enamoured with Hitler and his revolution despite the fact that Ingrid was a Maiden, a member of the female Hitler Youth.

Felix often saw her in the street wearing her knee-length black skirt, her white blouse and necktie. Felix hated the way his father placed him in the same bracket as himself; he was not one of *them*.

'How are you, Felix?' she said in her gentle voice.

'All right.' Despite wanting to know why Ingrid was here, in his house, he made to leave.

'Hang on,' said Gottfried. 'Don't you want to stay and say hello?'

'Already have.'

'I'm just teaching Ingrid here how to play the whistle.'

Oh, so that was it.

Felix knew his parents hoped to invite the Walthers round for dinner some time. But they never did. An innate sense of social inequality played its part – what if they said no, what if they didn't have much in common after all? So Peter was content simply to bump into Herr Walther outside his house and praise his car and ask after his family. Gottfried, in his headmaster role, declared Ingrid to be a 'clever girl'. How his grandfather knew this, on account he'd never spoken to her before as far as Felix knew, Felix didn't know but it annoyed him. His grandfather never called him clever, never said anything positive about him.

'Play him that tune, Ingrid,' said Gottfried.

Ingrid smiled weakly, flashed a sheepish look at Felix. She put the penny whistle to her mouth.

'Go on, don't be shy. Starts with an E. Remember?'

Felix groaned; did he really have to stay to listen to the stupid girl play her stupid whistle?

Ingrid played the opening notes of the 'Horst Wessel Song', the tune barely recognisable, littered with mistakes.

Ingrid had dusty blonde hair with dark eyebrows and a

"horsey" nose, as his father once called it, and a little but visible scar on the side of her chin. She was tall, lanky and awkward. Nice eyes, though; warm, honest, reassuring somehow. Be that as it may, Felix didn't like her while knowing full well it wasn't so much Ingrid he disliked, but because she was female and he had no idea how to talk to girls. It was rumoured she had a boyfriend, although Felix didn't believe it. What sane boy would want to hang out with a goody-two shoes such as Ingrid Walther? Luckily, she went to a different school, probably a *better* school, but at least it meant he was spared seeing her too often.

Fortunately, Ingrid's ham-fisted recital was mercifully short.

'Very good,' said Gottfried.

No, it wasn't, thought Felix. *It was rubbish.*

Ingrid placed the whistle down on the little oval table next to the settee. 'I ought to go,' she said. 'My mother will be worrying about me.'

She would, thought Felix.

Gottfried laughed. 'Nothing for her to worry about, surely. But if you say so. Felix, be so kind to see your guest to the door, would you?'

My guest?

'It's OK,' said Ingrid.

'No, no, I insist,' said Gottfried. 'You might get lost,' he added with a wink.

Felix sighed. 'This way,' he said. Ingrid followed.

He opened the front door for her. 'Thank you,' she said. 'He's very nice, your grandfather.'

'Is he? Can't say I've noticed.'

'Well, yes, he is, I suppose.' She seemed in no hurry to leave. 'Listen, Felix, I was w-wondering...'

27

'What?'

'I… We…' She pulled on a loose strand of hair. 'Oh. It… oh, doesn't matter. Sorry.'

He sensed her nervousness, recognised his old, recent self in her. He wanted to apologise, to reassure her that, like he, she'd be OK one day, that he also knew that feeling of awkwardness. But he didn't know how to express it, couldn't bring himself to reach out. Far easier, he thought, to brazen it out. 'You ought to go. Don't want your mother worrying about you.'

*

Sacrifice. The Hitler Youth loved the idea of sacrifice. Klaus knew Felix had sacrificed himself for him that day, had taken the plunge in that filthy, execrable water in his place. Felix emerged soaking and shaking with cold to a circle of snickering boys pointing their fingers at him, their loathsome laughs fluttering through the frigid February air. Yet, amongst them all, Klaus stood, his eyes fixed on him. And he wasn't laughing. He knew Felix could have won that race; he knew Felix purposely halted at the line. Felix went home that day cold and shivery but he went home happy.

The following day after school, Klaus paid Felix a call. Felix opened the door and simply stood there, not quite believing it was Klaus standing in front of him. Fortunately, Father was out at work. 'You gonna invite me in, or what?'

Felix hesitated. 'What? Yeah. Sure.' What did Klaus want? Had he come to offer the hand of friendship? After all this time wanting to be his friend, Felix wasn't sure if he could cope with the expectation. They went upstairs to his room.

Klaus stood at Felix's bedroom door taking it in, a few reproductions of famous paintings, a potted plant, his bookshelves, his board games, the Indian feathers. All so bourgeois. Felix stood to one side, not saying anything, as if waiting for Klaus' verdict. He needed something to impress him with. And he knew exactly what. Excusing himself, Felix ran downstairs to the living room, rummaged round in the back of a drawer in the dresser, found what he was looking for, and returned upstairs. 'Here, look at this. It's my dad's,' he said, handing over a rectangular cardboard box to his visitor.

'What is it?' asked Klaus, opening it. His eyes widened on seeing it. 'Wow, this is fantastic.' He removed the pistol from its wrapping and held it high. 'This is your old man's Luger, right? He mentioned it.'

'Yeah, from the war. 1915, I think. A P08, but look, it's inscribed. That's what makes it special.'

Klaus read out the inscription. '*Für den Gott und Land*.' For God and Country. 'Where did he get it?'

Felix shook his head. 'Don't know.'

'It's brilliant.' But then something else caught his attention – Felix's book of stamps. 'Hey, let's see that,' he said. 'You collect stamps too.'

'Yes. Why?' Klaus Beck, a collector of stamps? Surely not.

Klaus sat down at Felix's desk, the book open in front of him, and with Felix's magnifying glass looked through the collection.

And that is how Klaus Beck and Felix Stoltenberg became friends. An old wartime Luger and a book of stamps. Klaus exclaimed with delight on seeing Felix's 1928 Finnish stamp and his two 1932 French ones. And when Felix offered him the spare, Klaus seemed momentarily perplexed, as if no one had ever offered him something so precious. Klaus described the stamps he had at home and promised something in return. They talked for an age about the Olympic stamps and the athletes they depicted, tripping over their words with excitement. No mention was made of Felix's plunge into the lake but he knew Klaus appreciated it.

Felix's mother, on realising he had a visitor, came up with a tray of milk and biscuits. Please, thought Felix, please don't call me '*Bärchen*'. Not now. He turned red with shame – they were too old for milk. Klaus, he knew, could sense his embarrassment and covered for it – 'I love milk,' he said, thanking Felix's mother. Felix didn't believe him but he'd said it and he'd said it out of loyalty, to save Felix's blushes. He gulped down the emotion. 'Fancy a game of chess?'

'I love chess but...' Klaus checked his watch. 'I oughta go home. Don't want to worry my old man.'

From that day on, Klaus knocked on his door at eight in the morning, and together they walked to school. Then, come home time, they walked home together. Often, Klaus came up to Felix's room, and together they played chess. Being a year apart, they saw little of each other at school. Yet, somehow, the word got round that the two of them were the best of friends now. And overnight, it seemed, Felix gained respect from the boys in his year, and people suddenly wanted to be *his* friend. Klaus had given him credibility, something he'd never experienced before. Even Heinrich Richter, their HJ leader, treated him differently. Finally, having been on the outside for so long, he had *arrived*.

But, he wondered, why did Klaus never invite him back to his house? Was it important; did it matter? No, it didn't matter, it really didn't. Nonetheless...

One evening, his grandfather, on another of his weekend visits, presented Felix with another of his penny whistles, which he promptly ignored, and a copy of *Mein Kampf*, Hitler's autobiography. 'Here, read this,' he said. 'It has everything you need to know. But don't tell your father,' he added with a wink.

Felix ran his finger over the cover, over the Führer's fierce eyes, and he knew he had something very important in his hands. Every night, before turning off the light, he sat up in bed reading another chapter or two. He found a lot of it hard going and simply didn't understand much of it, especially his hatred of the Jews. He tried to understand why. There had to be an explanation.

The following day, he showed Klaus the book.

'I've had this for ages,' said Klaus with a dismissive wave of the hand. 'Surprised you've only just got it.'

'My dad...' He didn't need to say more.

'He still hasn't seen the light.'

Felix shook his head, the creep of shame inching up his body.

'You have to make him understand. You know that, don't you? It's your responsibility. You have to do it, and do it soon. Because one day, it'll be too late.'

Felix nodded, sagely, pretending to understand. But he didn't; he didn't understand at all. Too late? Too late for what?

*

Early evening. Felix was sitting on the settee, practicing the penny whistle while his mother busied around in the kitchen. 'Do you have to play that dreadful thing?' she called through.

'Don't you like it?'

She paused, as if thinking about this. 'Frankly – no. Why don't you learn to play the piano? Someone ought to play it.'

Felix ploughed on regardless. He was trying to learn the 'Horst Wessel Song', a Nazi favourite, an unofficial anthem.

His father came down from upstairs, decked out in a tweed suit and matching waistcoat and breeches. He'd waxed his

31

moustache, curling it upwards at the ends. He held his silver-topped cane and a hat with a couple feathers in its band. But what stood out most was his Iron Cross pinned to his lapel, the metal catching the glint of the side lamp. The occasion for this effort was a regimental reunion in a beer hall within the shadow of the Reichstag. Wives were not invited but, as his mother said in a whisper, an evening of middle-aged men talking about war didn't appeal.

'Is there nothing else you could play?' he asked.

'I don't know any other tunes. You look nice.'

'Hmm. Thank you,' he said, standing at the mirror, straightening his bow tie.

'Papa?'

'Yes?'

'That medal, the Iron Cross?'

'What about it?'

'Is it first or second class?'

Peter sighed as he sat in the armchair next to Felix. 'Sad to relate, only a second.'

'Still.'

'Yes. Listen, son. I know…'

Felix tensed up.

'I know you can't understand why I get angry about you and this Hitler Youth malarkey. I'm an old man, I don't appreciate what's going on. I know that's what you think. But the fact is, I *do* know and I can see where all this is leading. War is the most terrible thing. It reduces a man to a machine, without thought, without a personality. And this man you so adulate, he won't settle until he's got us into another war. And I… Felix, I don't want you, my son or any man's son, to go through what I went through. Whatever your comrades say, there's no glory in it, Felix. There's no glory when you're trembling in fear, put in situations you think you might not survive. You know, there's not a day I don't think about it. And yes, I have nightmares too. Because once you've lived it, it never leaves you. It scars you, Felix, and you'll never be able to escape it. So, that's why I get cross when I see what's happening to you. And I know there's nothing I can do to stop it. There's nothing you can do either. And it's that helplessness that's the worst.'

'No, Papa, you're wrong. The Führer's only wish is to have peace.'

'You believe that? You all believe that?'

'Yes. Yes, we do.'

'Then we really are lost.'

Felix tried to look at his father but found it too difficult. His father rose from the chair and returned to the mirror, checking his moustache. And it was at the mirror that the two of them caught each other's eyes.

The moment stilled.

Chapter 5

March 1933. A month had passed; spring had come. Granddad had returned home, thank God, and Felix and Klaus Beck were still the best of friends. Felix still hadn't been invited back to Klaus's and that rankled a little more each day. But, that apart, life was great. Felix was a different person. Gone was the shy boy looking in from the outside. He had grown in so many ways in such a short space of time – physically, mentally, he was tougher now in mind and body.

It was nearing ten o'clock on a cold, crisp evening, the night sky clear, a wind blowing down the avenue. Felix and Klaus marched down a deserted, cobbled Berlin street. Felix vaguely noticed the three boys at the far end of the street, lurking within the shadow of a shop doorway, but paid no heed.

It'd been a good evening: Felix and Klaus had been to the cinema and seen a great film called *Hitler Youth Quex*, about a group of boys just like them, about pride in the uniform, of finding acceptance. It was about sacrifice. Felix loved it – it was his story. He cried at the end, at the death of the hero,

Heini, a boy happy to forgo his life for the greater good and with Hitler's name on his lips as he drew his final breath. The lights went up, and Felix quickly wiped his eyes with his sleeve.

'You all right?' asked Klaus.

'Sure.' He swallowed. 'Yeah, it was good, wasn't it, Klaus?'

They skipped out of the auditorium. 'Yeah, that was some film,' said Klaus as they made their way home down an avenue flanked by trees and street lamps. 'Heini's last words, "The flag means more than death". He's right, it does. We have to remember that.'

He put his arm round Felix's shoulders, laughing. Klaus' contact stopped Felix short. That fleeting moment of affection, of camaraderie. The warmth of the touch seeped into him, reaching the depths of his heart.

'"The flag means more than death",' Felix repeated, punching the air. Just saying the words aloud made him tremble with excitement.

'That's what we need to make people understand – people like your old man.' Klaus stopped, and turning to Felix added, 'If you're not careful, mate, your father will get you all sent off to Oranienburg.'

'Oranienburg?'

'The camp there. Trust me, you don't want that.'

They walked in silence for a while. He'd heard of these new camps opening, places where they sent dissenters and people who criticised the regime. No one knew what happened in these places; one knew not to ask questions. Would they really send him and his mother to one because of his father? He shuddered at the thought. Klaus was right; he needed to do *something* before it was too late. But what? How could he persuade his father that he was becoming a danger to them all?

Felix half noticed a cigarette ahead on the pavement,

burning itself out. They heard nothing, saw nothing, no footsteps on the cobbles, no shadows hurtling towards them. The first Felix knew of the attack was the screaming behind him, followed swiftly by the ballooning sensation on the side of his head. His legs gave way. A heavy boot caught him in the ribs, a heavy crunch blowing the air out of him. He tried to get to his knees but another kick sent him sprawling, his palms scraped by the grit on the pavement. There seemed to be loads of them, the snakes. He scrambled up onto his feet, knew he had to. There were only three of them, boys a little older, dressed in black. His right fist shot out, the satisfying smack of his fist against bone. He saw Klaus from the corner of his eye, blood gushing from his mouth but he, too, had kept to his feet; he, too, was fighting back. Again, his assailant tried to hit him but, this time, his movements too slow, Felix parried the blow. Felix grunted as he took a handful of the other's jacket and tried to wrestle him to the ground. He punched out, surprised at the pain that blazed up his arm as his fist connected with a jaw.

Then something heavy whacked him on the back. A second blow sent him to the ground. Now, through the pain, the spiral of panic rose within him – the bastards had got bats; they didn't stand a chance. Then – a throaty shout – a couple of men's voices nearby. Men fast approaching. From his peculiar angle, his face against the ground, he saw the attackers' boots disappearing down the street, heard the rapid *click clack* of their soles on the pavement. He could hear Klaus shouting after them, his words distant somehow.

'You all right, lads?' said one of the men.

'Yeah, we're OK,' said Klaus, dabbing his bloodied nose. 'Thanks for your help.' His face wasn't too bad, just his nose and a cut above his eyebrow.

Klaus offered Felix his hand and pulled him up, first onto one knee, then the other before straightening up. He considered the blood on his knuckles and momentarily wondered how it got there.

'You did well, lad,' said one of the men, slapping Klaus on the back. 'Fought back like a lion.'

Felix rubbed the back of his head. 'Who were they?' he asked, conscious of the throbbing throughout his face.

'Communists,' said Klaus, brushing himself down. 'Scum of the earth. Bastards.'

'Well,' said the man. 'It was short and bloody but you got the better of them, all right. They won't be trying that again in a hurry. Heil Hitler.'

And with that, the two men sauntered off, their shadows disappearing round a corner. A tram passed, its wheels clunking on its track. Newspapers caught in the wind flared up like little ghosts. Somewhere a door slammed shut. Felix expected to be in pain but realised there was no pain, nothing; just a deep warmth as his skin tingled. He laughed. He knew, having taking a beating, he'd taken another step towards manhood. Klaus started laughing too, his face caught by the yellow glow of a street lamp. 'You did well, Felix, old man.'

'Not really. If you hadn't been there, I'd be dead meat by now. Scumbags.'

'Yeah, too cowardly to stand up to us like proper men. Had to sneak up on us like the scum they are.'

'Thanks, Klaus.'

'Hey…' He looked fondly at his friend. 'Don't mention it.' He slapped his arm again around Felix's shoulder. 'You'd have done the same for me. We're brothers, you and me.'

He squeezed Felix closer. He turned to look at Felix, his eyes boring into his. A charged silence zapped between them, an unexpected and uncomfortable intimacy, a hint of tobacco on Klaus' breath. Felix's heart contracted, the intensity too overwhelming. He saw something in Klaus' eyes he'd never seen before but he couldn't interpret it. He didn't like it. Instinctively, he inched back. The moment passed. Klaus let go, laughed it off. 'Blood brothers, that's what we are. Blood brothers. United we stand and all that.'

Felix couldn't prevent the sigh of relief. 'Bloody right,' he said, trying to cover it up.

They returned home. Having said their goodbyes, Felix trudged on alone, hands in pockets. The clouds parted, exposing the moon. Such a clear night now. He'd walked these streets his whole life, but now, tonight, everything looked different. The same mundane houses, the same drab streets, now looked like mansions on a street of gold. He was truly part of the brotherhood now; he'd spilt his blood for the cause, for the Führer. *The flag means more than death.* And he knew it to be true.

But his joy was tempered. Klaus had done something, shifted their relationship in a manner Felix didn't understand. He couldn't articulate his unease, but it was there, this unease, sitting in the pit of his stomach. And he didn't like it; he didn't like it one bit.

Chapter 6

Joseph Goebbels had deemed the day "the day of national awakening". Six o'clock in the morning: dressed, breakfasted and washed, Felix was ready to go. He was working as a helper at the polling station at school; for today, Sunday 5 March 1933, was election day and he risked being late. He didn't want to go, didn't want to see Klaus. But he had to, he knew that.

Peter, having his breakfast, was grumbling.

'What's that you're saying?' asked Klara, an undercurrent of irritation in her voice.

Peter stirred his tea. 'I said, what's the point? It's a foregone conclusion, isn't it? Bloody Hitler will win.'

'Dad, please,' said Felix. 'You can't say that.'

'I'll say –'

'Felix's right. You ought to be more careful, Peter. You can't say that outside; you never know who's listening.'

'I've got to go,' said Felix, adjusting his HJ cap. 'Dad, will you be voting today?'

'Of course.'

'But… but you said there's no point.'

'Still have to vote though; it's every man's duty.'

'And woman's,' added Klara.

'You won't…'

'What?'

Klara stepped up behind him, placing a hand on Felix's shoulder. 'I think what Felix is trying to say, Peter, is don't go and make a show of yourself. For his sake, don't. Please.'

'What is this? I will not be bossed around in my own home, thank you. Now, be off with you.'

Klara squeezed Felix's shoulder.

Felix pushed his bike outside, the heavy weight of dread within him.

'Hello there.'

He spun round. It was Ingrid, a satchel around her shoulder.

'Oh, hi,' he said brightly, ridiculously pleased to see her for some reason.

She was wearing her BDM uniform and had plaited her hair. She looked like every other girl but she had something about her, a coyness he liked.

'I've just come back from youth camp,' she said. 'Have you been yet?'

He shook his head.

'Oh, it was great. Singing songs and toasting bread over the campfire, riding ponies, hiking, games, it was such fun. You must go one day. Anyway' – she fiddled with the strap of her satchel – 'big day today.'

'Suppose.'

'We're giving out leaflets in the market and making sure everyone goes to vote.'

'Good.' He stared, transfixed almost by the glimmer in her eyes. He knew he wanted to say more but didn't know how to.

'Yes. We all have to do our bit. So, erm…' A flicker of an embarrassed smile flashed across her lips. 'How's… how's your grandfather?'

Felix shrugged. 'Still playing his stupid whistle.'

She laughed at that and he experienced a little ripple of pleasure. 'Good. Suppose I ought to go. Mustn't be late.'

'No.'

'Bye bye, Felix.'

'Yeah. See ya.'

He watched her walk away, her satchel bumping on her waist. He'd never heard her say his name before and there was something in the way she said it that pricked him. He found himself hoping she'd turn around.

But she didn't.

Bracing himself against the cold, Felix cycled to school. He still couldn't get used to some of the new street names, so many had been renamed in honour of one of the Nazi elite: an Adolf-Hitler-Platz or Horst-Wesselstraße here, a Goebbelsstraße or Goering Boulevard there, streets festooned with flags and banners. From every shopfront, every balcony, every lamp post or tree, swastikas and the national black, white and red flag flapped in the March breeze. Everywhere, posters of Hitler alongside the president, Hindenburg, posters proclaiming, *Adolf Hitler for peace! The Führer is our future! The future is here, vote National Socialism!* Felix had never seen the area so busy; everyone, it seemed, on their way to the school to cast their vote. People smiling and laughing. There was festivity in the air.

Then came the voice Adolf Hitler himself from out of nowhere, barking from a run of loudspeakers attached to lamp posts along the street. Felix cycled down the road, Hitler's voice chasing after him.

41

Already, a line of people queued at the school gates. A number of SA kept order, their hands behind their backs, some with pro-Nazi placards hanging in front of their tunics. 'Heil Hitler,' some said as Felix pushed his bike by. Returning the greeting, Felix left his bike against some railings and made his way to the gymnasium. He knew where to go but the route was lined with arrows for voters to find their way. All the usual equipment had been pushed to one side – the horses, weights and treadmills – but the smell of sweat and youthful exertion still lingered. Various adults sat behind tables, while dotted round the perimeter were a number of wooden voting booths. Felix found his HJ group gathering.

'Just on time, Stoltenberg,' said Heinrich, tapping his watch. 'Right, gather together. Stand to attention and listen up.'

Felix took his place next to Klaus. They exchanged muted "all rights". A stab of worry pierced his chest.

Heinrich looked at his watch. 'It's gonna be a long day. We open in ten minutes and we don't close until ten tonight. Your main job is to hand out leaflets to everyone who comes in, and I mean every single person, even their dogs. You have to make tea or coffee for the elderly or the crippled. After they've voted, you have to give them a button to pin on their lapels to show they've voted right. Buttons cost five pfennigs each. All for a good cause. Got it? Ain't too difficult, not even for a bunch of faggots like you lot. I've done a rota. Anyone not on one of these jobs has to loiter and make sure voters know where to put their cross, in other words, next to the name of Herr Merck, our National Socialist candidate.'

Klaus put his hand up. 'And what if they don't?' he asked.

'You politely point out the error of their ways, Beck. What d'you think? And if that don't work, there's always one of the

SA lads to give a hand.' Heinrich pointed out a stooped man with a large moustache. 'That, by the way, the one who looks like the grim reaper, is Herr Heinkel. He's the chief polling clerk.'

Felix and Klaus were given first shift at the gym doors, ready to hand out their leaflets.

'This should be fun,' said Klaus. 'You expecting your old man?'

'Unfortunately.'

Klaus rubbed his hands together. 'Even better. Listen, were you OK last night? You know, after I left.'

Felix rolled the leaflets tightly in his hand. 'Yeah, sure.'

Herr Heinkel did indeed look like he worked at a funeral parlour; the only dash of colour in his otherwise black suit and tie was his swastika lapel pin. He took his place in the middle of the gym. 'Right, gentlemen, ladies, brace yourselves,' he said, checking his pocket watch. 'It is time.'

Sure enough, the first voters emerged at the gym door, a scrum of people in black coats, men in bowler hats, women with berets. 'Heil Hitler, take a leaflet,' said Klaus and Felix, thrusting them into outstretched hands. 'Report to the clerks. Vote National Socialist. Vote Herr Merck. Vote Hitler. Heil Hitler, Heil Hitler, good morning; good morning, Heil Hitler.' And so it went on, more and more people.

Herr Heinkel dashed around between the voting booths. 'No, no, meine Frau, you should put your cross here. Next to Herr Merck's name,' he said in a sonorous voice, pointing his spindly finger at the right spot. 'That's the ticket. A nice, big X. Well done. Now, go collect your button from one of the boys over there. That's it, that's it.' 'That's it, sir. A vote for Herr Merck is a vote for Hitler, for peace and prosperity. Don't forget your button now. Five pfennigs.'

A solitary, glum-faced woman with wide eyes tried to shield her slip of paper from Herr Heinkel. 'Surely,' she said, 'I can vote for whoever I want. That's the point, isn't it?'

'Yes, of course, madam, you can vote for whoever you want. It's entirely up to you if that's what you want. Thank you.'

The woman marked her cross with a flourish. 'So now I see that spotty youth over there for my button.'

Heinkel cleared his throat. 'No, madam, I'm afraid not. You can't have a button because you didn't vote for Herr Merck.'

'But then those SA men will see.'

Heinkel shrugged his shoulders, moving on to the next booth.

The woman huffed, pressed her handbag against her bosom, and made to leave.

'Traitor,' hissed Klaus as she passed.

The woman stopped, glared at him, the uncertainty etched across her face, and left.

Felix chortled. 'Huh, she'll face far worse outside. Heil Hitler, please take a leaflet. Vote Herr Merck.' But, inside, his stomach churned with dread. That was nothing, he thought, he knew someone who would make a far greater fuss. Damn him.

Two hours later, and the initial rush of voters had died down. Klaus and Felix were on tea duty, making cups of tea in the little kitchen for those who looked like they needed sustenance. Klaus lit a cigarette. 'Fancy one?' he asked.

Felix did not. 'Sure. Thanks.'

But before Klaus had chance to pass Felix a cigarette, Heinrich's head appeared at the kitchen hatch, telling Klaus not to smoke.

Klaus threw his cigarette outside. 'The old woman.'

It was then Felix heard his father's voice. 'I do not want one of your stupid leaflets, thank you.'

Felix groaned.

Klaus' eyes lit up. 'Here he is,' he said.

The boys peered out through the kitchen hatch to find Peter arguing with a HJ boy who was trying to thrust a leaflet into his hand while Felix's mother tried steering him to the clerks. They gave their names, confirmed their addresses and took their voting slips.

Felix watched as his father went to a booth to be immediately pounced upon by Herr Heinkel. 'Here goes,' he muttered.

'Heil Hitler, sir. Good morning.'

'Good morning.'

'Now, if I may advise, sir, all you need –'

'I don't need your help,' said Peter too loudly.

Herr Heinkel cleared his throat again. 'You realise, sir,' he said quietly, 'you're voting for the Social Democrats.'

'As always. So what?' His voice echoed across the gym causing people to stop and turn in his direction. He marked his cross with two heavy, deliberate strokes.

Felix was dying while Klaus beside him lapped up the spectacle. 'Your old man's asking for it. Lucky for you Heinrich doesn't know he's your old man or he'd kick you out and you'd get the beating from hell from the rest of us.'

'Don't tell him. Please. I can't be expelled.'

'It's my duty, ain't it?'

Herr Heinkel took Peter by the arm with a bony hand. 'You should leave, mein Herr.'

'Let go of my goddamn arm, will you?'

'Stop shouting, you fool,' said Klara, placing her voting slip in the large, metallic box.

'I will not.'

'Please keep your voice down,' said Herr Heinkel, the colour rising in his cheeks. 'You're disrupting an election and influencing other voters.'

'Me? Ha!' Slowly, and with great show, Peter held up the election slip and tore it in two; the shreds floating towards the floor. A gasp of shock circled the room. 'This is no election, this is a farce.'

One of the polling clerks had alerted the SA men at the school gates. Two of them now appeared in their brown shirts and Sam Browne belts. 'What's going on?' grunted one, his hands on his hips.

'Nothing, n-nothing,' stuttered Herr Heinkel. 'This gentleman is just leaving.'

Peter eyed the two men, top to bottom, his face paling. Klara took his arm. 'Come, Peter,' she said quietly. 'Let's get you home. Heil Hitler,' she added for the benefit of the SA men.

Felix and Klaus watched them leave. Felix breathed a sigh of relief.

Klaus pushed him in the chest. Felix fell back. 'Who does he think he is? Your old man's really is a fucking traitor, you know that? A bourgeois traitor. He bloody deserves to be packed off to Oranienburg. And you? What are you even doing being with us? You *should* be expelled.'

'No, I'm not like him; we're nothing alike.'

'Like fuck. An apple never falls far from the tree.'

Heinrich burst in, a pile of leaflets in his hand. 'Right, time for you two to…' He stopped; looked at both boys, his eyes narrowing. 'What's going on here?' Neither answered. 'Well? Stoltenberg?'

'Nothing, sir.'

Heinrich looked from one to the other. 'Beck?'

Klaus threw a glance at Felix.

Don't tell him, don't tell him.

'I said, Beck, what's going on here?'

'Nothing, sir. Nothing at all.'

Chapter 7

Heinrich Richter had been given a job to do – an unpleasant one but, he knew, a necessary one. He had to ensure that all the parents of the boys in his HJ brigade were true believers. He was to give each boy a questionnaire which would ask directly whether their parents were good National Socialists or not. 'But they'll just lie, won't they?' he'd asked. Not if he had done his job properly and won their loyalty and total trust. Not if he had educated them into knowing that the nation and the party were more important than any family ties.

'And if they tell the truth and confess?' he asked. Simple, they said, the offending parents would be dealt with in the appropriate manner. Heinrich wasn't quite sure what the appropriate manner was but he could hazard a guess. So, he took the pile of questionnaires and just hoped, for their sakes, the boys had supportive parents.

The Hitler Youth brigade met twice a week in the municipal hall, a place that remained perpetually cold. They sat on fold-up chairs either side of a long wooden table under an arched ceiling with grand timber beams stretching from one side to the other, decorated with swastika bunting. One of the windows was still boarded up with a piece of wood, the result of a communist brick hurtling through the previous autumn. Above the main door hung the ubiquitous portrait of the Führer.

Heinrich distributed the questionnaires to his charges. It consisted of just five questions printed out on one sheet of paper. 'Right,' said Heinrich, his voice echoing within the hall. 'It's easy enough – just answer the questions as truthfully as you can. This is important. Remember, your first priority is to your country and to the Führer. However much you think you love your parents, it counts for nothing.' He shook his head. 'Soon, your parents will die. We all die. But the nation lives on. As individuals, we are nothing. But the nation and the Führer are everything.' Feeling hot, he pulled at his collar. 'If you do have anything to say, you don't have to worry. Nothing will happen. You have…' He scratched his face. 'You have my word. We just need to gage the temperature. Nothing more. OK, off you go.'

Felix, sitting beside Klaus at the front, looked down at the sheet of paper. He shifted in his seat, narrowing his eyes. The first question read, *Question 1: Do your father and mother support the National Socialists? If "no", please explain.* Felix closed his eyes. Just the night before, his father had seemed on the verge of tears. 'What's becoming of our country? Half the nation trembles in fear.'

'They tremble, Dad, 'cos they don't believe.'

'I keep telling you, the man is a tyrant. He's dangerous. He's mad.'

'He won the election, didn't he?'

'Yeah, right. Next time, he'll be voted out. Mark my words. This country will come to its senses.' He shook his head. 'It

49

has to, my God, it has to.'

Felix picked up his pen; his hand poised. *Does your father support the National Socialists? No, he bloody doesn't.* But what could he say? "Your first priority is to your country," said Heinrich. Easy to say. He'd said nothing would happen. Did he believe him? Yes, he did. Why would he lie? He put his pen to paper. But a little stab of fear stopped him writing the word *No*. The nation did take priority, for sure, but he couldn't bear the thought of his father having to answer for his lack of belief. And so, he wrote the word *Yes*. He just hoped the answers remained confidential, because Klaus knew. He knew exactly how Felix's father viewed the Nazis.

Question 2: Have you ever heard your father criticise the Führer or the National Socialists? If so, how? Yes, every single day. Felix shook his head as he wrote the word, *No*.

He glanced to his left. Klaus, his head bent in concentration, seemed to be smiling.

Question 3: How would your parents feel if you had a Jewish girlfriend?

Why would it matter? But he knew it did matter; he couldn't grasp why, but it did. So, instead, he wrote the single word, the only word he could think of: *Sick*.

Question 4: Do your parents think Jews should have equal rights with all other German people?

No.

Question 5: Do your parents interfere with your HJ duties? If so, how?

No.

He turned the page. *Name.* So no, it wasn't confidential, and he knew he'd done the right thing in protecting his father. He wrote his name.

He leant back in his chair. That was it.

Heinrich went from table to table, gathering the papers, briefly casting his eyes over the answers. He seemed pleased. It was only as he reached the back that he stopped. 'What's the matter, Hans?'

Everyone turned round, their eyes fixing on Hans, a weedy red-haired boy with large glasses, a squat nose and an abundance of freckles. He appeared to be crying. Heinrich read his answers. He looked down at the boy sitting in front of him and placed his hand on his shoulder. 'Don't worry, Hans. You've done well.'

'What will happen to them?'

'Nothing. It's down to you to re-educate them, make them see the error of their ways. You think you can do that? If so, it need go no further.'

Hans, sniffing, nodded.

*

Walking home, wrapped in their winter overcoats, Klaus stopped to light a cigarette. 'You didn't tell the truth, did you?'

'Might have.'

'So you're telling me your old man's suddenly become Hitler's greatest supporter. Like hell you did.'

'I can work on him.'

'What? Like little, meek Hans?'

'Yes, like Hans.'

Klaus kicked at a bottle lying on the pavement. 'Yeah, like fuck you can.' He stopped and looked at Felix. 'I'll come round yours after school tomorrow, OK?'

Felix caught his breath.

'I said –'

'Yeah, yeah. Sure.'

'I've got a new stamp I wanna show you. American.'

'Brilliant.'

A wintry sun had appeared, giving a pleasant orangey hue to the streets, but the cold still pierced. Felix wrapped his scarf tighter. A tram passed. A ring of its bell startled a flock of pigeons, noisily taking flight. Klaus was describing a rare Austrian stamp he'd seen in a shop he was saving up for, depicting a white-shouldered eagle.

They turned the corner into Friedrichstraße and, as one, stopped.

'Shit, what's happening?' said Felix.

There, fifty metres on, were a group of three or four SS men, shouting and yelling, kicking at something, surrounded by a small crowd of onlookers, equally vocal.

'Quick,' urged Klaus, picking up pace. 'Let's see.'

'Hang on a minute,' said Felix.

He followed his friend, running, his stomach for some reason heavy with dread. Something on the ground, a person, no, two people, a man and a woman, a couple perhaps. Boots flying in, the dull thud of kicking. 'Fuckin' Jews, bloody Yids.' 'Get them,' shouted the crowd. 'Beat them, get them.' The crowd squeezed in, the two boys at the back. Felix could see the couple's hats on the pavement, tossed to the side. 'Get back,' shouted one of the SS men, as if not wanting anyone to join in their fun.

'Georges,' shouted Klaus, spotting one of the SS men.

The man, Georges, heard his name, recognised the voice. He emerged from the melee, a good-looking boy, about eighteen, Felix reckoned, his hat at the back of his head, his blond hair tousled. 'Hey, Klaus, mate.'

'What's happening?'

'These two Yids,' he said, out of breath. 'Refused to return Schlecker's Heil Hitler. We're teaching them a lesson. Come on, give us a hand,' he shouted, returning to his friends.

'Us?'

'Yeah, you and your mate,' he said, motioning Felix. 'Why not? Fuck it, you're good National Socialists, ain't you? Prove it!'

'Yeah, fuck it,' said Klaus, barging through the crowd, following his friend. He looked back at Felix. Felix, trembling, shook his head. How could he kick at an old person? This, he thought, more than anything else, would prove his devotion, that he really did belong. But he couldn't; he couldn't do it. Klaus stepped back, grabbing his wrist. 'We must. We have to.'

The couple, middle aged, prostrate on the pavement, curled up, foetal, screamed as the boots reigned in. Felix hesitated; it seemed so wrong.

'Get on with it,' shouted Georges.

Their heavy outdoor coats gave the couple a degree of protection. But blood poured from the man's nose and mouth, blood encrusted the woman's hair. Felix stamped on the woman's hand, on her delicate ringed fingers. She screamed, her lipstick smudged. The bile rose in his throat. Suddenly hot, Felix removed his scarf, desperate to escape. A voice rose from the mayhem, 'All right, stop. Enough.' It was Georges' friend, perhaps Schlecker. On command, the kicking stopped. The men caught their breaths; the crowd broke into applause while the couple remained on the ground, crying, whimpering.

Schlecker leant over the man. 'Next time, Yid, you'll remember to return the salute, eh?' With that, he spat on him, turned and, acknowledging the applause with a hint of a bow, strode away. Georges, a smile on his face, called out to Klaus. 'See you later, mate.'

'Yeah, sure,' said Klaus, catching his breath. The crowd

watched them marching off down the street, a swagger in their step. Slowly, the crowd dispersed.

Felix felt a tug on his scarf. The bloodied woman still on the ground had gripped it. For a split second the woman and Felix locked eyes while both pulled on the scarf as if in a tug of war. She wasn't so old, after all; she looked a little like his mother. Her hair, dyed purple, positively shone. The sheer desperation in her eyes sliced into Felix, her confusion, the fear, the hurt. Felix staggered back, yanking free his scarf. Her hand remained outstretched, beseeching him, beseeching her god. His eyes pricked. It could have been his mother.

He ran. Klaus called after him. Ignoring it, he ran back down the street, tears clouding his eyes, round the corner, past a park. He ran and ran, where, he didn't know, didn't care, just as long as he escaped the shame. He turned another corner, still running, his eyes streaming, ran down a darkened alley between two blocks, alarming a cat, before finally stopping. Casting his eyes skywards, he clutched his heart. His head pounded; he feared he might faint. He propped himself up against a brick wall, weak with dizziness. His hand shot to his mouth. Too late, he leant over and vomited.

He heard footsteps approaching from behind. 'Felix, what's up?'

Felix wiped his mouth with his sleeve. 'Nothing,' he managed to croak.

He straightened. Klaus looked at him, his eyes clouded with confusion. 'You're crying.'

'No, no, I'm not, mate.'

'Fuck you, you are. I thought…'

'It's fine, mate. Really.'

'No, it ain't. You lost it, didn't you? You fag. I thought you were one of us, but you ain't.' Klaus' eyes reddened. He pushed Felix against the wall. 'I thought we were brothers, blood brothers,' he shouted. 'The flag means more than death – remember? Remember?'

'I still believe it.'

'No, you don't. You're crying over a couple of old Yids. Shit, man, what does that make you? You're worse than your old man. Shit, I trusted you, I thought you were my friend, but you're nothing but a faggot. Why are you even wearing that uniform?' he said, pulling at the lapel of Felix's tunic. 'You weakling, you bastard.'

'Klaus, no…'

'I fucking hate you.' Klaus turned on his heels and stomped away, kicking at the rubbish littering the alleyway.

Felix's knees gave way. The eyes of the bloodied woman filled his vision. The thought of someone, like him, doing that to his mother… He bit into the scarf and screamed.

Chapter 8

'All the nations of the east are there for the taking. We must and we shall subjugate them for our own purpose. It is the law of nature, the survival of the fittest.' Felix sat at the end of his bed, reading aloud, trying to memorise the words. 'It is the law of nature, the survival of the fittest,' he repeated, thumping his forehead, trying to drum the words into his memory. He put the book down on the bed with a sigh. Hitler's stern expression stared up at him from the cover. He gazed out of the window. It was a bright day out there, a perfect day, but he had no desire to step outside. His grandfather had set him this task, to memorise these three 'essential' paragraphs from Hitler's book. He heard the front door bell ring. Glad of the distraction, Felix went to his door, opening it a fraction.

'Heil Hitler, Frau Stoltenberg.'

Shit, it was Heinrich down there. He knew why he'd called. Felix had skived off the last two meetings, telling his mother he had a cold. He couldn't face going in, couldn't face seeing Klaus again. He kept seeing the woman's face again and again, her bloodied hand gripping on to his scarf.

'Yes? Can I help?' asked Klara.

'My name is Heinrich Richter, Hitler Youth leader. Is your husband in, meine Frau?'

'I – I think so. Who shall I say?...'

He heard his father's heavy footsteps coming through from the kitchen. Felix crept out onto the landing. 'Heil Hitler,' said Heinrich, shooting out his arm.

'What's all this about? About Felix, is it?'

'Your son has failed to turn up for the last two meetings, mein Herr.'

'So what?'

Please, thought Felix, *please, Father, be nice to him.*

'Mein Herr, attendance is compulsory. You know that, surely.'

His mother stepped forward. 'Felix has had a cold.'

Why, thought Felix, did she have to answer the door wearing her apron?

'Has he?' said Peter. Felix could see the back of his father's ears burning red.

'Yes, Peter. You remember?'

'It is my duty to report all absences, whatever the reason,' said Heinrich.

'No, please don't do that,' said his mother, her hands outstretched. 'It won't happen again. I'll make sure of it.'

'Compulsory, you say?' said Peter. 'Do I not have a say in this – as his father?'

Heinrich eyed his father. Felix had to admire his nerve. 'Frankly, no, mein Herr.'

'Be that as it may,' said Klara, talking quickly, 'cold or no cold, he'll be there. In fact, I'd call him down, but his grandfather has got him memorising vital passages from *Mein Kampf* as we speak.'

Heinrich's eyes flicked upwards. He caught Felix's eyes. Felix froze. He cursed himself for allowing himself to be caught out.

A glinting smile crossed Heinrich's lips. 'Good,' he said. 'I'm pleased we've reached an understanding. It wouldn't look good for your son to be reported for a lack of patriotism.'

'No, no,' said Mother. 'He's awfully patriotic.'

Heinrich bowed again. 'Thank you, meine Frau. As it is, I'm concerned about your apparent lack of enthusiasm. I see no portraits of our Führer in your house.'

Felix could sense his father stiffening, trying to contain his anger. 'I didn't realise it was mandatory.'

'It isn't. Nonetheless.'

'Yes, nonetheless.'

Heinrich clicked his heels. 'Thank you, mein Herr. I wish you good day.' He flicked his eyes upwards again. Felix's cheeks flushed. 'Heil Hitler.'

'Heil Hitler,' said Klara, as she closed the front door.

Peter waited for a few moments, waited until Heinrich was gone and out of earshot. 'My God,' he said. 'We've lost our liberties, our way of life, and now we've lost our children. That maniac wants them for himself. That's twice they've sent teenagers to intimidate me in my own home.'

'It's not that bad, Peter. Another three years, and Felix can do as he pleases.'

'You think so? You really think our wonderful Führer will let him go just because he turns eighteen.'

'Yes. Yes, I do.'

'I hope you're right, Klara. For all our sakes.'

*

Felix approached Klaus' home with trepidation swirling within

58

him. He'd put on his HJ uniform and looked at himself in the mirror. Where once he'd puff out his chest, now, instead, it shamed him. It's just a phase, he told himself. It would pass. In his pocket, a box. Inside it, a wartime Luger pistol. He'd taken it from the dresser drawers in the living room.

Twilight was fast approaching. He overtook a mother pushing a pushchair, a little gloved hand dangling from its side. The little hand dropped something, a toy of some sort. He reached down and picked it up – a knitted giraffe. The mother smiled and thanked him. He felt grateful for the smile, a dash of warmth. 'Heil Hitler,' she said. The greeting sliced into him, reigniting that sense of unease that rested in the pit of his stomach.

He reached Klaus' house but, instead of stopping, he walked on. He tried rehearsing what he wanted to say. He knew what he'd be expected to say – that if the situation arose again, he wouldn't hesitate. But he knew that wasn't something he could say because it wouldn't be true. Why would the Führer expect them to attack an elderly couple, Jewish or otherwise? Surely, they couldn't be seen as threats, just a harmless old man and his wife. He hadn't been able to stop thinking about it and it made him nauseous. He could still make no sense of it.

He paused at the end of the street. Opposite was a haberdashery with the word *Jude* emblazoned across the glass front. Slowly, he walked back down the street. He stepped up to Klaus' door and pulled on the brass ringer. He could hear purposeful steps from inside. The door opened. It was, Felix guessed, Klaus' father, chewing on a toothpick, his huge belly straining under a stained white vest and braces.

'What you want?' The man reeked of beer.

'I, er… Is-is Klaus in?'

The man shouted over his shoulder. 'Oi, laddie, some kid to see ya.'

Felix wilted under Klaus' father's scrutiny.

'Who are you then?' Tufts of grey chest hair poked out over the top of his vest.

'I'm Felix Stoltenberg, mein Herr.'

The man laughed, although Felix failed to see why. Finally, Klaus appeared from within the hallway. 'Have you finished the brass, like your mother said?'

Klaus turned red. 'Not quite, Papa. Sorry.'

The man shook his head. Turning to Felix, he asked, 'You, lad, any good at polishing brass?'

'Erm, no, mein Herr, no.'

The man tutted. 'Useless as this piece of shit then.' He laughed again, a loud horrible laugh.

Klaus took Felix by the elbow and pushed him away from the door, towards the street.

'Oi, where you think you going, laddie?'

'Won't be long, Papa.'

'Better not be.' The man slammed the door on them.

Klaus' cheeks reddened further as they walked down the street. Klaus was breathing hard, as if he'd just been running. He stopped and glanced back towards his house.

Felix wished he hadn't witnessed his friend's humiliation. 'I'm sorry, I didn't know about your dad.'

'You do now.'

They strode in silence, no destination in mind, simply for the sake of walking.

'What the fuck you doing here anyway?' said Klaus. 'Still wearing the uniform, I see. You're a disgrace to it and you know it. Heinrich doesn't know yet but when he does...'

'Don't tell him. Please.'

'You've been missing meetings. If you're not careful, you'll have Heinrich round.'

'He's already been.'

'You dad must've loved that. The others will tear you apart, you know that, don't you? The traitor in our midst. They'll fuckin' kill you. And so will I,' he added, shouting. Klaus pushed Felix in the chest. Felix fell back, caught his footing just in time. 'I'll fucking kill you too, because right now I fucking hate you, you know that?'

Was he crying? Felix cast his eyes down; if he was, he didn't want to see it, didn't want to embarrass his friend. 'You don't have to tell them.'

'That… that'd make me as bad as you. I've got no choice.' And with that, Klaus stormed down the street.

'Wait. Klaus, wait. I – I've brought you a present.' Klaus slowed down. Felix caught up. He offered the box.

Klaus wiped the back of his hand over his eyes. He took the box. 'What is it?' He opened it and peered inside. He raised an eyebrow. 'You're giving this to me?'

'Sure.'

'What about your dad?'

'He won't miss it.'

'*Für den Gott und Land.* For God and Country. You have to admire the craftsmanship. Thanks, Felix.' He almost smiled as he snatched it away in time. 'Listen, you tell anyone 'bout my old man, I'll kill you.'

'I won't.'

'He's not always so bad, it's…'

'I know, Klaus. I know what it's like.'

'Do you? Really?'

'Yes.'

Klaus seemed to deflate. 'I know you do, Felix. I'm sorry,

61

mate.'

'It's OK.'

'We're still mates, you and me.'

'Blood brothers.'

'Yeah.' He sniffed. 'Yeah, that's right. Blood brothers.'

The mother with the small child in the pushchair passed, rushing home, no doubt, before darkness fell. The child had his knitted giraffe clenched tightly in his podgy fist. Both boys nodded a hello.

Klaus sniffed again. 'I still have to tell Heinrich. It's my duty.'

'I know. I'll make it up to you. I promise.'

'How?'

'I... I don't know. But I will. I'll think of something.'

'You better. Before it's too late.'

Chapter 9

Felix was attempting a jigsaw puzzle. The cover depicted the Brandenburg Gate at the turn of the century with finely-dressed people riding by in horse and traps. He'd been working on it for three nights and he reckoned he was over halfway through. His mother sat knitting in an armchair opposite. Felix wasn't sure what it was she was knitting but he suspected a scarf. It usually was; jumpers were too hard for her.

It was six in the evening. Father was going out to his regimental reunion. He came down the stairs.

'You look nice,' said Klara, her needles clacking. 'Oh, I received a letter from my father today.'

'Oh yes? How is Gottfried, the old bastard?'

'Peter, please. He's not happy. He's retiring and he doesn't want to.'

'Retiring? He loves his job; he'd still be teaching till he was a hundred if he could.'

'Exactly. Most strange.'

'I saw Herr Walther today,' said Peter, standing at the

mirror, straightening his bow tie. 'A fine man. And, Felix, he's got a fine daughter. I think you should invite Ingrid round for tea soon.'

Felix muttered a 'no thanks.'

'Why on earth not? Lovely girl. You could do a lot worse than a young lady like Ingrid Walther. By the way, you're not still friends with that Beck boy, are you?'

'No.'

'Good, the little thug. Little thugs grow into big thugs, be very wary of him.' Satisfied with his bow tie, he asked, 'Klara, have you seen my Luger?'

Felix's heart plummeted.

'Isn't it in the drawer, as normal?'

'No, I looked earlier. Have you put it somewhere?'

'I've not touched it, Peter.'

Felix could hear the creep of desperation in his mother's voice.

'So you're telling me it's walked off by itself?'

Why did he want his Luger? He never wanted his Luger, had never asked for it before. So why now, for God's sake?

'L-let me have a look,' said Klara. She opened the drawer and rooted through its contents: books, papers, tea towels, a corn dolly, all hastily swept to one side.

'It's not there, I'm telling you. I've looked. You know how much that thing means to me.'

'M-maybe y-you took it upstairs? Have you looked?' she asked, her voice fading into nothing.

Felix cursed his stupidity. Why had he gone and given it to Klaus? Did he really think he'd get away with it?

'I did no such thing,' said Peter, scrunching his hat in his hand. 'I suppose it doesn't matter. I just wanted it tonight, to show… Not to worry.'

'Oh, Peter. It'll turn up. Have you taken it, *Bärchen*?'

Felix shook his head.

'Don't call the boy that stupid name. Maybe I put it somewhere; I can't remember.'

'It was me.'

His father spun round to look at him. 'What did you say?'

'I…' Felix glanced at his mother. 'I – I lent it to K-Klaus.'

'You Lent It To Klaus. I thought you said…'

'I'll g-get it back; I'll get it tomorrow.'

'Tomorrow? What use is that? I need it now. Tonight. You had no right.'

*

Peter went to his regimental reunion without his wartime Luger. He left behind a subdued wife and son and pieces of jigsaw scattered on the living room table. Klara and Felix spent most of the evening sitting in silence. Eventually, Felix went to bed. His mother stood as he left the room, an imploring look in her eye. '*Bärchen*…'

'Dad's right, Mum. Don't call me that any more.'

'Felix, you have to forgive him.'

'Why?'

'Because…' Her hands fell at her sides. 'He's worried; he's got a lot to worry about. His salary isn't enough for the three of us and this…' She waved her arms about. 'This huge house. But things may get better, *Bärchen*. Your father's got an interview, this week sometime. If he gets it, it'd be more responsibility, but more money. A lot more.'

Felix shrugged as if it didn't mean anything to him. 'Does he think he'll get it?'

'He's got a lot of experience, he could do the job, he's no doubt. But…'

65

'But?'

'He's not a party member and he knows that'll count against him.'

'And so it should.'

Later, Felix lay in his bed, waiting for sleep to come, knowing it wouldn't, his heart pumping with resentment. He tried to rationalize it, tried to understand it. His father had once been a good man, so 'kind and always so considerate'. The war had done this to him, had embittered him, had changed him. Felix was too young to understand what war could do to a man. But enough was enough. Something had to change. His mother couldn't do anything, he saw that now. It was down to him to do something before it was too late, before his father got himself arrested and sent off to Oranienburg. Or all of them.

Chapter 10

Felix jumped on a tram and made his way to the local HJ headquarters where Heinrich, as a full-time leader, spent his working day. He'd put on his uniform, thinking it best. The building in Haydnstraße was a half-timbered structure with a low, sloping tiled roof. Nearby stood a statue of some sixteenth-century Protestant theologian. A bunch of boys in HJ uniforms leant against it, sharing a cigarette. Swastika flags hung from every first floor window. Pine bushes flanked the main entrance. Felix entered the building and, having asked for Heinrich Richter at reception, was shown through to a large, high-ceilinged room. The place was bustling with several HJ leaders at work. A poster on the wall stated Jesus had "kicked the bucket" but the Hitler Youth marched on. The receptionist called out Heinrich's name. Heinrich looked up from his desk. Felix, standing there, clasped his hands and bowed his head.

'Well, well, look what the cat's dragged in,' said Heinrich, approaching. 'Come to explain your absence, have we, Stoltenberg?'

'I'm sorry, sir.'

'Well?' he said, his eyebrows raised. 'I've had words with your father. But we both know that, don't we? Between you and me, I don't reckon he likes me much. But who cares? It's not important. We know what's important. So, had a bit of a sniffle, did we? I trust, young Stoltenberg, we feel better now?'

'Sir, that questionnaire we did.'

'What about it?'

'Sir, w-with your permission, I'd like to do it again.'

Heinrich stared at him as if he didn't understand. 'I've already filed them. Yours was all right, if memory serves. You want to do it again?'

'Sir.'

Heinrich glanced left and right. Leaning in, he said quietly, 'Are you sure about this, Felix? I wouldn't want…' He waited a moment while a couple of his comrades passed, one slapping him on the back.

'Yes, sir. I'm sure.'

Heinrich seemed to deflate. 'OK. Wait…' He seemed lost for words for a moment. 'Wait here then.'

And Felix did wait, aware of the hubbub of noise, of people working, laughing, the quiet efficiency of Hitler's office workers, his future leaders hard at work. He wiped his forehead with a handkerchief. He still had time, time to change his mind, to apologise and leave. He'd look foolish, for sure, but if need be, he could say he'd made a mistake. It was hot inside the office. He pulled at his collar. Why had Heinrich used his first name? It didn't seem right somehow. Heinrich returned, the sheet of paper in his hand. 'You can still change your mind, Felix.'

Felix stared at him. His first name again. Was Heinrich trying to tell him something? He shook his head.

'As you wish. Do you want to sit at a desk for a minute?'

Felix nodded.

He sat down at a desk cluttered with paperwork and pens and sighed. Heinrich returned to his desk.

Question 1: Do your father and mother support the National Socialists? If "no", please explain. He glanced round the office, at all these fine-looking individuals and their self-confidence. How he envied them: to know your place in the world, to have the support of your friends and peers, to have the support of the nation, of the Führer. This is where he wanted to be, not cowering at home with his mother, fearful that Father's views could get them arrested and shipped off to a camp. He crossed out his 'yes' and in large letters wrote 'No'. He held his breath. He'd done it, he'd made his mark. *My father*, he wrote, *does not support the National Socialists because…* The words came easy, sentence after sentence, each one more damning than the preceding one.

Question 2: Have you ever heard your father criticise the Führer or the National Socialists? If so, how? Question 3; Question 4… He now wrote in minuscule letters, trying to fit it all in, this list of his father's heretical thoughts and traitorous deeds.

Then, finally, his hand aching, he placed the pen on the table. He'd finished.

He handed Heinrich the amended questionnaire. Heinrich cast his eyes over Felix's answers, his eyebrows rising. He looked at Felix with something bordering between disappointment and incomprehension. 'OK,' he said slowly. 'So this is what you wanted to see me about.'

Felix couldn't speak.

'Didn't think you had it in you, Stoltenberg.'

'Nor did I.'

'What was that?'

'I said I'm only doing my duty, sir.'

'So I see.' He rubbed his eyes. 'So I see,' he repeated.

'I have to do my duty, don't I, sir?'

It took a while for Heinrich to answer. Then, as if snapping out of a trance, he said yes. 'I trust we'll see you at tomorrow's meeting?'

Felix nodded. 'Sir, you said to Hans nothing would happen to his parents if he worked on them.'

Heinrich blinked several times. 'Why yes, that's right. S-so why you doing this if you're so worried?'

'I... I don't know.' It was true; he really wasn't sure – to get back at his father; to prove his loyalty? Yes, both, but he didn't want it to get out of hand.

Heinrich sighed. 'I saw the lack of portrait in your house; I heard your father's lack of patriotism for myself. You've got a mountain to climb there, Stoltenberg. Think you're up to it?'

*

Felix dreaded walking into the municipal hall, seeing all his comrades, dreaded seeing Klaus. He stopped at the door and took a deep breath. And it was Klaus he saw first on entering, at the centre of a group of boys, entertaining them, no doubt, with one of his tales. As soon as he saw Felix, his eyes dropped. 'Hey, it's Felix,' one of the other boys called out.

The boys erupted with cheers and a round of applause. Felix turned red.

Someone slapped him on the back. 'Been poorly, I hear.'

'I'm all right now.'

The boys took their places. Felix approached his friend. 'You all right, Klaus?' he asked quietly.

'Yeah.' Klaus flushed, showing a flicker of a smile. 'Yeah, sure. I, er... I showed my old man that pistol. He was

70

impressed.'

'Was he?'

Klaus shrugged. 'Almost.'

The door opened. Heinrich bustled in. 'Ah, Stoltenberg, good of you to join us.' he said. 'How goes it?'

'Very well, sir.'

The boys took their seats at the long wooden table. Heinrich paced at the front, his hands behind his back. 'Before we start,' he said, 'I'd liked to welcome our comrade Felix back to the fold. I trust, Stoltenberg, you feel better now. You've been missed.'

'Yes, sir; thank you, sir.' *You've been missed.* Had Heinrich meant that? Had they really missed him? A little shiver of satisfaction crept up his spine.

'Felix here is a brave man. He has put the interests of our Führer ahead of kin. Now, that's what we call loyalty. I applaud you, Stoltenberg. Well done.'

Felix glanced round, saw that every face was looking at him with smiles and admiration. 'Thank you, sir.' This, he thought, was acceptance; what he'd always wanted.

Tonight was collection night. Heinrich handed out the collection boxes and took the boys out collecting for the regime, obliging passers-by to relieve themselves of their change and contribute. No one refused. No one dared. The boys worked in pairs, competing to see who could get the most money. Felix was paired up with Hans – little, meek Hans – the red-haired boy who had also criticised his parents via the questionnaire. After an hour, Felix and his comrades returned to the hall, satisfied with their evening's work, their collection boxes rattling with coins. Who'd got the most? Who'd won this week?

Felix felt a tug on his sleeve. It was Hans pulling him back.

'What's up? You all right, Hans?'

Hans glanced round, as if making sure they were out of earshot of the others. 'Did you really shop your parents?'

'My old man. What about it?'

'You know Heinrich said nothing would happen to my parents?'

'Yes. It's up to us to –'

'They came for my father two nights ago. The Gestapo. They arrested him. They took him away.'

Felix stopped. 'What did you say?'

'You heard.'

'But Heinrich… He said, didn't he?'

'He was lying.'

The bile rose in his throat. He caught sight of his reflection in Hans' glasses. The boys ahead burst into song, singing the 'Horst Wessel Song' at the top of their voices as they made their way back to the hall, shaking their coin boxes in time. 'It's just a coincidence,' he said, aware of the tremble in his voice.

'You think so?' Hans shook his head. 'I was duped. You will be too.'

*

Felix returned home, his feet heavy on the pavement and his heart heavy in his chest, impervious to the cold wind whistling through his coat. Hans' words echoed through his mind. He liked Heinrich; he couldn't believe he would deceive them so. But what if Hans was right? What if he did pass on the questionnaires straight to the Gestapo? Back at home, he was greeted by an unusually jovial father, the pleasant smell of dinner and a dining table laden with food: a roast chicken, platters of vegetables, cinnamon bread. 'Have a drink,' said

Peter, pouring him a glass of red wine.

Klara pulled a face.

'Why not? He's old enough now,' said Peter handing Felix his glass. 'Aren't you, boy?'

'It's our anniversary,' said Klara with a smile. 'And...' She motioned towards her husband.

'And... I've just received a promotion. I'm not even a party member but they liked me so much, they overlooked that little inconvenience. Lucky me, eh? You're now looking at a senior sales director.' He waited for a response. 'Well? Aren't you going to say something?'

'Yes, sorry. Con-congratulations, Papa.' He took a sip of wine and tried not to grimace as its sickly warmth slipped down his throat; he tried not to cough.

'Come, let's sit,' said Klara.

And so on the one evening Felix needed to hate his father, Peter had transformed into a changed man right before his eyes, his cheeks flushed, an occasional affectionate pat of Felix's arm. It was strange how one can hate a tyrant and love him too. It wasn't his fault, he tried to remember this; the war had done it to him.

His mother served Felix a huge portion. Felix stared down at his plate and had to fight his nauseousness. He felt as if he'd walked into someone else's house, someone else's life.

His parents ate heartily, reminiscing about the day in 1915 when they met, about the awful but inevitable day a year later when Peter received his call-up papers. 'So,' said Klara, turning to Felix, 'we decided to get married.'

Peter laughed. 'Yes, I didn't want some wretched gadfly stealing my girl while I was away.'

'As if, Peter. Are you OK, Felix? Not hungry?'

Peter drained his glass. 'Look, Felix...' He hesitated, as if

73

trying to find the words.

Felix took his chance. 'I tried to get your pistol back, Papa, but I couldn't. I'm sorry.'

'It doesn't matter.'

'But... but you said –'

'It's just an old pistol. Trying to impress your friend, were you? I can always buy another, cheap as anything.'

'Felix, why aren't you eating? I thought...'

Peter interrupted. 'Look, what I'm trying to say is I know I've been a bit short with you, both of you. Sometimes you drive me to it. But I admit, I was struggling, financially. I thought we'd have to sell up, move to somewhere smaller, cheaper. But now, with this promotion, it's a huge salary increase. And what with today, being our anniversary, it's made me see things in a new light. Some of the boys I met at the reunion, well, let's say it made me count my blessings. There's many of them far worse off than me. The war...' He tapped his temple. 'It affected us all, but some of them, they don't have jobs, their wives have run off, all sorts of misfortunes.'

Felix laid down his knife and fork. 'I'm sorry, I don't feel well.' He coughed. 'Must be the wine.'

His mother reached out her hand. 'Felix?'

'If you'll excuse me.'

'What's the matter, boy? Where do you think you're going? Come back here this minute...'

But Felix wasn't prepared to obey. Not now. His father could shout and rant as much as he wanted; he had to leave. He heard his mother's soothing voice. 'Leave him, Peter. He doesn't look well. Something's ailing him.'

'Hmm. Got knocked back by Ingrid, perhaps.'

Felix lay on his bed, watching the minutes tick by on his

illuminated bedside clock. He could hear his mother downstairs clearing up, could imagine his father sitting in his armchair, puffing on his pipe, a contented grin on his face. He knew how the Gestapo worked, had heard about it often enough. They'd knock on the door in the middle of the night, stuff you in a car and whisk you away, no questions asked. He told himself his father hadn't really changed, it was simply the euphoria of the new job. Once the novelty had worn off, once his bosses realised he wasn't up to it, he'd revert back to his old self. A leopard doesn't change its spots, not that quickly.

It was almost midnight. He heard his parents go to bed, giggling as they came up the stairs. Felix tried to slow down his breathing.

He may have fallen asleep but then woke with a start. The clock now showed two in the morning. He heard the sound of a car slowing up, heard it come to a stop. His heartbeat quickened as he gripped his blanket. Doors opened and slammed shut. Footsteps sounded on the wet pavement outside. He held his breath, waited for the knock, listened out for the sound. Instead, the footsteps faded into the distance. He swallowed and realised just how hot he felt. Outside, it had started to rain again, the gentle *pitter patter* against his window. But the Gestapo didn't knock on their door that night.

Chapter 11

A week passed. Nothing happened. But the worry remained a constant, nagging at Felix at every turn, needling his every thought. Every night, he lay in his bed, fretting, unable to sleep. After a week, he began to hope. Surely, if they were to come, they would have done so by now. And surely, he thought, they had bigger fish to chase after; people who actively and vocally expressed their hatred of Hitler. Not someone like his father who ranted only within the privacy of his home, give or take the odd election. He attended a couple more HJ meetings where his comrades greeted him warmly, sometimes, Felix thought, with a degree of awe. Where once, recently, he would have enjoyed such attention, now it made him feel sullied. Only Hans looked at him sideways. Felix noticed Hans never said anything now, never contributed. His 'Heil Hitlers' were noticeably less enthusiastic.

His father, having started his new job, would come home exhausted but content. Klara cooked, made sure the house was tidy and that Peter had his slippers to come home to. They even talked about employing a new maid; they could afford it again now. Klara would speak to the Frau Walther, see if she knew of anyone. The image of Ingrid flashed through Felix's mind.

Felix agonised over whether he should say anything to warn his father of what he'd done. But the words, he knew, would never come. And anyway, what could his father do? He had nowhere to go, no place to escape to. Only his grandfather's place, and his grandfather had become even more of a Nazi, memorising Hitler's phrases, pouring scorn on the British and the French, hating the Jews. On a recent visit, Gottfried had complained bitterly about his Jewish neighbours, out in his small village. 'It's a blatant insult,' he'd said, 'to expect me, a loyal German patriot, to have to live cheek-by-jowl with a Jewish family.'

'Come on, Gottfried,' said Peter. 'Is it that bad?'

'Yes, absolutely. It's intolerable to have to look out my window and see those filthy Jewish kids playing in their garden. It turns my stomach. I'm telling you, Peter, it's making me quite ill.'

And so, Felix said nothing and just hoped.

And then they did come.

The first Felix was aware of it was the loud rap on the front door, of the doorbell ringing incessantly. He sat bolt upright in his bed, the sweat pouring down his back. He heard his father's footsteps, crossing the landing, going down the stairs. 'OK, OK, just coming.' Felix could hear the tremble beneath the words. His clock showed half past four.

He opened his bedroom door to see his mother gliding down the stairs, tightening her dressing gown. Peter had switched on the hall light and was about to unlock the door. Before doing so, he glanced back at his wife. The colour had gone from his face. It was like seeing a ghost down there. He opened the door. The hallway seemed filled with them. Three men, identical in their long coats and their hats and scarves. 'Peter Stoltenberg?' said one, thin lipped, a vivid scar near his right ear, eyes cold and hard. He stepped forward, a metal identity badge in his hand.

Peter nodded.

'Major Riegel of the Gestapo, Berlin East division. You're to come with us; you're under arrest.'

Klara's legs gave way. She gripped on to the banister for support.

Peter gasped. 'Arrest? W-what for?'

'You'll find out presently.'

Felix rushed downstairs.

'Go back to bed, Felix,' snapped his father.

'It's my fault.'

'I demand to know what this is about.'

'Demand all you want. You're coming with us. You have two minutes to get dressed. And you,' said the Gestapo man, pointing at Klara. 'Pack him a small case. Essential and warm clothing only.' The man's authority diminished them all, it filled the house.

The three Stoltenbergs stood stock still, staring open-mouthed at the three men in coats. The seconds seemed to tick by.

'Go on then,' shouted Riegel. 'Two minutes. Now!'

It was Klara who reacted first. 'Come, Peter. You must get dressed. Hurry now.' She took his hand and almost dragged him back up the stairs. Riegel clicked his fingers and his two henchmen disappeared into different rooms downstairs, leaving Felix alone with Major Riegel.

'It was my fault,' said Felix a second time.

'What?'

'But I didn't mean it.' He could feel his eyes watering.

The man put his hands in his pockets. 'I don't know what you're talking about.'

'What I wrote, it wasn't true.'

'Shut up, will you.'

He tried to hold the man's gaze; shuddered at the coldness he saw within. 'Please don't take him.'

'Fuck off, kid.'

Felix stepped back; the intensity of the man's words winded him. The man terrified him. The two henchmen continued their search, now traipsing upstairs, one of them entering Felix's bedroom. Riegel glanced at his watch. 'Hurry up,' he shouted. 'I haven't got all night.'

Felix turned on hearing his father's familiar footsteps on the stairs, his mother following, a small suitcase in her hand. Peter hooked his coat off the coat stand. He turned and gave his wife a hug, whispered in her ear. She nodded while wiping away her tears. He took the suitcase from her. The two men came back down the stairs, both shaking their heads – they'd not found a thing.

'Don't matter,' said Riegel. 'Right, let's go. Come on.'

The two men hooked their hands beneath Peter's arms, pushing him out of the door. And that was it; the door slammed shut and they were gone.

Klara and Felix stood, staring at the door as if expecting Peter to come right back in, the silence of the house pressing down on them. *I will not be bossed around in my own home.* Isn't that what his father had said once? Felix heard the sound of the car revving up, and driving away, away into the dark night to God knows where and God knows what. In his side vision, Felix saw his mother grip her hair and realised she was shaking, huge convulsions that racked her whole frame. Doubling over, she reached out for the stairs and sat on the bottom but one step, her head in her hands.

'Mama?'

She looked up, gasping for breath, her eyes clenched shut, her whole face a mess of tears and snot. He didn't know what to do, what to say. Felix remained standing, not wanting to look at her, his arms hanging limp at his sides, his stomach empty. And all he could think was, that in his leaving, his father never looked at him; never said goodbye.

It was almost as if he knew.

Chapter 12

Those first few days following his father's arrest had been the darkest Felix had known. He'd wake up to the sound of his mother crying in her bedroom, sometimes gulping for air as she struggled with her tears. She rarely got dressed, instead trudged round in her dressing gown and slippers as if a heavy weight, like a ball and chain, inhibited her progress. She didn't go out. Her skin seemed tinged with yellow, thin as a sheet of parchment. She said nothing, wanted nothing from her son. Occasionally, he'd ask if she was OK, if there was anything he could do, and she'd stare at him, her head tilted to one side, as if she'd forgotten who he was or as if he was speaking in a foreign tongue. On the whole, though, he tried to avoid her, feeling ill-equipped to deal with her distress. He hid away in his bedroom or went out.

There were moments when the guilt threatened to crush him. If only he hadn't believed Heinrich, if only he hadn't been so drawn to Klaus Beck, if only he hadn't been so desperate to belong, if only... if only. Oftentimes, he tried to rationalise it – it was bound to happen, almost inevitable given his father's antagonism towards the regime. He'd known of the risks, yet he maintained his solitary protest. Had he given voice to his opinions at work, with his friends, at his regimental reunion? He liked to show off, his father, Felix saw that now; confident of himself, confident of a sympathetic if not appreciative audience. He was always going to push it too far, like taunting a tiger, there was only ever going to be one winner.

Meanwhile, Felix learnt to scramble an egg, to boil an egg, to heat up beans, fry a sauerkraut. His mother refused to eat and he hardly dare ask her to cook. Then, on perhaps the fourth day, perhaps the fifth, it struck Felix that his mother hadn't gone out to find out about her husband. They had no idea where he was, what was happening to him, how long he'd be away. It was at the same time, Klara finally got dressed, even applied a little make-up and smiled. It was almost as if she didn't care – no, that was too strong. But whatever it was, Felix couldn't fathom it out. The emotion, the outpouring of grief, stopped as abruptly as a full stop at the end of the sentence. He couldn't put his finger on it but there was something rather unseemly about it, this discarding of the stricken persona, the shredding of skin.

But what are we going to do, he wondered? They needed money, a wage earner in the family. But Klara waved his concerns away; they'd be fine, they had some savings to keep them going, she said. He didn't believe her; how would she know? Still, worse comes to worst, she said with a wave of her hand, they could always sell the house and live somewhere a little more 'modest'. This house, it was far too big for them. Felix wondered how she defined 'them': the three of them, or just the two?

Felix still attended his thrice-weekly HJ meetings; he had no desire to but knew he couldn't not attend. He had a reputation now; the other boys, especially the newer, younger ones, looked up to him. He'd done something extraordinary in their eyes, had truly proved himself worthy of the cause. And once there, he rather enjoyed it, enjoyed the attention and muted admiration. He always walked back with Klaus. They talked of how much they hated the British and the French, and, behind cupped hands, repeated jokes about fat Goring, the half-blind Himmler, the club-footed Goebbels. But never Hitler. Oh, no, the man was a living god, and you never mock the Führer. They talked lewdly about girls, about the pretty ones, about the ones they fancied, about the ones rumoured to have done 'it'.

And then, one day, his father was back. There was no announcement, no fanfare. He just arrived. By himself. Unescorted. He'd let himself in, he must have kept his key all along. How long he stood in his coat in the hallway, clutching his hat, silently taking everything in, Felix didn't know. Did he hear his wife up in their bedroom humming to herself, did he sense anything had changed at home? It was Felix, bounding down the stairs, on his way out in his HJ uniform, who first saw him and let rip with an involuntary 'FUCK!' The two of them stared at each other and, for a moment, standing on the bottom step, Felix thought it was a stranger standing there, a stinking, unshaven man with a sharp, pointed nose, hollowed-out cheeks, invisible lips and thinning, white hair. And then his father spoke. 'Hello, son.' His voice. Felix hadn't realised how much he'd missed it, the sound of his father's familiar, reassuring voice. It'd lost much of its strength, was imbued with an ingrained sadness, but it was still unmistakably his father's voice. And when Felix opened his mouth and tried to say 'hello' in return, he couldn't; the word remained stuck behind an abrupt cascade of tears.

Felix's father said almost nothing during his first few days back. He angled his armchair in the living room to face the window and sat there for hours at a time simply staring out onto the street as if he were expecting someone. He read the sports pages of the newspapers but certainly not the news, which was full of Hitler and his unending achievements and the nation's grievances, which seemed to be many. He picked at his food and drank small glasses of beer. Once, Klara ventured to ask what had happened to him. He couldn't say, he said. He'd taken an oath. Klara washed his clothes, and afterwards, he insisted they'd be folded and put back in his suitcase, which he then kept next to the hat stand – just in case.

On his first day back, Peter declared he needed a bath and a shave. He certainly needed it, thought Felix. The smell was starting to pervade into every corner of the house. Klara helped him. He stayed in the bath for over half an hour. When, finally, he decided to get out, he couldn't manage it, even with Klara's help. They called Felix. Felix braced himself. The water was a horrible murky brown colour. His father sat with his knees up. 'You take one arm,' Klara said to Felix. 'I'll take the other.'

Felix nodded. This was not something to relish.

'Ready? One, two, heave...'

Peter clenched the side of the bath while Felix gripped his arm below the armpit. Between them, they got him to his feet.

'Let me get you a towel,' said Klara.

Felix caught sight of his father's penis, the mass of grey pubic hair, and shuddered. Now, with a towel around his waist, Peter stepped out of the bath. How thin he looked, so fragile.

'Thank you,' he said.

'How about that shave now?' said Klara. 'And then we'll get some ointment for your back.'

'Yes.' He turned to face the washbasin and it was then that Felix saw his father's back. He gasped; his knees gave way. Peter's back was lined left to right, top to bottom, with livid red scars. His mother shook her head at him, as if to say, 'Don't say anything.' What had they done to him, he wondered? What pain he must have endured.

One morning, Felix awoke to hear the sound of someone playing the piano, a gentle lilting tune. He came downstairs to find that it was his father, his eyes half closed, stooped over the keyboard. He remembered his mother said his father used to play. His hands glided effortlessly over the notes. Felix was impressed. If only he played more often. Later, Klara told him Peter was playing Schubert's *Winterreise*. He'd never heard the piano played before. He never heard it again. But whenever he heard *Winterreise*, he would always visulise his father playing it on this mournful morning.

Three weeks later, they came for him again. This time, they came in the morning. This time, it was someone different, a politer man, but the end result was the same – they took Felix's father away. Klara cried and begged them not to take him, that he was too weak. Peter said nothing, merely took his coat and his small suitcase. It was almost as if he'd been expecting it and had resigned himself to his fate.

This time at least, Klara went to the local Gestapo headquarters to find out where they'd taken him. They'd taken him to the recently-opened concentration camp at Oranienburg, thirty kilometres north of Berlin. They never saw him again.

Two weeks later, Klara received a letter from the camp authorities. Felix was upstairs, getting dressed into a pair of shorts and T-shirt. It was a beautiful day and he was about to meet up with Klaus and friends for a game of football in the local park. The sudden sound of his mother's howling ripped through the house. Felix raced downstairs to find Klara in the living room, her face in her hands, her body racked with sobbing. 'Mama, what's…' But he knew. The letter lay on the floor in front of her. He knelt down and picked it up, his fingers trembling. "For your information…" Peter Stoltenberg, aged forty-three, had been shot "while trying to escape". While trying to escape. Felix repeated the words again and again. He went to the cupboard under the stairs, fished out his football boots and left, quietly closing the front door behind him.

Stepping outside, he heard his name. He turned to see Ingrid trotting up the street towards him, her coat flapping open. 'Hello, Felix. Long time no see. How are you?'

He stared at her, unable to speak.

'Off to play football?' she asked.

'Maybe.'

'I, er, I wanted to ask… Would you, I mean, my dad said… Would you care to come round one day, tea perhaps…'

'What?' The idea appealed yet the words came out wrong. 'No. God, no. Too, too busy.'

She almost fell back, rubbed her scar on her chin. 'Oh, yes, of course. Silly idea. I'm sorry. You… you all right? You look…'

'What?' he snapped. 'I look what?'

'I… I don't know. How's your grandfather?'

'Don't know. Don't care.'

'Have I… Have I said something wrong?'

'Oh, shut up, Ingrid. Just leave me alone, will you?'

She stared at him, her eyes clouded by hurt, by confusion.

He pushed past her, stormed down the road. She hadn't deserved that; she was nice really, but he didn't care. He really didn't care.

He stood at the entrance of the park, the sun on his back. Two women passed, one pushing a pram, both talking at once. A doddery man in an ankle-length coat shuffled by, leading a dog, a corgi, who, in dog years, seemed even older. His father was dead. Dead. 'While trying to escape'. But it made no sense, it didn't register. It was as if he'd been anaesthetised somehow. He could see his friends in the middle of the park, kicking a ball round at each other on the lush green, their shadows dancing behind them. He loved his father. Despite everything, he loved him. But it was too late now. He'd never see him again.

That didn't seem possible. Surely, he'd be at home when he returned from football, sitting in his armchair with the paper and his pipe. How could he not be? His father had paid a heavy price for not believing. He, Felix, would not make the same mistake. He did believe. Germany was changing; it was for them to follow Hitler's lead. The future belonged to us, he thought, the youth, the strong, the loyal. It belonged to him. He was part of it now, truly part of it. He glanced over his shoulder, down the road he'd just come along.

He heard his name. Turning back, he saw Klaus waving at him from the middle of the park. 'Oi, Felix! Don't just stand there, you idiot,' he yelled. 'We're waiting for you, mate.'

Felix smiled. He waved back. 'Just coming.' Then, under his breath, he added, 'Heil Hitler. Heil fucking Hitler.'

PART TWO

Chapter 13

Berlin, September 1942

Felix and former captain Rudolph Karstadt have been in this cell for a couple of days now. There is no day or night here, no passing of time. Just a bright light bulb screwed into the ceiling and four blank walls made up of breeze blocks. Not knowing the time, not even having a sense of it, is difficult. Felix is disorientated by it. The grill on the door remains permanently shut. He is cold, they both are, constantly cold. There is no escape from it. The blanket offers nothing in the way of warmth. He is tired but it's usually too cold to sleep.

Whenever they hear footsteps outside in the corridor, their attention picks up; their nerves stretch. They watch the door, frightened lest it should open, lest they should be summoned... summoned to their deaths. Once a day, the cell door opens, and an elderly orderly will hand them each a metal tray of food, indeterminate in its nature, and a beaker of water.

A corporal with a bulbous nose and a Führer-type moustache stands guard at the door, his rifle visible, just in case the prisoners are foolish enough to try something. They've seen him before and they've taken to calling him Corporal Bulbous. The orderly is old, shuffles with a hunch. He looks like a man that hasn't seen sunlight for a long time. Once someone came and emptied their stinking bucket. No one ever spoke to them despite Rudolph's best efforts to engage them in light conversation. Each time, the relief floods through Felix: *it's just the orderly, it's not my executioner*, he thinks, *not this time at least*.

They have become invisible, stripped of their insignia and rank, stripped of their dignity, branded traitors. It doesn't matter. What does matter, thinks Felix, is trying to come to terms with what he is now. For so long, he'd been enthralled by the regime, convinced it was on the side of God. For so long, he'd been determined to play his part, to further its cause – because its cause and his cause were one of the same. And now, at long last, he knows the truth. But truth brings him no joy, no redemption. He has no one to share the truth with, apart from a disgraced homosexual captain, a soldier who once looked at joining the priesthood.

He is as alone now as when he was a boy, living in the house shrouded inside and out by mists of fear. His father had been right about the regime, time had justified his hatred of it. The thought brings no consolation. His father had also been right about Klaus Beck. It must have been hard for a forty-three year-old man to be cowed by a boy not yet out of his teenage years, but that was the power of Hitler's uniform. Klaus Beck had the authority of the state to back him up. He knew it, and so did Felix's father.

Rudolph Karstadt, true to his word, has been a good listener. But Felix is not sure he wants to continue. There is still so much to tell, to confess, and he's not convinced he has the strength for it. He closes his eyes and tries to hide his expression behind his hand. Rudolph stands, paces the length of the cell and stretches.

'Are you OK, Felix?' he asks.

'Yeah. Yeah, I guess so.'

He leans back against the wall, contemplates the bucket perilously full of their excrement. 'Must've been difficult.'

'Yes, the cancer spread.' He pulls on his beard.

'That's right, that's what it was, and...' He pauses. 'And it still is.'

'After Dad's death, people in the street spat at my mother, called her names, names that pierced her. The kinder ones simply ignored her.'

'Christ, that's even worse than a man who happens to love another man.'

'I guess so. Then we received another visit from the Gestapo. They wanted our house. Our home was to be requisitioned for a *loyal* German family. Twenty-four hours later, we found ourselves rehoused in a tiny, dirty apartment that once belonged to a Jewish couple before they, also, had been "moved on".'

'You had to grow up quickly.'

'Yes, I lived under a camouflage. I put party ahead of family; my mother, thank God, never knew. And you know, I almost believed it. I went through a few years when I was able to separate my home life from what I thought was my real life. I *was* loyal, I *was* a good National Socialist. When we invaded Poland, I cheered. I got drunk that night.'

'Lucky for you. I was there. I was a soldier, but, I admit, I enjoyed it. I was doing what I'd been trained to do. Then I heard about the killing squads right behind us, the

Einsatzgruppen. I pretended not to know that they entered the villages we'd secured, and shot the Jews, the communists, the intellectuals. I closed my ears to that, pretended not to know. We all did.'

'Yes. We all did.'

'Fighting was a good place to hide. I had a lot to hide. I'm considered an abomination. So, I had to hide. And where's the best place to hide? In plain sight, of course. So, I joined the party, became a soldier for Hitler. It almost worked; I got away with it for years. After Poland, I saw action in Belgium and France. Was made a captain, earned an Iron Cross, second class. I am a soldier of distinction. I began to believe it after a while. I was like you, Felix, enthralled by the regime. I was married for a while. Lovely woman, beautiful, educated. But, alas for me, she also loved sex. I'd get back on leave and she'd want it every bloody night. Exhausting for any man but even more so when… you know. I couldn't wait to go back to action. I found killing easier than fucking. Then, one day back home, this is about nine months ago, I met a man and… well, I fell in love. He was a fair bit younger than me. I'm forty-three now –'

'Forty-three? My father was…'

'Yes?'

'It doesn't matter.'

'And he was about your age, I guess. I knew my luck wouldn't hold, that I'd be found out one day.' He squeezes the bridge of his nose. 'And that's exactly what happened. You know in the camps, men like me have to wear a pink triangle.'

'I know.'

'A few years ago, the triangle had the letter "A" on it, meaning *Arschficker*, ass fucker.'

That, he didn't know. The image of Klaus Beck pops into

his mind. He pushes it away.

Rudolph sits again. 'Do you want to tell me the rest of your story?'

'No.'

'But you have to; I don't think you have a choice.'

Felix puffs out his cheeks. 'Maybe you're right. I have no choice.'

Chapter 14

Four years earlier: Berlin, October 1938

Felix Stoltenberg considered the rows of twelve-year-olds sitting in front of him, saw their expectant faces. His stomach churned. As a part-time member of Hitler's SA, he had fought communist thugs on the streets of the capital, had withstood the bullying tactics of his SA commanders and squared up to older, tougher recruits. But this was something entirely different and, frankly, far more intimidating. Twenty-five pairs of eyes focussed on him. Most of the boys wore their Hitler Youth uniforms, and the girls, their Maidens uniforms. He'd been told the ones not in uniform were the Jewish kids, soon due to be expelled, although they weren't to know yet.

Sitting in the corner of the classroom at the back was Herr Fromm, his assessor, his eyes magnified by his thick glasses, poised with pen and paper, ready to mark Felix's performance and his every word. Felix's remit for this, one of his first classes as a twenty-two-year-old trainee teacher, was to illustrate the difference between Aryans and Jews. Herr Fromm, with his swastika pin on his lapel, was a passionate

Nazi. Felix knew he was being tested not only on his teaching skills but on his dedication to the National Socialist cause. He turned to the blackboard and wiped away the faded but still visible writing from the previous day's lesson. 'G-good morning, class.' He swallowed. 'My... my name is Herr Stoltenberg.' He wrote his name on the blackboard.

He'd been told that this class were a decent lot, attentive and keen to learn. That was good. But it meant that if here, he failed to impress Fromm, what hope did he have as a teacher? His previous classes had not gone well. The kids had fed off his nervousness and run roughshod over him. So now it was vital he stamped his authority or at least get the kids on his side. Fromm hadn't said it, but Felix knew he was living on borrowed time. He needed to impress Fromm, to show that Germany's youth could be entrusted to his care.

'Good morning, Herr Stoltenberg,' came the slow, uniform reply.

So far so good, he thought. But why was it so hot in here? Glancing out of the window, he saw the church spire, its slate roof reflecting the sun. He loved this school. It had been founded in 1786, the year Frederick II died, the greatest of all German kings. Its history seeped from its very fabric and its walls, infusing the whole school with a warm, musty fragrance. Gottfried, his grandfather, had been a teacher, a headmaster of supposedly fine repute. Teaching was in his blood, surely. So why, he wondered, did he feel so ill at ease.

'Right. So, yes... Now, as I'm sure you're aware, we hear a lot in the news today about the Jews and their malign influence upon our nation.' He hooked his thumbs into the sides of his waistcoat, hoping it made him look more authoritative. He paced up and down, stopping occasionally to look out the window. 'Now, it worries me sometimes the young may not fully appreciate what the fuss is all about. After all, aren't we all, essentially, the same, you ask. We all have a brain, a heart, two legs, two arms, well, most of us.' He waited for a laugh that never came. He glanced up at Fromm, with his ill-fitting suit and the oversized knot in his tie, who was already scribbling notes on his pad.

'Charlotte's grandad only got one arm, sir,' said a bespectacled boy pointing at a girl next to him.

'Is that so? Is this true?'

The girl, Charlotte, one of the Jewish kids, answered in the affirmative. The poor girl trembled like a frightened rabbit, her cheeks flushed red. From the corner of his eye, he could see Fromm watching him with his huge eyes.

'And how did he lose his arm? Got it chopped off maybe while stealing money from good, honest Germans?' His jibe struck her like a fist. He caught a glimpse of Fromm writing something down and managed to stop himself from apologising to the girl.

'No, sir. He lost it in the war.'

Felix was immediately impressed but managed to huff. 'Did he indeed? What a hero. So, what was I saying? Yes, we are all essentially the same – but are we? Are we really? I think we all know the answer to that. We are all moulded by our history, and the history of the Jew is one of perfidy and deceit.' He cast his eyes over the assembled children. He had to find someone who wouldn't give him gyp, who wouldn't show him up in front of the assessor. His eyes settled on a rake of a girl with bright blue eyes, an intelligent-looking girl with long braids. Her name, she said, was Hannah.

'Could you come up to the front, please, Hannah?'

Obediently but slowly, she made her way to the front.

'Come on, come on, girl, stop dragging your feet. Stand

here,' he said, taking her by the arm and placing her in front of the blackboard. The girl stood, arms at her side, feet together, back straight, head up, looking straight ahead. Picking up his cane from his desk, Felix waved it vaguely at her. 'Now, Hannah here is a good Aryan specimen.'

'Why, thank you, sir.'

'Pleasure,' he said, not sure whether she was playing with him. Pulling on his lapels, he cleared his throat and continued. 'Please observe, class, the fine bone structure. Hold your chin up, girl. Her features, typical of an Aryan, are quite symmetrical, nothing too big or out of place. She stands straight like a proper Aryan person should, she's good and tall, and her legs aren't bowed. Now please note, class, Hannah's got good eyesight, her lips aren't too fat, her nose not too big. Hannah is the sort of girl this country needs, a future mother of many children, a servant to the Führer. OK, Hannah, you can sit down now. Thank you.'

Hannah did so, a swagger in her step, a supercilious smile on her lips.

'Right,' said Felix. He pointed his cane at the girl called Charlotte and immediately wished he'd picked on someone else. Too late now. 'Up here, please, Charlotte.'

Charlotte blanched, glancing left and right as if someone might help her out. In her anxiety, she dropped her pencil. A boy, a large lad sitting at the adjoining desk, leant down to pick it up as it rolled towards him.

Felix saw Fromm shake his head. 'Stop, boy!' shouted Felix. 'Let the Jew pick up her own pencil.' Fromm smiled to himself and scribbled something down.

The fat boy straightened, a look of embarrassment on his face. 'Sorry,' he mouthed at her.

The whack of the cane on his desk made the boy jump,

made most of them jump. Watching Charlotte, they hadn't seen Felix glide across the room. 'Don't you apologise to a Jew, young man.'

The boy slumped further in his chair while Fromm made another note. He was liking this.

Felix continued. 'Never. Apologise. To. A. Jew,' he said, conscious of Charlotte quivering next to her desk, her hands behind her back, tapping its wooden lid. Felix ordered Charlotte to the front, following her, clutching his cane behind his back. He dreaded this, hated having to humiliate her, but Fromm with his huge eyes had him in his sights. He couldn't afford to mess this up.

Charlotte took her place where, moments before, Hannah had been. She stood with her eyes cast down, her shoulders slumped, her hands clasped.

'So, let us observe again, class, and compare and contrast. You saw Hannah as a fine example of how we define an Aryan, and now we have a Jew. And by her very misery, she makes an equally fine specimen of Jewishness. Look up, girl.' She did; her eyes clouded with fear.

Again, using his cane, the teacher pointed things out. 'See here, her little, crafty eyes, pupils like pin pricks. Now, this is typical Jew – little eyes always on the lookout for a quick buck, the means by which to benefit from someone else's misfortune. And look at the nose...' The tip of his cane pushed Charlotte's nose up. 'See how big it is and see how hooked it is. All the better for sniffing out the next, devious scheme, eh, Charlotte? I mean,' he said, turning to the class, 'what more evidence do we need? Don't be fooled by her, class. Yes, she looks all meek and mild, and yes, she probably is. Butter wouldn't melt. But she'll grow and she'll learn, and she'll learn to hate us and she will, like all her kind, try and dupe us at every turn. Mark my words.' Fromm was nodding his approval.

He continued. 'I said look up, girl. How can we assess you if you keep staring at the floor? What's the matter with you? Worried in case you dropped a pfennig down there?' He paused, waiting for a round of laughter. Again, none came. The girl bit her lip, a little gesture that, for some reason, moved him. He had to fight through it; he knew that. 'Now, class, consider her lips; look how big and puffy they are. Again, this is typical Jew. Now, for all we know, Charlotte might be good at something. Perhaps she's a good runner or a fine painter. Don't fall for it though. Do not be deceived. There are always going to be Jews who are good at something, just as there are Negroes who can excel. We all saw what Jesse Owens did at the Olympics. Three gold medals, for heaven's sake.'

'Four, sir,' said Charlotte in a quiet voice.

Felix couldn't afford to let her correct him. He spun round to face her. 'I didn't ask you to talk,' he said, raising his cane. Charlotte flinched.

'She's right though, sir.'

'What? Who was that?'

'Me, sir,' said the fat boy, his arm raised. 'Jesse Owens won four gold medals. He won the hundred metres in ten point three seconds, the two hundred metres in –'

'Yes, yes, all right, no need to go through all of it. The man won four gold medals, he beat some of our finest Aryan specimens but, so what? As the Führer says, aberrations can and do happen. Jesse Owens was one; Charlotte maybe is another. And that is why we must be vigilant at all times. We must not bow to these false gods.' He paused, allowing his words to sink in. Addressing Charlotte directly, he lowered his voice, asking, 'Where did your grandfather fight?'

'Passchendaele.'

'Passchendaele, eh? I had an uncle who died there. A sea of mud. Nothing but mud. Men drowned in it, horses drowned in it. We lost many good men at Passchendaele. Your grandfather lost his arm there?'

'Yes, sir.'

'Hmm. Terrible times, terrible.'

He heard a cough from the back of the class. It was Fromm, shaking his head. 'Anyway, back to your seat, girl.'

'Right,' he said, taking a deep breath. 'I was asked to mark your most recent homework assignment.' On the table next to the door sat two piles of exercise books. He instructed two boys at the front to take a pile each and distribute them back to their owners. 'The plant cell,' he said as the boys did their task. 'Not such a difficult assignment I would've thought, but by gods, most of you employed your baby brothers or sisters to draw the diagrams; I'm sure of it.' Fromm smiled. That was good.

'I've asked some of you, too many for my liking, to try again, to improve on your abysmal attempts. I expect your completed assignments here on this desk by morning break tomorrow. And this time, put some effort into it. Any questions?' His eyes darted round the room before settling towards the back. 'Good god, you have the gall to ask a question. I give it to you, Charlotte; you don't lack courage. What is it?'

'Please, sir, you've not marked my homework.'

Felix straightened his tie, trying not to sigh. 'New policy, my girl. The teaching staff have unanimously agreed that from now on we shall continue to expect homework from our Jewish pupils but that we refuse to mark it. Any more questions?'

There were no more questions.

The children quietly went to their next class. Charlotte was last to leave. She paused at the door and looked straight at him. 'Thank you, sir,' she said in the softest of voices. Inside, he screamed. The door closed behind her. Felix puffed out his cheeks, strangely exhausted.

'Not bad, Herr Stoltenberg,' said Herr Fromm, rising from his chair at the back. 'I thought, though, you were a bit soft on the Jew girl. So what if her grandfather fought in the war?'

'A lot of Jews did, sir.'

'Please, do not interrupt me, Herr Stoltenberg,' he said, his magnified eyes boring into Felix. 'First of all, why would you believe her? She was lying, no question about it. She was trying to win your sympathy, and for an awful moment, I thought she had. Never give them the benefit of the doubt. Give a Jew an inch, even a child, and they'll take a mile. She almost had you on her side there. That diminishes your standing in front of the others, makes you look soft. Secondly, never forget, we are all foot soldiers marching for the Führer. And for that, we need to be tough. Never allow yourself to feel sentimental even for a child such as Charlotte Wolff. You're still young; you'll learn.'

'Yes, sir.'

'I was reading your report, Stoltenberg. I'm sure you're nothing like your father.'

'No, sir.'

'Some say an apple never falls far from its tree. Let's hope, for your sake, that's not the case in your instance.' He clicked his heels. 'Good day to you. Heil Hitler.'

'Heil Hitler.'

Felix slumped in one of the children's chairs, loosening his tie. He never thought it'd be so difficult. He rubbed his eyes and concluded that, yes, fighting street brawls was infinitely easier than humiliating schoolchildren. And again, his father came up. He always did, this huge black mark against his name. He had to carry the responsibility for his father's dissent. *An apple never falls far from its tree...* the same words Klaus had thrown at him all those years ago. His father's traitorous beliefs still haunted him. It was like when he was a kid all over again – being on the outside, looking for a way in. He couldn't risk staying on the outside; it was too dangerous. He saw what they did to his father.

Chapter 15

'But, Felix, it's pouring with rain.'

He tried not to laugh. 'So?'

'Well...'

'Mum, you know the deal. There are certain things I have to do on occasion. Is my tie straight?'

'I know but...'

'I can't exactly say, "I'm sorry, I can't come out today, it's raining". Please, Mum, don't fuss. I'm twenty-two years old; you don't need to fuss over me.' The conversation was all too familiar. He stood at the mirror hanging over the mantelpiece, making sure his cap was at the right angle, the knot in his tie just so. His mother hovered behind him, that anxious look in her eyes. Please, he thought, please don't launch into the *your father would have hated to see you in this uniform* speech. He could recite it by heart. He always wanted to shout back, *yes, and look what happened to him.* But it seemed too cruel.

He was dreading the day ahead, standing around for hours. It was time to go. He batted off his mother's questions. Yes, he had his sandwiches, yes, he had everything he needed. But no, he wasn't going to take an umbrella. Who ever heard of a SA stormtrooper with an umbrella? He ran down the stairs, amidst the smell of boiled vegetables and dirty diapers.

Felix hated the boycotts. He and his colleague, Ernst Gluck, had been given a list of six premises to visit, all within a mile of each other. They were to spend up to an hour at each and warn people they should not patronise Jewish shops and businesses. A fine way to spend your Saturday off, thought Felix. These were the things he had to do but he wasn't happy. For one thing, he and Gluck were not friends. Gluck was your typical SA man, a barrel-chested, overweight thug in a shit-coloured uniform. He was much older, in his mid-thirties, was uneducated and proud of it. He had a scar down his left cheek which he was equally proud of. No one was sure how he got it. Gluck's version of events changed with every telling. Felix knew he was no more than a sissy in Gluck's eyes, one who had joined the Party for no other reason than career advancement. He couldn't deny it.

Felix bumped into his neighbour, Frau Pappenheimer, outside his block. The woman, a widow, was rumoured to be Jewish but people left her alone for they thought her mad. She owned numerous cats, had a stoop, and local kids called her a witch, though she was only about fifty and always wore white. 'Hello, lad,' she said cheerfully in her scratchy voice. 'Still wearing that uniform of yours.' She was always scathing about Hitler.

'Yes, Frau Pappenheimer.'

She approached him. Talking quietly, she said, 'He'll be the death of us all, you know. You think I'm crazy, I know, but your little man with that moustache, he's going to hell and he'll take us all with him. You'll see.' People said she went mad after her husband died. Others, including his mother, thought she'd killed him by plunging a kitchen knife into his eye.

Anyone else, he would have done something about it but, like the village idiot, it was best simply to humour her and hope she'd go away. 'Please, Frau Pappenheimer, you shouldn't –'

'What do I care? I worry for you, though, lad. You're young. You be careful now.'

He tried not to laugh. 'Thank you, Frau Pappenheimer.'

He made his way to his rendezvous, a ten-minute walk. The tops of the buildings were bathed now in sunlight but down here, at street level, it was dingy. The rain had ceased. He arrived shortly before eleven, not wanting to be late, not wanting to incur Gluck's wrath. Having got there, he ambled round outside like a spare part. Gluck was nowhere to be seen. The shop had the words *Wolff's Flowers* painted in white letters in a sloping curve across its window, bookended with little flower-shaped stencils.

Next door, at the butchers, the butcher boy stepped outside and, shielding a match between his cupped hands, tried without success to light a cigarette. The boy tried again and eventually managed to light his cigarette. He'd barely lit it when a voice bellowed at him from inside. 'Arthur, get back inside; you've got work to do.' Arthur rolled his eyes, took a last puff of his cigarette before throwing into the gutter. On seeing Felix, he smiled, revealing a mouth almost devoid of teeth. It was not a friendly smile.

It was eleven. Gluck emerged in his uniform and his heavy boots carrying two placards on the ends of long wooden poles. 'One for me, one for you,' he said passing one to Felix, the words written clearly in black on a red background. *We buy nothing from Jews*, it screamed, while Gluck's placard had *Jews are our misfortune*.

'So now what?' asked Felix.

'We hit passers-by on the head with the placards, what d'you think? Typical of you lot – all education and no bloody sense.'

Taking a placard each, Gluck and Felix paced up and down in front of the florist, Felix wishing he'd brought a pair of gloves. Ten minutes passed and not a single customer had turned up. Felix shivered. A couple of people stopped some distance away from them, read their placards and moved on. 'See, it's working,' said Gluck.

Finally, after twenty minutes, a woman in a pink-spotted headscarf approached, head down, carrying a wicker basket, accompanied by a little dog, *some sort of mongrel*, thought Felix.

Gluck stepped in front of her. 'Stop!' he shouted, startling the woman. 'Heil Hitler.'

'What?' Her dog yelped. 'Shush, Bruno,' she snapped to no effect. 'Heil Hitler. What is all this nonsense?' she asked, peering up at Gluck's placard.

'Madam, it is not nonsense. Do not go into this shop. It is owned by a Jew and true Germans don't buy from Jews.'

'But I need to buy a couple of plants. I've got my sister coming to stay and the apartment looks –'

'Find another florist,' said Felix.

'And tell your mutt to shut up,' said Gluck.

'But there isn't another for miles,' the woman shrieked.

'Shush,' said Felix, aware that a small crowd was gathering. 'There's no need to shout.'

'What?'

A man in a duffel coat appeared by her side. 'What's up, Mildred?' he said.

'They won't let me in.'

'True Germans don't buy from Jews,' said Gluck. 'Heil Hitler.'

'Yeah, Heil Hitler,' said the man, reaching down to stroke the dog.

'There's no other florist for miles,' said Mildred. 'I just want some plants and I'm cold; I just want to get home.'

'Let her in, will you?' said the man. 'This is ridiculous.'

'Ridiculous, is it?' snapped Gluck. 'You think working for the Führer is *ridiculous*?'

'She only wants a bloody plant, for god's sake.'

'It's the principle,' said Felix, pleased to have contributed.

'Yeah, it's the principle, so get out of here.' Balancing his placard in the crook of his arm, Gluck produced a camera from his pocket. 'One step closer and I'll take a photo of you. You really don't want to see your picture in the *Völkischer Beobachter*, do you? Labelled as a Jew lover.'

The man eyed him out while Bruno resumed his barking. 'Come on, Mildred. I've got a plant I can spare you.'

Mildred and her friend strolled off, pausing while Bruno cocked his leg against a lamp post.

'It works,' said Felix.

'Yeah. That's one customer Herr Wolff has lost today. Imagine if we kept this up, he'd soon have no customers and we'd have driven another Jew out of business.'

'Not much of a business anyway. He's only had the one customer.'

'People know, that's why,' said Gluck, tapping his temple. 'They've wised up and know what's right. We'll give it another ten minutes, then we'll head off to the next one. Listen, I so need a piss.' He passed Felix his placard. 'I'm gonna ask the butchers next door.'

Felix blew into his hands. He hadn't heard the woman approach him from behind. She read one of the placards out loud. 'We buy nothing from Jews. Are you boycotting this shop?' she asked in a matter-of-fact tone.

Felix turned to face her. Like Little Red Riding Hood, she wore a bright red overcoat, was tall, had vivid blonde hair under a jaunty hat with a feather in it, arched eyebrows and, *rather incongruous for the time of day*, thought Felix, full-bodied red lipstick, as red as her coat. The faintest of lines either side of her eyes betrayed the first hints of age but she was stunning, nonetheless, quite the most beautiful woman he'd ever seen. There was a perfect symmetry to her face, but a sorrowful kind of beauty. Her face was stern though, her eyes hard, and for some reason he shuddered. 'Yes, madam.'

'Because it's Jewish? A bloodsucking Jewish capitalist, taking jobs from good honest Germans? Is that it?'

'Something like that.' He guessed her to be about thirty. She had the confidence of an older woman.

'You speak very nicely for an SA man. Are you sure this sort of work becomes you? Is there not something more *important* you could be doing for the Führer?'

He stuttered, unable to form a sentence.

She laughed, but it was, thought Felix, a cold laugh. To his surprise, she offered him her gloved hand. 'The name's Stella. Stella Hoffmann. And you are?'

He told her. 'Nice to meet you, Frau Hoffmann.'

'Fräulein, please.' And with that, she turned and headed straight for the florists. He should have stopped her; after all, that was why he was here. But he couldn't.

Gluck returned, still buttoning his fly. 'Why you let her slip through?'

'She told me her name for some reason. Stella Hoffmann.'

'Eh? I know that name,' he said, taking back his placard. 'She's some degenerate artist or something. Nice arse, look at it. You shouldn't have let her through though. Doesn't matter.

Come on, let's go.' He blew into his cupped hands. 'Hang on, who's this?'

Felix groaned. Coming towards them, slowing up with each step as she read the placards, was the Jewish girl from his class, Charlotte. 'Hello, sir,' she said.

'Who's this?' asked Gluck.

'One of my pupils.'

'I'm Charlotte Wolff,' she said looking Gluck firmly in the eye. 'My granddad owns this shop.'

'Does he indeed?' said Gluck.

Turning to Felix, she asked, 'Have you been stopping people from coming into my granddad's shop, sir?'

'No. I mean, well, no one c-came in anyway.'

Herr Wolff had emerged from the shop, waving a tea towel. Sure enough, he had only one arm. 'What's going on?'

'Stay right there, Jew,' said Gluck, pointing at him.

'Are you OK, Charlotte?' asked her grandfather.

Charlotte nodded. 'How did you get the scar, mein Herr?'

'Mind your own business.' Gluck made to leave, bracing his placard against his shoulder. 'Come on, mate,' he said behind his shoulder. 'Let's get outta here.'

'You should be ashamed of yourself, boy,' said Herr Wolff, addressing Felix. 'I fought for this country while you and most of your Nazi pals were still in your diapers.'

Charlotte held Felix's gaze. 'It doesn't matter, Granddad,' she said. She shook her head, a look of disappointment on her face.

Felix so wanted to apologise – to apologise for standing outside her grandfather's shop, to apologise for humiliating her in class. But the words simply wouldn't come.

Chapter 16

Only the teachers and a few parents and relatives had turned up for the winter sports day, the chill cutting through people's coats, the clouds heavy and grey. The conditions, in late October, were far from ideal for sprinting. Eighteen schoolgirls on a damp playing field wearing their black shorts, plimsolls and white vests adorned with a triangular Hitler Youth badge were present, the mist shrouding them, the drizzle dampening their hair. Even the PE teacher, Frau Junge, looked miserable. But it had to be done right and properly; the headmaster, sheltering under a black umbrella, expected nothing less.

Felix wrapped his arms around himself and stamped his feet, trying to keep warm. The girls had dumped their tracksuit tops in a pile on the damp grass behind him. The boys were already gone – sent off on a cross-country run, not expected back for a good hour, poor lads. The girls were expected to race the 100 metres, six at a time. Frau Junge had split the girls up in a series of heats. All the girls who were expected to win, did win, including Charlotte who came in first at a relative canter while Hannah won her heat with equal ease. Strange, thought Felix, how the two girls he picked for his Aryan/Jewish comparison happened to be the year's best girl sprinters. The headmaster glowered. Charlotte shouldn't have been allowed to win; she was a Jew, for God's sake. Still, it was the final where it really mattered.

Six girls remained for the final. Once finished, warm showers awaited them. The other girls would have preferred to have gone straight indoors and not watch the final – no one gave a hoot about it anyway, apart from Frau Junge and the headmaster. But Frau Junge, Felix knew, enjoyed the spectacle and would not be denied standing at the finishing line with her stopwatch. The girls gathered their tops from the heap behind Felix and took their places alongside the track to watch the final, none of them filled with any semblance of interest or anticipation.

The six girls lined up, ready at the starting line, the vapour of their breaths visible. Some stretched their leg muscles, others just shivered. Felix experienced a flutter in his stomach. He was worried about Charlotte, what would happen to her if she dared win.

Frau Junge took her place at the finishing line and waved at a girl called Helene, whom she designated as her starting judge. Everything was ready. Charlotte and Hannah occupied the middle two lanes. The four other girls were there, by and large, to make up the numbers and fight for third place. Frau Junge blew her whistle, indicating to Helene that she was ready. Helene, one could tell, was rather enjoying the moment. 'On your marks,' she ordered, her arm in the air. The girls did as told. Felix noticed Charlotte offer Hannah a hint of a smile but received nothing in return. There were no starting blocks, no finishing tape; the race wasn't important enough to warrant such an effort. 'Get set.' Someone shouted out Hannah's name by way of encouragement. The drizzle intensified. Frau Junge held her thumb over the knob of the stopwatch.

'Go...' Helene's arm came down and they were off.

The girls and teachers and the few visitors cheered Hannah on, the headmaster especially so; after all, no one wanted the embarrassment of a Jewish girl upstaging the year's top Aryan sprinter. It'd be like Jesse Owens all over again.

Within the first twenty metres, Charlotte and Hannah had already put daylight between them and the rest of the field. Hannah took the early lead. Half way, she was still in front but Charlotte was catching up. Seventy-five metres and the two girls were neck and neck. The cheering for Hannah intensified. Not a single person cheered for Charlotte. Felix wondered whether, amongst the visitors, her mother had come. With the finishing line within sight, Charlotte edged forward. Surely, Hannah couldn't be beaten? Then, with less than ten metres to go, Charlotte seemed to tire while Hannah found an inner strength, stepped up and overtook. Hannah romped home the easy winner.

Her victory was greeted by a healthy round of applause, led by the beaming headmaster. Charlotte took second while the girl in third finished quite some distance behind.

'Well done, girls,' said Frau Junge. 'Fifteen point two seconds, Hannah. Not bad considering the conditions. Well done, you can stand proud today. Not bad, Charlotte, you run fast for a Jew but you will never beat Hannah, a true German sprinter.'

Charlotte shook Hannah's hand but no words were exchanged. The girls ran over towards Felix to gather their tracksuit tops. Hannah arrived first, a smile on her face. 'Congratulations, Hannah,' said Felix. 'Well run.'

'Thank you, sir.'

He offered his congratulations to the other girls as they collected their tops. Not one took any notice of him, too eager to get back inside and out of the cold. The headmaster and others were already leaving. Frau Junge stood by herself with a clipboard, still at the finishing line, making notes.

Charlotte arrived last.

He edged towards her, his hands in his pockets, not wanting to be overheard. 'Well done, Charlotte,' he said quietly, aware that perhaps he shouldn't be seen congratulating her.

Charlotte flashed him a smile and he knew in that moment that she'd thrown the race.

'You...' The aching memory came back to him, the race around the lake all those years back, pushing Klaus Beck over the line.

'Sir?'

He didn't want to say it. 'Charlotte, about the other day...'

'Yes, sir?'

'When I made you stand up in class.'

She looked at him with expectant eyes. He hated the way she reduced him to such wretchedness, her mournful, detached expression. He hated the doubt she stirred in his heart. She was just a kid, she meant nothing to him, yet... He glanced over at Frau Junge, making sure she was far enough away.

'I'm sorry I had to pick on you.'

She didn't respond, didn't give him her benediction, the blessing he so craved. He realised then just how much he did crave her forgiveness, to be rid of the guilt stirring within him. She slipped on her tracksuit top and, turning, jogged back towards the changing rooms.

It was properly raining now. Looking around, he realised Frau Junge had gone too. He was quite alone.

Chapter 17

Another Saturday, another day of duties with his rotund, scar-faced SA comrade, Ernst Gluck. It had begun to rain so Felix and Gluck decided to have a mid-morning coffee in Café Flamingo on the corner of Hitlerstraße. They'd had a busy morning pasting up posters round the district encouraging young men to join the ranks of the SA. *The National Revolution awaits* screamed the headline above a picture of a muscular, squared-jaw man in a SA uniform.

Now sitting at a small round table, with their rolled-up posters and bucket and brush on the floor, they ordered and paid for two coffees and a pastry each. The place was half full of men smoking and reading their newspapers. A middle-aged couple at the next table chatted in whispers. They were dark, thought Felix, they had that look of Jew. Was there not a 'No Jews' notice on the door? There usually was. The woman shifted her coffee cup from hand to hand, betraying her unease.

Sipping their coffees, Felix and Gluck didn't speak. Instead, Gluck smoked a cigarette and read a newspaper someone had left behind.

Behind the counter, a waiter was chalking up the day's specials on a blackboard while whistling *Ode to Joy*.

Felix eyed Gluck with flecks of pastry in his little moustache and wondered how his life had come so low. There had to be something better he could doing, rather than this mind-numbing donkey work. The doubt had sagged at the edges of his mind for a while, but it was that woman in the red coat, Stella Hoffmann, who had brought it to the fore. What was it she'd said? *Is there not something more important you could be doing for the Führer?* And she was right. The work was demeaning but there was no way out of it. He was committed. *Are you sure this sort of work becomes you?* Damn her.

Two SS officers swaggered in and, standing at the café entrance, looked round. The Jewish couple fell silent.

Felix swirled a spoon round his cup while eyeing the Jewish couple as they quickly gathered their things, aware that they were being carefully watched by the SS men. Gluck, noticing too, stubbed out his cigarette. The couple, their eyes to the floor, scuttled past the men, ignoring the waiter's goodbye, and quickly left, leaving behind their newspaper on the table. Felix could imagine them on the other side of the door, out on the street, breathing a collective sigh of relief. Gluck and Felix gathered their posters and buckets while the two SS men sat down in the Jewish couple's place, both huffing in their tight uniforms. 'Good morning, gentlemen. Welcome to Café Flamingo,' said the whistling waiter. 'What can I get you?'

'Two black coffees,' said one in a booming voice as if wanting the whole café to hear him. 'First off, though, get rid of this stuff,' he said, waving his hand over the Jewish couple's coffee cups and plates. 'Make sure you properly sterilise it all. Jews have had their grubby little fingers all over it. In fact, better still, throw it out. It's been contaminated. No one should be expected to touch this filth now.' His colleague laughed heartily as Gluck and Felix made their exit.

'We should be doing more of that,' said Gluck once outside, turning up his collar. 'Making a point like that. It's good to see.'

'Where now?' asked Felix. The rain had stopped; dark clouds scudded across the sky.

'Somewhere where the sun's shining. The Bahamas maybe. Wait up, look at that woman. That one over there,' he said, pointing. 'The one with the hat.'

Felix followed Gluck's gaze and saw a woman he recognised sheltering from the rain under the awning of a chemist's, wearing a bright-red coat and a jaunty hat with a feather in it.

'Oh god, it's her,' he said.

'So it is; that artist woman with the nice arse. The bitch has got a fag in her mouth.' With that, Gluck strode towards her with a determined step. 'Hey, you.' The woman, Stella Hoffmann, turned to face him just as Gluck reached her. She had no time to react as Gluck snatched the cigarette from her lips and, with exaggerated movements, threw it to the ground where it sizzled in a puddle.

'Hey,' yelled the woman. 'What the hell –'

'Women are not to smoke in public,' said Gluck, loudly, as he dramatically stamped on the cigarette. 'Have you not seen the signs?'

'Why, you –'

'It's an insult to the Führer. He does not approve of the habit, especially amongst women.'

The woman, her hand on her chest, gaped at him, open-mouthed, as Gluck marched back to Felix.

'That's what you call making a point,' he said, grinning. 'Let's go, we've got work to do.'

Gluck, picking up his bucket and brush, marched ahead but Felix remained rooted, the rolled up posters beneath his arm, looking across at the woman. She caught his eye and he knew she recognised him. 'Herr Stoltenberg,' she said, approaching him. 'We meet again.'

'Frau Hoffmann,' he said with a bow, conscious of the colour rising in his cheeks.

'Fräulein, please,' she chortled. 'Still doing the Führer's lowly work, I see. Maybe you should consider a career with the SS instead. I hear they're a little more refined up here,' she said, tapping her temple. 'Unlike your ruffian colleague with a scar who seems to think my smoking is a personal affront to the Führer.'

'He tells me you're an artist.'

She smiled, a smile that didn't reach her eyes. 'I am, yes. Do you like art, Herr Stoltenberg?'

'Yes,' he lied.

'Oi, Stoltenberg,' shouted Gluck from afar. 'Hurry up, will you, you stupid ape.'

'You'd better go,' she said with a wink. 'Your bloodhound awaits you.'

'It was nice meeting you again, Fräulein.' As he said it, he realised just how much he meant it. There was something rather fierce about her, but he liked her. A lot. He was about to offer his hand but stopped himself in time. Instead, he made his leave.

She called after him. 'Herr Stoltenberg?'

For some reason, his heart faltered. 'Yes?'

'Tell me, have you ever been inside an artist's studio? No? I didn't think so. It's about time you did. Brucknerstraße, number 110, fourth floor. Come see me. Tuesday. Anytime. I'll be in all day. Smoking.'

He nodded.

'Oh, Herr Stoltenberg, if you do come visit, and I hope you will, please…'

'Yes?'

'Ditch the uniform.'

Chapter 18

'Quieten down, quieten down. OK, so this is your assignment,' said Felix, using his cane to point at the words written up on the blackboard. 'In 1933, the year the Führer was appointed chancellor, there were sixty-six million inhabitants living in Germany. Of these, five hundred thousand were Jews. So the question is this: what was, in 1933, the percentage of aliens living in Germany?' He waited for the class to absorb the question. 'You have two minutes. Put your hand up when finished. Two minutes starting from...' He looked at his watch. 'Starting... now.'

Felix stood at the window and gazed out at the church spire. A crow glided down, landing on the apex of the church roof. It was a Monday, the day after his second encounter with Stella Hoffmann and he couldn't stop thinking of her, kept replaying their conversation in his head. Did he want to visit her? No. The thought terrified him. There was something about her, something wrong, and a voice deep inside his head told him to stay away from her. She was not part of his life and it'd be better for it to remain that way. And yet...

Less than a minute had passed when the first arm went up.

It was the meek Jewish girl, Charlotte Wolff. Her desk had recently been painted yellow, yellow for Jew, presumably on the orders of the headmaster. Hannah's hand went up next. A couple more hands followed. He checked his watch. A knock on the classroom door interrupted him. Felix sighed. 'Yes, come in.'

'So sorry to disturb you, Herr Stoltenberg,' said the school secretary, peering round the door. 'The headmaster wishes to see you.'

'Now? Why?'

'Straightaway. He didn't say why.'

Felix turned to the class. 'Excuse me, children. I shouldn't be long.'

Felix followed the secretary down the corridor. She stepped aside at the headmaster's door, motioning him to step inside. He hesitated a moment on seeing the headmaster on his feet in front of his desk, flanked by two men in long, black coats. 'Ah, Stoltenberg, Heil Hitler. Come in,' said the headmaster. 'Shut the door, there's a good chap.' Felix returned the salute but was immediately disarmed by the head's kindly turn of phrase. This wasn't like him. The office smelt of old books and stale smoke. A large map of Germany shared wall space with a coloured print of Hitler. The headmaster's bald head, reflecting the light, shone through his thinning hair. He removed his glasses and Felix noticed the shaking of his hands. 'These two men are from the Gestapo,' he said with the slightest quiver in his voice. Felix realised the headmaster was frightened of his two visitors; they had stripped him of his usual venom. Felix bowed his head at the two men. Both were mirror images of each other, tall, pale, thin and intimidating. 'They are here on official business,' said the headmaster, lowering his eyes. The air crackled with tension.

'You have a student in your class by the name of Charlotte Wolff,' said one in a predictably shrill voice.

He thought of Charlotte with her expectant, doleful eyes, sitting at her yellow desk. 'Y-yes, that's right.'

'Bring her to us. Tell her to bring all her things – coat, bags, whatever else.'

Felix glanced at the headmaster as if seeking his approval, but the head couldn't look him in the eye. He wanted to ask why, but he knew it wasn't his place.

He returned to the classroom, his polished shoes clicking down the corridor, his limbs heavy. This was part of the process, he knew that, and he was part of it too. It was easy castigating the Jews *en masse* and hiding behind the anonymity of the state. But this was personal, not a statistic or a percentage, this was different; this was so much harder.

He paused at the classroom door, his hand on the knob, and breathed in. He was aware of the secretary waiting behind him. He walked in, conscious of every set of eyes upon him, aware of the nervous expectancy that hung in the air. He walked over to her. 'Gather your things, Charlotte,' he said in a whisper.

Charlotte stared at him, the colour draining from her face. 'Everything, sir?' she asked, a tremor in her voice.

'Yes, and your coat.'

She hesitated, her lip trembling. This wasn't his doing; he was just the messenger. So why this urge to put his arm around her, to tell her everything would be OK?

'Please, Charlotte.'

She did so, her face white. She looked round her as if someone might help.

'Hurry up, girl,' said Felix, desperate for this to be finished, to wash his hands of it.

Slowly, Charlotte lifted open her desk lid, aware perhaps of every pair of eyes upon her – aware of the total silence – and carefully placed the items one by one inside her satchel: a pencil case, a ruler, maths compass, ream of paper, a folder and a paperweight. She worked slowly, her hands shaking. Having emptied her desk, Charlotte picked up her coat from the back of her chair. How small she looked, thought Felix. Charlotte walked down the central aisle, towards the secretary holding the door open. Hannah, sitting at the front, stopped her, placed a hand on Charlotte's sleeve. Her eyes had turned red. 'Good luck,' she whispered. Charlotte tried to smile.

At the door, Charlotte stopped and turned, casting her eyes over the class. Her gaze stopped on Felix causing him to flush. 'The answer is zero point seven five per cent, sir.'

'What?'

'The number of Jews here in 1933.'

'Right. Yes. That is correct.' He almost laughed. 'Well done, Charlotte. Go on now. Don't keep the headmaster waiting.'

'Thank you, sir,' she said.

'What for?'

She shrugged. 'For being a nice teacher.' She bit her lip.

What did she mean by that? He hadn't been particularly 'nice' to her and yet she'd said it and she'd meant it. He'd wanted to say thank you in return, to wish her luck, but he found himself bereft of words.

Still not a sound as she left the room. He could hear her footsteps, along with the secretary's, echoing down the corridor, fading away. He closed the door and, almost as one, the class breathed again.

*

'May I see you for a moment, Herr Strindberg?'

School had finished for the day. The children had gone home, as had most of the teachers. But Felix had found the art teacher crouching on the floor facing the wall in the corner of his classroom. 'Who is it?' said Strindberg, without looking up. He seemed to be praying or up to something odd.

'Felix Stoltenberg, mein Herr.'

'Ah, one of the trainees. What is it you want, Herr Stoltenberg?'

'I, er…' It was as if he was speaking to Herr Strindberg's bottom. 'Are you OK, mein Herr?'

'I've got mice. I'm trying to set a trap. Pass me a piece of that cheese on my desk, would you? What is it you want?'

'I wanted to ask you about art. I know there're many we call degenerate but I confess I wasn't paying much attention and –'

'Ha, don't tell me, you're frightened of saying how much you like the work of so-and-so, only to find out they're Jewish or something.' Still without looking at him, the art teacher held out his arm behind him, waiting for his cheese.

Felix handed him it. 'Exactly.'

'Chances are, if they're still breathing, it's degenerate and you don't like it. If they aren't breathing, as in dead, you should be on safe ground. Now, if I…' He tried balancing the square of cheese onto the one side of a mousetrap, while holding down the other side. 'So, you can safely dismiss the Expressionists, the Fauvists, the Cubists. As for the Surrealists – huh!'

'I don't understand.'

'Listen, if you look at a painting and you can't see what it is or you think it indecipherable, you don't like it. Or if you

126

think it's morally suspect in some way or it makes no sense to you, you don't like it. You don't like Otto Dix; no one does, nor George Grosz, trust me. They're considered degenerate and for good reason. Their work is grotesque in the extreme. Not that you'll see them; they've been banned and rightly so. The Führer knows his art. As for Max Beckmann, well…' The mousetrap snapped shut. 'Damn it,' shouted Strindberg. 'That's the third time it's done that. But you like anything classical, especially if it's got a Roman or Ancient Greek influence.'

'So, what actual artists do I like?'

'The cheese's crumbled. Pass me another square, would you? Let's see now, for starters, I'd say you like Albrecht Dürer, Rembrandt, Caravaggio, a bit of Michelangelo, and you can't go wrong with Turner, even if he is English.'

'Thank you, mein Herr.'

'Yes! I've done it. Right, it's all set. Let's see the blasted mice survive that man-eater of a trap.'

*

Felix returned to his classroom to fetch his coat. He paused in front of the blackboard. He'd been at the school a couple of months now and, after a shaky start, things had improved. The children seemed to like him, the headmaster seemed to have confidence in him, and Herr Fromm's assessment had been quite glowing, all things considered. He enjoyed teaching. He could see why his grandfather had stuck in for so long, becoming a headmaster and forcibly made to retire.

He peered across at the empty chairs and tables, could hear the excited gabble of the children in his mind. His eye was drawn to the back, to the yellow desk where Charlotte sat. Where Charlotte *used to* sit. He'd humiliated her, that first lesson. But since then, she'd become his favourite. She was polite, attentive, intelligent, obedient. She was every teacher's dream pupil. And now she was gone.

He knew why it had to be; after all, he'd grown up with it. But he still grappled to *understand* why it had to be, why a twelve-year-old girl could be seen as a threat to the nation, to him, to the Führer. The school was virtually *Judenfrei* now, free of Jews. Charlotte was among the last. They said they were all sent to 'Jew only' schools. The more fanatic teachers reckoned that even this was too good for them, that as Jews they were not deserving of an education at all.

Two minutes later, Felix found himself knocking on the headmaster's door, without any remembrance of why he was doing this.

'Enter.'

He found the head poring over a sheaf of papers, fountain pen in hand. 'Yes, Stoltenberg, what is it?'

This unnerved him. The diminished man of earlier, cowed by the presence of the Gestapo, had gone. The normal headmaster had returned, sharp of tongue, coldly efficient.

'Sir, I wanted to ask, if I may...'

'Yes? Spit it out.'

'About Charlotte Wolff...'

'Who?'

'The...' Had he really asked who? Why? Was he playing a game? 'Charlotte Wolff, sir.' Felix lowered his voice. 'What will happen to her?'

The head carefully placed his pen down on his desk and looked up at him with piercing eyes. 'Just this once I shall pretend you never asked that question.'

'S-sir?'

'Ask me again and I will report it. Now, get out.' He

128

returned his attention to his paperwork, strands of loose hair falling out of place.

Felix's mouth gaped open.

The head looked up again. 'Oh, and never assume to walk into my office again without the proper greeting.' He shot his arm out. 'Heil Hitler.'

Felix staggered back. 'Of course. My apologies, sir. Heil Hitler.'

*

Felix trudged home, his head down, nestling into his scarf. A cloak of misery had wrapped itself around him and he couldn't shake it off. He couldn't bear to think of Charlotte, the poor girl. What future lay ahead of her. He tried shaking her from his mind and thought of Stella instead, but somehow that didn't work either. So, instead he thought about art, trying to remember the names Strindberg had recommended – Albrecht Dürer, Rembrandt, Caravaggio, Michelangelo, Turner, 'even if he is English'. Up ahead, he could see the butcher's, next to Herr Wolff's florist with a large swastika daubed across its windows. Again, he saw the butcher boy, Arthur, smoking a quick cigarette outside. The butcher's door opened; a woman appeared. The boy put his hand behind his back, hoping to hide the fact he was smoking. 'Thank you, ma'am,' he said to her. 'I hope them there pork cook good.'

'I'm sure they will. Good day.'

Felix narrowed his eyes. He recognised that voice, a voice from a long time ago. The woman strode along the pavement, stopped and pulled out a pair of gloves from her handbag. And then he recognised her. He hesitated, wasn't sure whether to say hello. The way he'd treated her when they were kids still shamed him. All the better, he thought, to show that he'd changed.

He ran over. She looked up, a flash of concern. 'Ingrid, hello.'

'H-hello.' She didn't recognise him.

'It's me. Felix.'

'Oh my, so it is.' She looked him up and down, taking in his uniform. 'Hello, how are you?'

'Yeah. Great, thanks. And you?'

She still had that coyness about her, that warmth in her eyes. But the warmth quickly disappeared. She glanced round the street as if embarrassed to be talking to him. 'Yes, fine, I guess.'

'It's good to see you again, Ingrid.' They stood, looking at each other, unsure where to go next. That little scar on her chin was, if anything, even more obvious now.

'Where…' She cleared her throat. 'Where do you live now?'

'We moved just a few streets away. The house was too big, you know, after Dad died. So, we sold up, and my mother got an apartment instead. And you? Still in the same house?'

'My parents, yes. But I'm… I'm married now.'

Lucky man, he thought.

'But, like you, I still live nearby. How is your mother? Is she OK?'

'Yeah. Not the same, of course, but she copes. I think the reason she wanted the smaller apartment was so that there'd be no room for my grandfather to visit.' He laughed. Of course, she'd know the real reason, forced to 'move on', to give up their family home to a *real* German family, a loyal one.

Ingrid fiddled with her gloves, trying, unsuccessfully, to slide them on. 'Your grandfather. Of course, how could I forget? The old man and his penny whistle.' She stuffed the gloves into her coat pocket. 'Still with us?'

'Yes, he lives out in the country.'

'Hmm.'

'You OK, Ingrid?'

'Yes, of course. I… I must go.' She patted her shopping bag. 'Got to get dinner on before His Highness gets home.'

He smiled, trying to disguise his disappointment. 'Of course.'

'Lovely to see you again, Felix. Give my love to your mother.'

'I will. Thank you.'

Felix watched her leave, wishing she hadn't had to rush off so quickly.

Chapter 19

Felix stood outside the block of apartments at 110 Brucknerstraße, home of Stella Hoffmann. It'd just gone five o'clock Tuesday; school had finished for the day. A strange day. It was as if Charlotte Wolff never existed. No one mentioned her, not one pupil asked what had happened to her. They, at least, knew when to hold their silence. She was already forgotten by staff and pupils alike. If he knew how to, he would pray for her.

The air quivered with the sharp breaths of early winter. He wasn't sure whether he wanted to be here. Part of him simply wanted to turn round and go home. A woman pushing a pram said hello with a Heil Hitler. He returned the greeting. He wore a tweed jacket and a checked shirt, hoping he had neither overdressed nor underdressed. He had, as she had instructed, 'ditched the uniform'. His hand clutched a bunch of flowers he bought at Wolff's Flowers. He took Herr Wolff's advice and bought yellow carnations and white alstroemeria. He wasn't sure whether presenting her with flowers was appropriate. She might read something into it. He was tempted to bin them. But then to arrive empty-handed seemed even worse.

Why had he come? He really didn't know. She intimidated him both times they met… yet there was something about her he liked. He sensed she was perhaps not as tough as she made out to be. And the mere fact she was an artist appealed. He'd never met anyone 'bohemian', as his mother would say. Everyone in his life was like him, strait-laced, people who did and said the right thing. So, with heavy feet, he pushed open the door to the block and presented himself to the block warden, who, admiring his bouquet of flowers, directed him to the fourth floor.

He ambled down the corridor, still wondering whether to do this. Number 110. He knocked on her door and waited. He waited a while. Perhaps she was out, he thought, hoping it to be the case. And then she was there. And she looked stunning with her lipstick, and her neatly-plucked eyebrows and her vivid green eyes.

'Herr Stoltenberg, what a delight. Do come in. Nice jacket. Tweed, lovely. My, are those for me?' she asked, taking the flowers. 'How divine. Thank you.'

'A pleasure, Frau Hoffmann.'

'Fräulein, please.'

He walked straight into what seemed like a living room turned into a studio. The room was dominated by a large table laden with boxes and jars, full of paintbrushes and tubes of paint, with pots of white spirit and large sheets of thick paper. To one side stood an easel with a blank canvas on it. Every inch of the four walls was covered in paintings, some big, some small. The place smelt of turpentine and paint and stale cigarette smoke. He'd never seen a place like it.

Wow, he said to himself.

She waited in silence, holding his flowers, as if allowing him time to absorb his surroundings.

He examined some of the paintings on the walls. There were landscapes painted in oil, or so he guessed: rolling fields under thunderous, multicoloured skies, distant forests, lakes rendered dramatic by splashes of red and yellow, as if on fire. There were paintings of buildings, churches and palaces, only she hadn't portrayed them as the majestic buildings they were, but humble… reduced, even. They seemed imbued with a personality and again streaked with unusual colours. There were portraits of men and women with long faces, wide faces, huge eyes, wild hair, red cheeks, huge lips, vivid and frightening.

'You seem a little perplexed,' said Stella.

'No. Not at all. It's wondrous, it's… it's…'

'You like art, Herr Stoltenberg?'

'Felix, please. Yes, I love art. I like, erm… I like Turner, even if he is English, and er, Dürer, Rembrandt, Caravaggio and a bit of Michelangelo.'

'And what bit of Michelangelo do you like?' She was laughing at him, he could tell, but somehow he didn't mind.

'What? Oh, the later stuff mainly.'

This time she laughed out loud. 'Yes, I know what you mean. The later stuff. That early stuff, well, it was a bit rubbish really, wasn't it?'

'I don't like Otto Dix so much, let alone Max Beckmann.'

'No? That is a shame, I love their work.'

'You… you do?'

'Not that we ever see it now, you know… Times change.'

He didn't want this conversation, too dangerous. 'What's this one called?' he asked.

'I call her my *Blue Lady*.'

The Blue Lady was, thought Felix, an astonishing work. It

depicted the head and shoulders of a woman lying down, her skin a blue-grey colour, her eyes closed, a slight hint of a smile, a blissful expression. Her wild hair fanned out behind her, painted in such a way one couldn't be sure if it was hair or, in fact, swirling water.

'It's beautiful,' he said in a whisper.

She smiled and he saw that it was the same smile as *The Blue Lady*. He looked at her and she held his gaze. His heart fluttered. He was scared of her, of her art, of this apartment. He'd never met anyone like her. Her individuality frightened him. There was something untamed about her, a freedom in her soul. And he didn't like it, found it too difficult to understand. He wanted to leave, to escape her. He wanted to fuck her.

She excused herself, saying she'd find a vase for the flowers.

He stood there, next to the table, in the middle of this chaos, awkward, adrift in a sea of unknowns. He didn't know what to do with himself. Dozens of pairs of eyes stared down at him from the walls, defiant, angry eyes, mocking him, daring him to judge them. And it was at that moment he realised he knew nothing about life, that the Party had taught him all he needed to know. But it was only a slither of what the world had to offer. A crack of an existence that only allowed one to see what was straight ahead, that didn't allow one to look left or right, to see that things could be different. That a lake, a church, a face, might have a thousand and one different meanings. Too much, it was too much for him. He needed to leave, to escape, to go back and find the familiar, to anchor himself in a world that made sense.

He put his hand to his heart. She seemed to be taking a long time finding a vase for his flowers. It would look rude just to up and leave. But he had no choice. He spun round, dizzy with the assault of so many different colours leaping out at him. He couldn't breathe. He'd found freedom and freedom was suffocating him.

'Sorry to take so long,' she said, gently, her voice behind him, sounding as if she were miles away.

'I have to go.' He said it in a whisper but in his head he was screaming. 'I have to go.' He turned to face her, to offer his apologies for his abrupt departure. He opened his mouth to speak. But the words stuck in his throat. She was standing at the door to her kitchen, leaning against the door jamb, arms folded, a wry smile playing on her lips. She was wearing only a dressing gown, its cord hanging loose, its front gaping open.

Chapter 20

Felix thought the idea appalling but Stella had set her mind on it – she wanted to go boating. Felix tried to object – it was late October and, despite the sun, it was cold out there, even more so on an exposed lake. But his objections fell on deaf ears. And so, against his wishes, they set out early and they made their way across the city, made their way to Lake Tegel and hired a rowing boat. Felix paid the half-hour fee to a sour-looking woman sucking on a clay pipe in a wooden booth, flanked by a sign that stated that Jews were prohibited from hiring boats or using the lake.

Stella stepped into the rickety wooden boat, giggling as she tried to maintain her balance. 'Sit down, Stella, before you fall over.'

Felix had never rowed before, but he managed to steer the boat out onto the lake albeit in a rather circular route.

He had to admit, the day was idyllic: the gentlest of breezes, the lake mirroring the sky above, its silvery-grey surface as smooth as a sheet of glass. Felix rowed gently while Stella, sporting her sunglasses, lay back and closed her eyes, breathing in the cool air, the very image of serenity. The world smelt fresh and new, the air fragranced with pine. He could hear the call of the birds, the lapping of the oars in the water. Stella drooped her hand in the water, forming V-shaped ripples. A family of ducks swam past, the mother duck calling out, her young trailing behind in an orderly fashion.

'We should have brought some bread,' said Stella.

A light grey mist hung over the far end of the lake. A wave of happiness washed over him. Once they'd reached the middle of the lake, Felix stopped rowing and reached over and kissed her.

'Listen to the silence,' he said. It was as if the rest of the world had melted away.

'I never want this day to end,' she said.

He smiled at her. 'Neither do I.'

They weren't the only ones to enjoy the bucolic, autumnal day. They waved at fellow rowers in their boats, some painted in stripes of white and blue, and traded cheery exchanges. Coniferous trees cast shadows across the shore of the lake. A flock of geese wheeled noisily above them, their shadows flitting across the water.

'Did you see that sign?' she asked. 'The one about Jews not being allowed on the lake? Why? That's what I want to know – why?'

'I don't know.'

'But you're a proper German, you're a Nazi; you should know.'

'We ought to head back. Don't want to be charged twice.'

She removed her sunglasses. 'You're changing the subject.'

'It's because I haven't figured it out yet.'

'You haven't figured it out? You'll let me know when you have, will you?'

He closed his eyes, listened to the gentle rush of sounds,

the ducks, the geese, the sound of the oars on water. He opened them. Stella was gazing across the lake, her eyes glazing over, but there was no serenity in her expression any more; there was anger in there. He wanted to speak, to reassure her somehow, but couldn't. As so often, he lacked the words, didn't know what to say. Why did it always have to come back to politics? Why did she have to go and spoil it?

*

Stella Hoffmann possessed Felix's thoughts. He'd never met anyone like her before. She possessed a spirit that was both liberating and intimidating. He lost his virginity to her. Not that he hadn't the opportunity before, but he always considered himself rather old-fashioned in that regard. He wanted to meet an attractive, normal German girl his own age, get married and have children, lots of them, for the Führer. He didn't reckon on falling for a sexually assertive, peroxide blonde, almost a decade his senior, a woman who painted her lips, painted her nails, plucked her eyebrows and much else besides and shaved under her arms. And an artist to boot; an artist who painted paintings he didn't understand. Thus, if he didn't understand it, to follow Herr Strindberg's logic, it had to be 'degenerate'. He wondered whether Herr Strindberg had caught his mouse.

Stella had made him realise how empty his life had been hitherto. Everything he did, everything he had ever done, was in the name of the nation, the Party, the Führer. The children he taught were cast in the same mould, as were his colleagues and his friends, all of them.

Stella was different. She thought for herself and carved out a life of her own. But she was poor, barely had two reichspfennigs to rub together. He even offered to lend her

139

some money, but she said no. He realised too how dull his existence had been, everything measured out and controlled. Yet, for its dullness, it was safe. Being with Stella, he knew somehow it was unsafe, as if she was a danger to him. Yet, she never uttered a derogatory word, never cast aspersions on the state, on anything or anyone. He wanted her to, was desperate for her to criticise the regime in an articulate and processed way – simply because he couldn't, didn't know how to. Like anyone his own age living in Germany, he'd never experienced anything different, had no more than a vague concept of what democracy meant, and he knew, because he was told over the years, that democracy was inherently weak. If everyone had power, it meant that, in effect, no one had power. He knew there had to be an alternative to the National Socialists but he lacked the ability to visualise it or to put it into words. Not that he would dare with anyone else, but he would have with Stella.

After all, how could a man visualise an ocean when he's only ever seen a puddle? He knew Stella would know; she was older, possessed a strength he'd never known before, but she refused to be drawn in. Why, he didn't know. But he feared it was because she didn't trust him enough, and that hurt. He supposed trust was not something you could simply turn on like a light switch. It had to be earned.

Yet, he always went back for more. It was as if he had no choice in the matter. He knew nothing about her beyond the walls of her cramped apartment. She mentioned her father once, but when he pressed for more, she clammed up as if she were already regretting saying too much. One afternoon, as they lay in her bed enjoying the warm afterglow of sex, he foolishly invited her over for dinner. He regretted it the moment the words tumbled out of his mouth. But no worry, he thought, there was no way she'd accept. To his shock, she not only accepted, but seemed delighted by the prospect.

His mother, when he told her, was equally delighted. He'd never brought a girlfriend home before. 'So, what's she like then?' she asked several times. 'Will I like her? What do her parents do?' All the sort of questions he expected but had no answer for. How does one explain a woman like Stella Hoffmann? 'How old is she? What does she do?' She was expecting a wholesome girl with her hair in braids and wearing a dirndl. He was dreading it, for he knew his mother would be shocked by the age difference and much else besides.

Felix went to see Stella, determined to withdraw the invitation. But the first thing she said as he stepped into her apartment was how much she was looking forward to meeting his mother. He opened his mouth to protest but she took his hand and pulled him into the bedroom.

And so the appointed time came, six o'clock, one Sunday evening in early November. Klara had prepared a lavish pork casserole, far beyond what she could afford. But it was, she said, a special occasion, and merited the cost.

Stella breezed in fifteen minutes late, which Felix knew would not impress his mother. She wore her bright red coat, Little Red Riding Hood. Klara put her hand to her chest on seeing Stella, as if confronted by an alien. If Stella noticed, she didn't show it. 'Delighted to meet you, Frau Stoltenberg. I've brought a present for you both,' she said, handing Klara a picture frame wrapped in brown paper.

'Oh, I say. T-thank you.' Klara unwrapped it. It was *The Blue Lady*. Felix groaned. 'Oh my!' said Klara. 'It's… it's… Did you *buy* this…?'

'No,' laughed Stella. 'I painted it.'

'You *painted* this… this painting?'

'Is it so strange?'

141

'Stella is an artist,' said Felix, taking Stella's coat. 'Didn't I say?' She wore a dark-green dress with a bright-red necklace that matched her lipstick. He saw his mother appraise her outfit and she was clearly not impressed. But, for him, she looked gorgeous. No woman he'd known had ever dressed like Stella.

'An artist? I-I didn't know women could paint.'

'Yes, they do. I do. I paint for a living. Odd, I know. You can hang it next to your Führer portrait,' said Stella helpfully. 'The two would go well together, don't you think? Beauty and the beast.'

Klara gawped at her guest as if she couldn't believe what she just heard. 'I-I think what Stella means, Mama, is that our Führer is so strong, he is like a beast, strong as a bear or an ox or something.'

'Of course,' said Stella with a grin. 'That's exactly what I mean.'

The meal was as awkward as Felix had anticipated. Klara asked several questions of her guest and received unsatisfactory answers to all. No, said Stella, she had never joined the female Hitler Youth; no, neither she nor her parents were party members; no, she didn't approve of what Hitler was doing for the country. Felix blanched. To say such words aloud could land you in a concentration camp. Stella had shown considerable faith that Klara wouldn't report her. But she was right: as much as Klara thoroughly disproved of her guest, she would never report her scandalous opinions; it would reflect too badly on her. Nonetheless, Felix kept trying to steer the conversation to less contentious topics. He talked about his grandfather, the former headmaster, who now lived in a pretty village called Bad Bernsdorf, west of the capital. 'Let's not talk of your grandfather, please, Felix.'

'I must go see him one day.'

'I'd rather you didn't.' Changing the subject, she asked Stella whether her hair was naturally blonde.

'Can't you see my roots,' she said, lowering her head.

'Yes, I suppose I can.'

'You ought to dye your hair, Klara. A little bit of colour, it takes years off a woman.'

'W-would it? Yes, I suppose... I-I hadn't really thought about it before. Can I ask, forgive me, but... but do people buy your... your paintings?'

'Once upon a time they did. I was quite famous. Not so much now, not since –'

'How's your dinner?' asked Felix, conscious he was almost shouting. He couldn't let her loose on her favourite grievance, of how the Nazis labeled her work as degenerate and banned it.

'Yes,' said Klara. 'Is it OK? You've not touched your pork.'

'It's lovely, thank you, but I'm a vegetarian.'

'A vegetarian?' Klara could not conceal her distaste. 'Felix, you didn't tell me.'

'It's my fault,' said Stella. 'Felix didn't know, did you, my love,' she said, sliding her hand over the tablecloth towards his. Felix abruptly removed his hand. 'I should have mentioned it. But the vegetables and potatoes are lovely. Thank you, Klara.'

'I suppose the Führer is a vegetarian,' said Felix.

'All the more reason why I shouldn't be, I guess,' said Stella.

'Felix, pass me the water, would you?' said Klara.

'And of course the Führer was a painter. Something else we have in common.'

Mercifully, the meal came to an end. 'I'll give you a hand

clearing up,' said Stella.

'No, there's no need. I wouldn't want you to miss your last tram home.'

'It's only half nine, they run for hours yet.'

'Nonetheless.'

'Yes, I suppose…'

'I'll escort you out,' said Felix.

They stood outside the apartment block. Stella buttoned up her coat. It had begun to rain.

'Whoa,' said Felix. 'That was hard. I knew it wouldn't work. I should've warned her. I'm sorry, Stella. I didn't mean it to be so…'

Stella threw her arms round him and kissed him on the mouth. After, she whispered, 'I've been wanting to do that all night. Come back to mine and I'll rip your clothes off you.'

'Frau Hoffmann, you shock me.'

'Fräulein, please.' She eased her hand down the back of his trousers, grabbing a buttock. 'I can shock you a whole lot more if you want.'

'Oh, yes, yes. Erm. Wait a minute, I'll get my coat and find us an umbrella.'

A voice shot through from the night. 'Hello, lad.'

Felix jumped. 'Oh, Frau Pappenheimer, you gave me a jump.'

She emerged like a ghost from the dark, dressed in her habitual white, her hair grey and brittle. 'Who's this then?' she asked, addressing Stella.

'This is…'

Stella stood frozen as Frau Pappenheimer ran her scaly fingers down the side of Stella's cheek. 'She's all right this one,' she said. 'But it won't save her.'

'What… what do you mean?' asked Stella.

'That false idol your lad worships, he'll be the death of us all.'

'Yes, thank you, Frau Pappenheimer,' said Felix.

'I tell him all the time but he don't listen. That man of his is the devil and he's taking us to hell, every one of us.'

'I know. You're right,' said Stella.

'Won't save you, though, unless you run away. You won't beat them, you know. Your only hope is to flee.'

'Flee? But where?'

Felix couldn't bear it any more. 'Frau Pappenheimer, if you'll excuse me…'

He rushed back to the apartment, taking the stairs two at a time. Whenever he saw Frau Pappenheimer, the witch, he couldn't help think of the woman stabbing her poor husband in the eye. She'd rather dampened his ardour but, no matter – Stella would soon put him right. He charged back into the apartment. 'Mum, I'm going to… Mum? Mama, you all right? Is there anything wrong?'

Klara was sitting at the dining room table, the dirty dishes piled high, a handkerchief scrunched up in her hand. She was crying.

'Why, Felix? Why?'

'What's the matter? What do you mean?'

'You're a good-looking boy; you could have the pick of anyone – but of all people, you choose *her*.'

'Yes, I know. Mum, look, I know she's a bit different but you'll like her when you –'

'How can I like a woman who gives me such a monstrosity,' she said, pointing at *The Blue Lady* resting against the sideboard. 'It's so ugly. How can anyone paint such a thing?'

The heat rose within him. 'I'm not staying to listen to this.'

I'm going out.'

'What for? Where are you... No, please don't go back to her's. She's not –'

'Enough,' said Felix, slicing the air with his hand. 'I love Stella and that should be good enough for you.'

'Love? You love her? You love a Jew?'

Felix staggered back. 'A Jew? What do you mean? She's not a Jew.'

'Ask her, Felix. Ask her if she's not a Jew.'

Chapter 21

However many times she dyed her hair, she still disliked the pungent smell of the peroxide. She had long hair now, so it was always a lengthy and messy process. She sat in front of her bedroom mirror, carefully applying the hydrogen peroxide with a small brush. Still, needs must. Men liked it, especially the Nazi men. They were surrounded by solid-looking Gretas and Helgas who all looked the same with their braided hair, square shoulders and flat chests and their sexual passivity. Worse still, they all thought the same, not an original idea between them. Their Führer frowned on women wearing makeup and prettying themselves, let alone dying their hair. So, of course, the men outwardly agreed while inwardly fantasizing about fucking a proper woman.

Her father hated her hair too. 'Made her look brazen,' he said. She could hardly tell him that was the idea. She'd been to visit him that afternoon in his synagogue. Dreadful place. She hated it, always had, even as a child. Hated the cloying smell, the subdued, reverential atmosphere. She didn't believe in God, Jewish or otherwise. She hated the people at the synagogue with their expressions of frightened rabbits and their eyes full of sorrow. She hadn't wanted to go, but she needed some money. She admired her father's strength to carry on in spite of the rabid anti-Semitism all round him. While she, Stella, went to huge lengths to conceal and deny her Jewish roots, her father was still there, preaching in his synagogue, studying his Torah and wearing his skull cap. That, she had to admit, took courage.

She asked how he was but her attempts to remain civil faltered, as always. He asked whether she was still plying her trade as an artist. The way he said *plying your trade*, it made her sound like a prostitute. And he positively spat out the word *artist*. She was always a disappointment to him; she knew that. She pointed out, as she had many times before, that as a Jew, she had limited job offers. She once worked as a textile designer, a job she loved. The boss had to sack her because she was Jewish. He cried, said he had no choice. His tears didn't stop her from calling him a spineless bastard. But later, when she reflected on it, she knew she'd been too harsh on him.

The Nazis were passing a new law with each passing day, each one designed to make life harder for the Jews. Now, legally, as a Jew, she couldn't work for an Aryan, she couldn't go to the swimming pool, to the library, was barred from all non-Jewish restaurants and cafés, couldn't own a dog, couldn't walk in certain sections of the park. The list was endless. Perhaps she should flee; perhaps that crazy woman outside Felix's apartment block had a point. But how?

One couldn't just up and leave. It was a lengthy and expensive process, and liable to fail. So now, without a job, she had to rely on selling a painting every now and then. For a while, she did OK. But then the Nazis labelled modern art as 'degenerate', and that fairly well screwed that up. Still, she managed occasionally to sell the odd piece to a private collector, as long as it was traditional and anemic. Meanwhile, her father lent her a few Reichsmarks, although he could hardly afford it and knew full well he'd never see it again. Oh well, these are the things we do for our children. It's called sacrifice, Father.

Her own daughter had gone out with her little friend. Poor little mites. They'd be sitting on the yellow bench in the park, the one specifically reserved for the Jews, hoping not to be subjected to abuse. It always bothered her that Charlotte looked so damned Jewish. She, Stella, had escaped that misfortune but not poor Charlotte. She had that dark Jewish look, the shallow skin, the dark eyes. She tried to get Charlotte to dye her hair but she wouldn't have it. She could understand. You can't really appear at school one day with peroxide blonde hair, especially at a Jewish school.

So, what about this new Nazi in her life? Felix Stoltenberg. Well, he was tall, deliciously good-looking with his kind eyes, square jaw and blond hair, and energetic in bed and he was in love with her. His mother was a bitch, but that was neither here nor there; she was used to Nazi boys and their overprotective mothers. She liked him, he was intelligent and knew how to talk to a woman. But none of that mattered. Not one bit. Sadly, she came to the conclusion she'd have to ditch him, just as she ditched her husband five years before. It was a shame because Felix had invited her out for a meal at the Schlossgarten, quite one of the most expensive restaurants in the district. She had a horrible feeling he might ask her to marry him. The poor, deluded boy.

Felix was still in the SA, not the SS, and it was the SS that had clout these days. The SA was finished, anyone could see that. Furthermore, he was no way senior enough. But there lay the perpetual problem. She could always twist the younger ones around her finger but they lacked power. While the older ones, the ones with influence, were too Nazified to fall for her charms. Felix Stoltenberg looked like the sort of man who'd go far, but that was too long-term. She needed someone with influence now. The previous one, a chap called Dieter, had started off charming, but soon proved to be a bully and he certainly didn't love her. She didn't need that.

Ideally, what she needed was a high-ranking Nazi to be utterly devoted to her so that when the time came, she had someone to protect her and protect Charlotte. And the time would come. It always did for the Jews, even the ones who dyed their hair.

Chapter 22

No Jews Allowed.

The sign on the restaurant door was clear enough but Felix took no notice; he had no need to. Stella was not Jewish.

The restaurant, The Schlossgarten, was the most expensive in the district: low ceilings, an amber light and thick carpet. Stella arrived almost half an hour late, as he'd expected. A waiter took her red coat and hung it on a coat stand near the door. She was wearing that wonderful green dress she'd worn to his mother's. Until that evening, Felix had decided that as much as he liked Stella, he didn't love her. But his mother's dislike of her made him see her in a new light. He realised Stella probably had to contend with people like his mother every day of her life, people unable and unwilling to accept her. It made him realise just how precious she was, and that perhaps after all he was in love with her.

Indeed, he'd bought a small ruby ring, spending a whole week's wages. For tonight, he was going to ask Stella Hoffmann to be his wife. Stella Stoltenberg. He rolled the name round his mind, trying it on for size. She was in a talkative, excitable mood. She'd started on a new work, she

151

told him, a painting of the Reichstag with lots of people passing by its front, tall, thin shadows with bowed backs, a small army of burdened men and women, while the Reichstag, painted Nazi red, loomed over them. 'Sounds nice,' said Felix, immediately regretting his choice of words.

'Ladies and gentlemen,' came the booming voice of the compère over the microphone, making them both jump. 'Please welcome the beautiful, the exotic, the mysterious, Berlin's very own black beauty with the voice of a dozen black angels, the wondrous Miss Angel...'

A round of applause greeted the African singer to the stage as the band struck up the opening bars of Lili Marlene. Miss Angel, tall, slender and elegant, her dress decked with sequins, sang of her longing, her crimson red lips pouting against the microphone... *"Underneath the lantern by the barrack gate, Darling I remember the way you used to wait."*

Felix tried to relax but it was all too lush for him – the white tablecloth, the rich food, the candles and the overly-attentive staff. Whenever he half finished his red wine, a waiter would be on hand to top up his glass. He couldn't very well 'pop the question' while the singer was still singing.

A group of men laughed at the next table, puffs of cigar smoke floating above them.

'How was your lamb?' she asked. She'd managed to find something vegetarian on the menu.

'Lovely.' In fact, it was about the nicest thing he'd ever had; the food, though rich, positively sung on his tongue. 'Tell me, have you always been an artist?'

'For as long as I remember.'

'Did you have to train?'

'No.'

For now, no one noticed or heard the rhythmic, rumbling

roar out on the streets, the roar of hundreds — hundreds of men chanting and stamping their boots on the tarmac.

'So… so, you like painting.'

'Yes.'

'I wish I could paint.'

'It's not difficult.'

Unlike this conversation, thought Felix. 'Shall we have pudding?' he asked, having to raise his voice to make himself heard above the singer.

'No, I think we should go. I don't like it here.'

'You don't?' Felix couldn't help but take that personally. 'Stella, there's something…'

'What? I can't hear you.'

'I said there's always room for a pudding. Let's see what there is.'

Felix ran his finger down the dessert menu, his lips pursed in concentration. As he did so he heard the chink of delicate crystal as the table next to them toasted good health to the beloved Führer. Stella, her elbows on the table, pretending not to hear, listened as the singer sang of her forbidden love, the feathers on her crown catching the beams of light. *'Time would come for roll call, time for us to part,'* sang Miss Angel. *'Darling, I'd caress you and press you to my heart.'*

'Have you decided?' asked Felix.

The briefest hint of impatience passed over her features but she quickly smothered it with a smile. 'You choose for me.'

'OK, if that's what you want,' he said reaching for his wine glass. Everything felt wrong. He should never have brought her here; it wasn't her sort of place. Problem was, he didn't know what *was* her sort of place. And he realised there was still so much he didn't know about her.

A waiter attended the next table, his back to them. The

diners, a middle-aged couple, gave their orders. The woman, with a butterfly bow laced into her hair, caught Felix's eye. She raised her glass. He turned away.

'Felix, I'm tired. We ought to go.'

'What? Miss out on pudding? Come on.'

A crash of glass at the next table made him jump.

'Oh, I'm so sorry,' screeched the waiter who somehow had knocked a wine glass off the neighbouring table. 'I do apologise.' He knelt down to pick up the shards of the wine glass but, in his haste, cut himself. Felix stared as the waiter drew the gashed thumb to his mouth and sucked off the blood.

It was only when the band stopped playing and the African singer had taken her applause that everyone in the restaurant was strangely aware of something. Something that didn't feel quite right. A hush swept across the restaurant. 'What is that?' asked Stella in a whisper.

'I don't know,' said Felix, rising from his seat. 'But I don't like the sound of it.'

No one else moved. They watched as Felix made his way to the entrance, passing the waiter wrapping a handkerchief around his thumb. He opened the door to the street, feeling the blast of the cold November air. But it wasn't the cold that made him tremble. It was the sound of all those deep voices chanting and the stamping of feet. *Jews out! Jews out!* There was hatred in those voices, pure hate. People began talking in hushed tones, asking questions. What *is* that noise? Where's it coming from?

Felix returned to the table. Stella had turned white. 'My father,' she said, getting to her feet. 'I've got to check on my father. He'll still be there.'

'Your father? Where?'

She didn't answer and was already heading towards the

154

door, reaching for her coat.

'Stella. Stella, wait a minute. Where you going?'

He counted out a few notes and, returning to his table, threw them down on the tablecloth. The waiter nodded his thanks.

Outside, they stood on the pavement. Felix, shivering with the harsh bite of the night, listened to the noise. It sounded so primeval, so malevolently sinister. He couldn't tell where it was coming from; it sounded as if it was everywhere: in the air, echoing down the streets.

'Go home,' said Stella. 'Come see me tomorrow if you like.'

'I don't understand. What's the matter? Where are you going?'

She kissed him on the cheek. 'Some things you don't need to know. Goodbye, Felix.'

Felix had forgotten his scarf. 'Wait for me,' he said. He rushed back inside the restaurant to retrieve it. The waiters, the singer and her band, the customers – everyone was watching him. The woman with the butterfly bow smiled at him again, a fleeting acknowledgement. And at that moment he knew with a dreadful certainty that his life was about to change, that he would never again sample the delight of such a simple, pleasurable evening, even if at times it had been a tad strained.

He rushed back outside. She'd gone. Looking up and down the street, he saw her distinctive coat, momentarily illuminated by a streetlamp. He had to follow her. He rushed down the street and saw Stella take the first left onto Friedrichstrasse. He heard the sound of breaking glass coming from somewhere, and still that chanting noise getting louder and more intimidating. *Jews die! Jews die!* On and on it went, a constant drone filling the air. He passed numerous people, their heads down, rushing to get home. No one wanted to be out on a night like this – unless you were one of them.

And he was one of them. Any other time, he might have rushed home, put on his uniform and joined the fun. But not tonight. From Friedrichstrasse he saw Stella reaching Kolberger Platz up ahead. And that's where they had gathered. Stella had stopped. Felix hung back. You could see them – dressed in their brown uniforms with their peaked caps and swastika armbands. Most appeared to be armed with sticks and cudgels, many carrying firebrands, the macabre dance of the flames. He should have been there, he thought.

She ran down various streets, a left here, a right there, a winding detour to avoid the main thoroughfares. Felix kept up, following her red coat. Each street was festooned with swastika flags hanging from first-floor balconies, fluttering in the breeze. An upright piano lay on the road, smashed up, stray notes of ivory littering the pavement.

He caught sight of a group of Hitler Youth boys halfway down one street throwing bricks and stones at a window emblazoned with the single word: *Jude*. The glass shattered in an explosive arc, a thousand shards of glass. Strangely mesmerising. The boys cheered. Stella took the first left in order to avoid them. And still, in the background, that noise, the swirl of hate. The chanting erupted into a cacophony of cheers and Sieg Heils, unending Sieg Heils: *Sieg Heil, Sieg Heil, Sieg Heil*. Stella paused to catch her breath.

She turned into Kranzerstrasse and Felix following found himself stepping over a carpet of glass. So many of the shops had broken windows. A bakery, a grocer, a delicatessen, all of them vandalised. A truck passed by before skidding to a halt. An SA man jumped out from the back, followed by another and another, a whole mob of them.

He could hear the sound of marching feet. It still seemed to be coming from everywhere, behind him, in front of him, like an invisible army on the march.

Stella took the next right. Felix followed, determined to keep her within his sight. The noise was still there, the sound of leather boots on cobblestones. Somewhere nearby, an explosion ripped through the night.

He followed her as she turned into Elsterplatz. The square was clear of Brown Shirts, yet that noise, increasing in its intensity, threatened to wash over him any moment. Stella quickly crossed over the square, her shadow dancing behind her, Felix in her wake. She seemed to be heading towards the synagogue. Why the synagogue? What would Stella want with a synagogue?

Chapter 23

The synagogue, painted white with a blue dome, was small and – although attractive – was rather unimposing compared to some of the huge ones Felix had seen in the centre of town.

Stella tried the main door but found it locked. She scurried round the side of the building. Felix crept after her, the grass sodden with the damp of the night. Peering round the corner towards the back of the building, he could see her, thumping on the door. 'Dad,' shouted Stella. 'Open up, it's me.'

Felix fell back against the wall. Why would her father be in a synagogue?

Finally, the door opened. 'Stella!' he heard a man say, clearly delighted to see her.

'Dad, we've got to get you home.'

'Why? What on earth –' He stopped on hearing a round of boisterous cheers coming from the square. 'What's happening?' he asked, his voice edged with the tremor of concern.

'God, they're here already,' Felix heard Stella say. 'Quickly, let's go back in.'

Felix waited a moment before trying the door. They hadn't

158

locked it. There was a bolt. He engaged it, securing the door. He was amazed by the space of the interior. Most of the lights had been turned off, yet even in the semi-darkness, it seemed so much bigger from the inside. There was a mystical enchantment to the place: the yellow walls, the Doric columns, the interior stained-glass windows set back in arches, plus the inherent peace within its walls. He saw Stella's shoes running up a spiral staircase. He hid behind one of the columns.

'Are you alone, Dad?' she shouted up.

'Yes, I was just preparing –'

'Oh shit. Come to the window, Dad. There are hundreds of them. Look.'

Felix could hear them out in the square, yelling their threats and invective, a diabolical wall of noise. Then came the chant again: *Jews out! Jews out!*

'Dad, is the door double at the front locked?'

'No, only single locked. But look, Stella, it's all bluster. We've seen it before. They'll get bored in a minute–'

'No, this is different. The whole city's erupting. They're everywhere.'

'What can we do?' he asked.

'Double lock the front door and escape from the back. Where're the keys?'

'In the office. Do you want –'

'Yes, Dad, yes. Quickly.'

Felix could hear Stella's father scuttling off.

'For pity's sake, hurry up, Dad,' she shouted.

Felix jumped on hearing a huge bang against the main door. Then a second. The Brown Shirts outside were ramming the door. The thunderous sound of metal on wood reverberated round the synagogue.

Felix heard the dangling bunch of keys. He saw them

coming back down the staircase, Stella and her father, Stella taking two steps at a time.

Then came the second blow to the door, the sound of wood splintering.

'Oh hell, it's not going to hold. One more hit and they'll be through. Dad, we'll go out the back. Hurry.'

But no sooner had they reached it, they heard the pounding of fists on the back door.

'There isn't another exit, is there?' asked Stella.

'No.'

'We're trapped. We're totally at their mercy.'

Fear seeped into Felix like a cold liquid.

'We've got to hide you, Dad.'

'There's only the office upstairs,' said her father.

They rushed back upstairs. This time, Felix followed, calling out Stella's name as he reached the top.

'Felix, what the…'

'I followed you. I'm sorry.'

They heard the door downstairs shattering and the cheers and shouts of the men as they breached the entrance and stormed into the synagogue. Felix closed the office door behind them and turned the key. He knew that the lock to the office would offer no protection. He tried to calm his breathing, to quell the swelling panic. Stella quickly introduced the two men, then forced her father to hide behind the table. The rectangular room was small and without windows, bare apart from the solid table pushed up against the far wall. Felix switched the light off, plunging them into total darkness except for the thread of light beneath the door. Stella and Felix leant against the wall. Stella's father, reverting to Hebrew, began praying, his voice muttering, trying to maintain his composure.

'Why did you follow me?' asked Stella. 'You had no right.' But she was too frightened to be angry; he could hear the timbre of fear in her voice.

He had no answer. He wished he could see her. All he knew was that he had somehow found himself on the wrong side and, if discovered, they'd lynch him. They'd send him to a concentration camp, they'd kick him out of the party, sack him from his job and evict him and his mother from their home. He couldn't stop himself from trembling, his legs weak. The noise outside was unbearable to hear: the screams, the hysteria, the sound of furniture being upturned, of things being thrown round, the sound of devilish laughter.

'How can they do this?' said Stella.

Felix flinched on hearing the sound of something crashing, followed by an eruption of cheers. 'What was that?'

'The chandelier probably.'

'I think I'm going to be sick.'

'I know. I feel the same.'

They were like wild animals, he thought, men gone mad. Would I have behaved like this? he thought. Stella's father carried on praying, his voice stuttering with fright.

'Oh shit,' said Felix.

'What? What is it?' And then she heard it too – they were on the stairs.

'I'm sorry, Felix,' said Stella. 'I should have...' She stopped. Someone was rigorously rattling the door handle. Her father stopped praying.

They could hear the shouting immediately outside the door. "*It's locked.*" "*Smash it in then, you idiot.*" "*It's not worth it.*" "*It bloody is; it's probably where they keep all their stash.*" They were kicking at the door, aiming for the lock.

'It's not going to hold,' said Stella, the terror in her voice

161

evident.

He heard Stella speaking quickly and quietly to her father in the pitch black. 'Dad, whatever happens to us, we can take it. We're young. Do not show yourself, OK? You stay there. Don't make a sound.'

'I will.'

'I love you, Dad.'

'And I love you, my girl.'

Felix felt Stella's hands reaching out for him. The door flung open. Splinters of wood flew. Stella cried out. Two silhouetted men stood at the door, laughing, sticks of some sort in their hands. One found the light. The unforgiving glare made Felix blink.

'Hey! What have we here?'

'Two Yids for the price of one.'

'We're not Yids,' said Felix as firmly as he could muster. 'We're just making out.'

They guffawed at that. 'In a synagogue? Like fuck. Get out of here.'

Felix took Stella's hand. Just in time, he stopped himself from checking on Stella's father. They emerged from the office to find Brown Shirts everywhere, like savages in a playground: shouting, swearing, kicking at everything in sight, pushing things over. He viewed the scene of utter devastation: windows smashed, broken furniture, prayer books in shreds, ripped carpets. They had destroyed so much in so little time. Yet none paid them any attention. He could see the hatred in Stella's eyes. He glanced over the balcony. Men, working in relays, were carrying armfuls of things outside, their boots crunching over glass and bits of wood. And there, at the centre of it, the skeletal chandelier, neatly surrounded by millions of dazzling bits of glass. Coming down the stairs, floating almost, he saw the stained-glass windows and the Doric columns disfigured by huge splashes of bright red paint. It was hard to reconcile this diabolic image with the serene beauty he'd seen just a few minutes earlier.

They descended to the ground floor, and still no one took any notice of them, it was as if they'd become invisible. The shame bit into him, hurting him within, as acute as any physical pain. He knew that any other day, he would have been in his uniform, one of them. Stella looked drained but then he saw her stiffen. Following her gaze, his stomach turned. Two Brown Shirts, their shirt sleeves rolled up, were emptying large jerry cans of petrol over the pews, the carpets and round the altar. Stella ran towards them. 'No, you can't do this.'

They laughed. 'Try stopping us,' said one, reaching into his trouser pocket. He held up a box of matches.

Stella yelled. She made to grab the man but the other landed a heavy punch into her stomach, doubling her over. The first one lit a match and, lifting his arm, held it high, laughing. Felix, with his hand over Stella's mouth, watched the scene play out. Stella freeing herself from him, beseeched the man not to do it. But he did, he dropped the match. The burning match fell to the ground. The two men ran. It took only a second for the flames to take hold, swiftly sweeping across the central carpet and licking at the pews. Felix screamed for Stella to get away. But she stood rooted, as if transfixed, not noticing the heat that was already building up. The Brown Shirts were making their way out, slapping each other on the back, cheering and shouting. A good job done. 'Stella, your father,' he shouted. And still she did not move. The flames had turned her into a statue.

Felix sprinted back up the spiral stairs, now free of Brown Shirts, and ran to the office. 'Rabbi Hoffmann, it's me, Felix.'

Stella's father emerged from behind the table. 'Have they gone? Is it safe?'

'No, they've set the place alight.'

He grasped his constricting heart. 'No, surely…'

'We've gotta get out of here. Quickly, mein Herr.' He took his hand. The poor man trembled.

They reached the bottom of the stairs. Stella was there, waiting for them. 'They've barricaded the back door,' she said. 'We'll have to leave by the front.'

'No, we can't,' said Felix. 'They'll still be there, hundreds of them.'

'We don't have any choice. Dad, hold on to me. Don't let go.'

Stella's father nodded. Already, the synagogue had filled with smoke, getting denser by the second. Felix could feel it at the back of his throat, the smell of charcoal in his nostrils. At the far end, near the altar, the fire, crackling and fierce, was spreading up the walls, bubbling the paint, then across the pews.

'How can they do this?' asked Stella's father.

Stella, her eyes smarting with tears, began to cough.

The doors at the main entrance were smashed open, hanging on by their hinges. Beyond the thickening veil of smoke, Felix could see the dancing silhouettes of the Brown Shirts gathered around a bonfire. The three of them stopped. With the fire building up behind them and the heat intensifying by the second, they knew they had no choice. The sweat drenched his clothes. Stella kissed the side of his head. Then, taking her father's arm, she said, 'Let's go.' Felix nodded.

Chapter 24

Stella walked in the middle, holding her father's hand to her left, Felix's to her right, still wearing her red coat. Behind them, the altar, racked with fire, collapsed on itself. Together, they strode towards the entrance, the sweat pouring off them. They paused just outside the burning synagogue and cast their eyes over the scene of bedlam before them: a throng of jeering Brown Shirts joined now by a host of ordinary citizens, people drawn from their homes by the noise and spectacle. The mob parted, providing them with an impromptu passageway that led towards the middle of the square and the bonfire that had just taken hold. With no option but to furrow the route before them, Stella, Felix and Stella's father took one careful step after another, the taunts and shouting ringing in their ears. A tall Hitler Youth boy armed with a drum kept a steady beat. The crowd clapped in time with his rhythm.

Felix wanted to scream *I'm not a Jew,* but that would be worse; he'd be pulled to the side and questioned and, once they realised they had a 'traitor' in their midst, they'd kill him. Unexpectedly, amongst all the people, he saw a familiar figure, a ghostly woman. 'There's Frau Pappenheimer,' said Felix, delighted and hugely relieved to see his neighbour, a familiar face, even if she was mad, even if she was a witch dressed, as always, in white. What, he wondered, was she doing here. He caught Frau Pappenheimer's eye. She shook her head, the look of despair in her eyes. Women with expensive-looking coats had joined the throng, a few with small children on their shoulders: all the better, thought Felix, to see the fun, to see history in the making.

They approached the bonfire. 'So, what have we here?' said a deep, guttural voice from a man in a long trench coat, silhouetted by the fire behind him.

'Colonel Telemann,' said Felix.

'Good god, it's you, Stoltenberg. Have you brought me two Jews?'

'No, sir.'

'Yes,' said Stella loudly. 'Yes, he has, the bastard.'

'Good man, Stoltenberg.'

The bonfire, circled by the gathering of brown-clad spectres, had been made up of pieces of wood, segments of pews and hundreds of prayer books, the pages and covers disappearing into the flames, its dry heat burning Felix's face. 'So, what do you think?' said Telemann loudly to a round of cheers, waving his hand around. 'Germany has spoken, and this… this is the result.'

'My synagogue,' said Stella's father, jabbing his finger at the Nazi. 'You philistine, you'll burn in hell for this.'

Telemann laughed and in a sweeping movement removed his gun from its holster and aimed it at the rabbi's head. The circle of onlookers cheered and stamped their feet. Behind them, the synagogue roared with flames, black smoke rising into the night sky and blotting out the moon.

'Are you with them?' asked Telemann of Felix, a sneer on

his face.

'No, he's not,' said Stella. 'He's nothing to do with us.'

'Throw the Jews into the fire,' someone shouted, a phrase picked up by others until it rapidly turned into a chant that kept time with the drummer boy's beat. *Throw the Jews into the fire. Throw the Jews into the fire.*

A young Brown Shirt ran up to the colonel. 'Sir, I've got them.'

'Aha,' shouted Telemann, taking his revolver from its holster. Holding up a rolled-up scroll in his hand, he addressed the crowd, 'See what we have here?'

The crowd cheered with fresh gusto. Stella's father leapt towards the colonel. Telemann pushed him away.

'The Torah scroll,' shouted Telemann, waving the scroll above his head. 'Sacred to the Jew. I wouldn't want to wipe my arse with this. I feel dirty even touching it.'

People hooted and cheered.

'Give it to me, give it here,' shouted Stella's father.

Stella, pushed and jostled, pleaded. 'Please, don't...'

Throw the Jews into the fire. Throw the Jews into the fire.

Beneath the noise and shouting, Stella shouted at Felix to leave. He shook his head, realising it wasn't bravery that kept him there but the fear of being alone. So much noise: the cheering, the shouting, the drumbeat, the chanting, the crackle of the bonfire, the synagogue burning behind them... Felix put his hands to his ears, desperate to block it all out, to transport himself away from this hell.

Then, amidst it all, Telemann threw the scroll high above his head. It all happened as if in slow motion. The crowd drew its breath as the scroll spun in the air. Stella's father, sidestepping his daughter, threw himself at the Nazi. The two men fell back. Stella shrieked. Someone caught the flailing

Nazi, while Stella's father fell to the ground. A crowd of men moved in, blocking Felix's view, kicking at the stricken rabbi and hitting him again and again. Telemann emerged from the scrum, a smile on his face. He removed his revolver from its holster and winked at Felix as if trying to capture him within his complicity. Felix felt the tight pull of fear in his bowels. Telemann disappeared back into the melee. Felix's knees gave way. Someone scooped him up from under his arms. He heard a woman's voice, not unkind. 'Careful now, lad. Let's get you out of here.' It was Frau Pappenheimer, smelling of almonds, reassuring somehow. 'It's time we left,' said the scratchy voice.

'Stella. Stella needs me.' He said it despite the spiralling of panic within him.

'There's nothing you can do for her now. These devils have got her.'

Defeated and weakened, he allowed himself to be led away.

A shot rang out in the air. There followed a deep moment of silence. Felix froze. The crowd erupted again into cheers. Felix heard Stella's wailing and knew his heart was breaking. He screamed her name but Frau Pappenheimer, more determined than ever, pulled him away. Felix tried to escape her determined grip but Frau Pappenheimer wouldn't let go, digging her long fingers into his flesh. The last of his energy drained away, then a darkness descended. Frau Pappenheimer draped her coat over him, and he smelt that scent of almonds and, for a cowardly moment, felt safe. But he'd let her down; he'd never see her again. He'd let his uniform down; he'd let his comrades down, he'd let his Führer down.

Chapter 25

Felix woke up to find his mother sitting at the end of his bed. 'What happened last night?' she asked, her voice laced with anger. She threw a newspaper at him.

It took a second but then it all came flooding back. It'd been easily the most frightening experience of his life. He'd come home near midnight. His mother was waiting up for him, furious, worried sick and relieved to the point of tears when finally he walked through the door. He remembered Frau Pappenheimer guiding him away from the square, away from the mob, but had no recollection of how he'd got home. 'Did you not think I'd be worried?' she asked. Frankly, he hadn't. He was twenty-two, a member of the SA; he could do as he pleased.

But she too had heard things that night, she said, seen things from her window, and her son was out there somewhere and she had no idea where. She was terrified. Felix had almost fallen through the door and hadn't been able to stop shivering. His mother made him a hot water bottle. He jabbered and screamed, told her of the mayhem, the violence and the glass, but that was it. Telemann had murdered Stella's father there on the street, in cold blood.

'The papers say thousands of Jews have been arrested and sent to the concentration camps. Listen: "The German people have risen up against the scourge of Jewry, they have sought their own justice against the wicked Jew. Synagogues, Jewish businesses and homes throughout the country have been targeted and destroyed. There was so much broken glass on the streets, glittering like so much crystal, they're already dubbing it the Night of Broken Glass, *Kristallnacht.*"'

Felix shook his head. 'It was the work of the mob; Hitler would never condone such violence.' He did draw a degree of comfort from that. Hitler, once he knew, would be appalled that his men had behaved like savages in his name.

'I know, Felix,' she said, resting her hand on his sleeve.

He shook it off, he had no need for his mother's cloying concern. Felix knew it was more essential than ever that he held firm to his belief and show the country that it was people like him, not the uniformed thugs, that truly represented the party and everything that was good about it.

'I'll leave you to get dressed. You've got school today.'

His mother had been right after all, damn her; Stella *was* Jewish, she'd lied to him. He'd had sex with a Jewish woman. There was a law against that; she would have known. His blood ran cold. If he'd been found out… if someone he knew had seen them together… His head pounded. Her father had been killed, right there in front of her. He was sorry about that but…

'She lied to me,' he said, sitting up in his bed. She'd lied, she'd bloody lied. He walked across his room, feeling as if he aged a hundred years overnight. He looked out of his bedroom window down onto the street, the early morning blanketed by mist. A couple of boys were playing football. In the distance he could see plumes of smoke. He heard the sound of a siren, a fire engine on its way somewhere. He saw people rushing by. The world looked different. He was different. He shivered.

He'd been on the verge of asking her to marry him. What a fool. *Kristallnacht*. The biggest event of his life and he had missed it, too dewy-eyed over a peroxide Jew. He clasped his hands to his head. It still seemed wrong somehow. If he'd been there, in his SA uniform, he might not have thought twice about it. The Jews, they deserved whatever they got. But instead, he'd seen it all unravel from their point of view, had tasted their fear, their incomprehension, their utter defencelessness. He was tainted by the experience. He didn't know what to think any more. But there was one thing he was sure of… he'd been betrayed and he never wanted to see Stella Hoffmann again.

He had to get to work. Last night's clothes were heaped on his wicker chair, the stench of smoke filling the room. He found the velvet box in the inside pocket of his jacket. He flipped open the lid to reveal a silver band with a small ruby nestled on top. A week's wages, and for what? He'd have to sell it, see if he could claw the money back. The bitch, to have led him on like that, to have allowed him to think he had a future with her. How dare she? 'Damn you,' he said aloud. All that hope, all that emotional investment, and for what? For nothing, absolutely nothing. Except a well of emptiness in the pit of his stomach, knowing he'd been thoroughly duped. How she must have laughed at him, mocked his naivety.

He wondered momentarily where she was now, whether she too had been arrested and sent to Sachsenhausen, the concentration camp just outside Berlin. The place was one of unimagined horror. No one knew for sure what went on there, but occasionally you'd hear of someone coming back, young men turned old, fit men turned crippled. To think his relationship with Stella might have landed him there. He shuddered at the thought. He threw the velvet box across the room. 'You bitch,' he screamed.

He stormed through to the kitchen, still in his pyjamas. His mother was there, stirring a simmering pan of porridge, the kettle whistling on the stove. 'I was just… Felix? Felix, what's wrong?'

He pulled open the cutlery draw, found the sharpest knife.

He yanked the picture off the wall where, despite his mother's objections, he'd hung it a few days before. 'Bitch,' he seethed as he sliced the knife through the canvas. 'You bitch…' He attacked it again, tearing *The Blue Lady* in half, slashing at her, destroying her smile, ripping through her face. He pulverized it, smashed its frame, reduced the painting to nothing but shreds of canvas, devoid of meaning. Satisfied, he threw the painting on the floor – panting, happy, exuberant even. Then, as quickly as it came, his anger and his strength deserted him, leaving him weak and empty. The knife slipped out of his fingers, falling to the floor.

He fell to his knees, his heart hollow, his vision clouded by tears.

PART THREE

Chapter 26

Berlin, September 1942

It's a strange existence, knowing you could be executed at any moment. It could be next week, tomorrow, within the hour. Time creeps slowly. There are footsteps outside in the corridor. Rudolph Karstadt stands; they strain their ears, hoping that whoever it is goes away. But there's a small part of him that thinks, let them come, get it over and done with. This life, in the cell, it's like living in a netherworld, not really living, not quite dead, somewhere in between. The footsteps fade away.

'When I was a young man,' says Rudolph, sitting on the bench, 'back in the days of the Weimar Republic, being a homosexual in Berlin was deemed quite fashionable. Hard to credit it now.' His eyes drift away. He shifts his weight on the bench. 'I saw Marlene Dietrich sing once. What a woman. You know the Nazis tried to persuade her to star in their films, offered her a lot of money. That's why she emigrated to the States. She knew what it was all about; she saw what was happening.' He leans forward, his elbows on his knees. He looks up at Felix who is still standing next to the cell door. 'Unlike you.'

The accusation stings. But he's right, of course. Even as a twenty-two-year-old man, he feared being left on the outside. The spectre of his lonely childhood still haunted him. Klaus Beck had saved him. He thought Stella Hoffmann had saved him too – for a while. He had to belong, to be on the inside. But being on the inside didn't mean you were one of the thugs, ransacking synagogues, blighting the lives of those deemed impure. Stella had been right about that; he was destined for better things. What a fool he'd been.

Rudolph speaks. 'We hovered on the precipice for a long time. That night, *Kristallnacht*, that was the day we stepped over. That was the night evil emerged from the shadows.'

'But you were part of it too; you are as guilty as me.'

'I can't deny it.' He sighs. 'I wonder why they haven't come for us yet.' He stands, paces the length of the cell and back again. 'We're both walking dead, you and me.'

'How did they find out?'

'You mean me and my man? We thought the office where he worked was empty, we both did. It was late at night. Everyone had gone home. Everyone, that is, except the janitor. The look on his face. I could almost laugh. He tried blackmail. I paid him too. But of course, the price went up and I told him to fuck himself. And so, one day, unbeknownst to me, he followed me home. And then he told my wife.'

'A bit of a shock for her.'

Rudolph laughs, shakes his head at the memory of it. 'Telling me. She went mad. A bit like you with that painting. And' – he sighs, his face scrunching up – 'being the good Nazi frau that she is, she did her duty and reported me.'

He recounts the tale as if he's telling a lighthearted anecdote: the flippant tone, the facetious turn of phrase, the wave of his hand. But the pain is there for Felix to see, etched in his eyes. 'And now you're here.'

'And now I'm here.'

He wants to ask the man a question but isn't sure how to frame it. He tries nonetheless. 'Can I ask, what was he like, your...?' He doesn't know what to call him – his lover, his boyfriend... companion maybe?

'Anton. That was his name. Anton was... he was great. He was beautiful, intelligent, generous, good fun, and... and he was a bastard.'

'Oh.'

There's a quiver in his voice now. He forces a laugh, the means to cover it up. It doesn't deceive Felix; it hardly deceives himself. He may be a good listener but he's not good at unburdening his own story.

'Like I said, he was much younger than me, not much older than you really. He claimed he was half blind, and that got him excused from active service. He wasn't blind; he merely seduced an optician into vouching for him. Clever chap, you see. He was as poor as a church mouse and that's where I came in. Oh, I knew I was being taken for a ride; I wasn't born yesterday, and he knew I knew. Still, we maintained the charade. I still had money to buy things that most people couldn't afford because of the war. And I knew the people to go to, people who had access, connections, the black market.

'Sometimes it was simply a case of bribery; you know how it is when you wear the uniform. I bought him things – food, clothes, decent shoes, I even offered to pay his bloody rent so he could live somewhere better, but he was a mummy's boy at heart, didn't want to leave his mother. He had me twisted round his little finger. It was a price worth paying, I loved him so. It was hard work though. I was usually away on service somewhere, and when I was back, it was difficult finding places to… Like I said, Anton lived with his mother, and me with my sex-crazed wife.'

'What happened after the janitor discovered you?'

'Nothing at first, not while I paid the beastly man his pound of flesh. But when my wife found out, my lovely Anton saw the writing on the wall, and he scarpered quicker than a sewer rat.' He shivers. 'Is it me, or is it getting colder in here?'

'Have you seen her since? Or him?'

'No. Guess I never will again. Anyway… And your Stella… I don't suppose you ever saw her again.'

'Ah, as a matter of fact…'

'Yes?'

'As a matter of fact, I did…

Chapter 27

One year earlier: Berlin, December 1941

It was three o'clock on a freezing-cold morning. Behind him stood two of his Gestapo subordinates – hefty, bull-necked men who said nothing and understood even less. It was quite the seediest part of the capital. The air positively hummed with a seething sort of menace: the lack of light, walls marked with graffiti, a metal fire escape to the side of a building, a pile of wooden pallets, the smell of cooking coming from the back of a restaurant mingling with the smell of rotting rubbish. His shoes squelched on something unpleasant. Two cats scattered as he passed.

Number eighteen. Felix Stoltenberg thumped on the apartment door. He lifted the flap of the letterbox. 'Open up,' he shouted through. 'SS. Open up now.' He knew all the neighbours would have heard him but no one would show their face; they wouldn't dare. He knocked on the door again. He knew how they were feeling in there; he remembered it all too well. Eventually, he saw a light come on, then, through the letterbox, saw a pair of female slippers shuffling along the tiled floor. He straightened. 'Coming, coming,' said a terrified-sounding voice from within.

The door opened a slither. A middle-aged woman stood before him, her fingers visibly shaking, clutching her dressing gown, her unruly hair streaked with grey, her eyes wide with dread. 'Frau Wankel?' She nodded. 'Let us in, please,' he said, holding out his identification papers. He walked in, pushing past her, the two muscle men following. He introduced himself and his colleagues and found himself in a cramped hallway, its walls lined with peeling wallpaper, a hat stand, a pile of old newspapers, a broom. 'Where's your husband?' he snapped.

The woman mumbled something, unable to catch his eye.

'What? I didn't hear you. Speak up.'

'I said I don't know where he is.'

He barked a load of questions at her from which he gathered that the woman hadn't seen her husband for a while and she had no idea where he'd gone or when he'd be back. She was lying of course. They always lie. Her husband, she said, was a ne'er do well; he owed her almost a month's housekeeping, reckoned he had another woman on the go.

'When was the last time you saw him?'

'Here. About a week ago.'

'Did he say anything about going away?'

'No. Why you asking anyway? What's he done now?'

He marched through to their living room, his men remaining at the door. The room stunk of greasy food, piles of clothes, an ironing board propped up.

'I need a photograph.'

'You think I've got a photo of that old git? You ain't half stupid for such a grand man in his dandy uniform.'

If she didn't look so pathetic, he'd gladly have slapped her.

Instead, he said, 'I'd advise you to be more circumspect with your words, Frau Wankel.'

'Circumspect? Such big words. Want to check the rest of this shithole? Check under the bed, why don't you? In the wardrobe. You won't find him.'

He was impressed by her ability to maintain eye contact, by the strength of her voice. But he'd seen it before, the *you can't intimidate me* attitude. It never lasted; an hour at SS headquarters soon diminished them to quivering wrecks.

Felix heard something, his boys too. They froze a moment. The expression of horror on Frau Wankel's face confirmed it. He sprang into action, pushed at a door. Locked. 'Stop,' he shouted.

One of his men shoved him to one side and, with a heavy boot, kicked at the door. Two, three kicks. Splinters of wood flew. A fourth kick, the door gave way. The bathroom. A man trying to squeeze through the window, but stuck. Felix laughed on seeing the impossible position the man had got himself in: half in, half out, one leg in the wash basin below the window, his other knee against his chest, unable to move. The window was simply too small. 'Oh dear, oh dear,' he said. 'What a pickle. Otto Wankel, I presume?'

*

Four o'clock and still not even a hint of light. Felix and his bull-necked colleagues took Wankel back to base in Prinz Albert Strasse. Time to go home; it'd been a long day. At this hour, the SS bosses had their drivers take the night-shift workers home in their cosy cars. Felix was about to order his driver for the night to take him home. Instead, for reasons he couldn't articulate, he wanted to return to a place where, momentarily, a long time ago, he'd been happy. But why now, at such an improbable time of day? His mind empty of thought, he ordered his driver to take him there.

They drove through the empty streets of the capital, the German eagle pendant on the bonnet fluttering in the wind. Twenty minutes and they were there. He stepped out of the car and rubbed his hands, his breath visible in front of him. 'Give me five minutes.' He knew his driver had also come to the end of his shift and would be wanting to get home: home to a wife, his children, a warm bed, normality. The driver switched off the headlamps, already dimmed because of the blackout, plunging them into the night. Felix blinked, allowing his eyes to adjust to the darkness.

Hands in pockets, he stepped along a path, the damp leaves squelching beneath his feet. He reached the edge of the lake just as the dawn chorus had started. How deafening it was, he thought, how utterly reassuring somehow. Lake Tegel stretched ahead of him beneath the first glaze of light, the early morning mist hovering above its surface. The surrounding trees seemed alive with invisible life, heaving with thousands of birds singing, heralding the new day. He breathed in the crisp air, relishing the coldness as it hit his lungs. He breathed out vapours of icy breath and drew in the scent of damp leaves and musty wood, of bark and pine.

The last time he'd been here, was with her. Flashes of images came back to him – her hand in the water, the V-shaped ripples, waving hello to fellow rowers. He remembered her words: *I never want this day to end.*

But it had ended; it had all ended that terrible night of breaking glass. *Kristallnacht.* Three years had passed. Love had turned to resentment, resentment to disillusionment, disillusionment to anger.

And now he was here, three years on, wedded to a life of

hate. It was everywhere now, no longer lurking in the shadows, but fully visible in the expressions of people on the street, on the U-bahn, in the markets and churches. So ubiquitous, one had almost become desensitised to it. And he embraced it, the hate. It protected him from his heart, gave him a reason to carry on, a direction he could follow. Where it might take him, he didn't care, didn't think about. It wasn't important. What was important was to put as much distance between now and his time with Stella. Stella Hoffmann had killed something in him that night – hope, humanity, love, whatever you wanted to call it. He cared little for humanity now; that had died on that night three years ago, on *Kristallnacht*. He had had a plan, a ring, a dream. All of it involved her, Stella. And she'd killed it, all of it. And yet, he was here, at the lake, Lake Tegel, shivering with cold, alone, very much alone, thinking of *her*.

A skittering interrupted his thoughts: a couple of squirrels. He wondered, as often he did, what she was doing now, indeed whether she was still alive, whether she was managing to keep her head above the hatred that he was helping to engineer. He picked up a small, flat stone and bounced it up and down in his palm. He hoped, against all probability, that she was doing OK, surviving somehow amid the chaos. He knew he would never see her again. He knew equally he'd never forget her, not now, not ever.

He checked his watch. Half past six. Time to get back, time to allow his driver for the night to go home.

He skimmed the stone across the lake, watched it zip away into the murky light.

Chapter 28

Felix Stoltenberg arrived for work at the SS headquarters at number eight Prinz Albert Strasse near Potsdamer Platz at noon. He had a meeting in the colonel's office first thing.

He found Colonel Friesler on his feet, his hands behind his back, gazing out of his window. 'Ah, Lieutenant, come in.' The colonel was about forty with a shaved head that glistened under the chandelier, and metal-rimmed glasses that magnified the dart of malice in his eyes. Felix glanced up at the colonel's Führer portrait. 'Well done for arresting Otto Wankel last night. Good work.'

Felix tried to control his beaming smile. 'Thank you, sir.'

Friesler was a man imbued with an aura of authority, from the shine of his leather straps that criss-crossed his spotless tunic to the glittering gold of the elaborately-patterned braids that sat on his shoulders. A party man through and through. 'Now, I want you to deal with him, Stoltenberg. Get him to reveal where he's hiding these bloody Jews. Make sure he talks. Think you can manage that?'

'Sir.'

Felix was told the suspect was waiting for him in Room 2J,

one of the basement rooms.

Otto Wankel came across as a weedy little man with his crew-cut hair, his catlike eyes furtive behind his round glasses, and his ill-fitting jacket. But Felix knew him to be a tough, sinewy operator who knew everything that went on within the district. Whether it was prostitution, gambling or thieving, Wankel either had a hand in it or he knew who had. And now, he had turned his hand to hiding Jews. And his clients, the Jews, were usually desperate enough to pay a high price to be hidden.

The war had been raging for two years. Joseph Goebbels, Hitler's propaganda minister, wanted Berlin to be free of Jews. They had just started deporting them. Hence, scum like Otto Wankel saw the chance for a fast buck and offered to hide Jews desperate enough to pay his extortionate fees.

The guard, waiting outside Room 2J jerked to attention and, unlocking the door, allowed Felix through. He found Wankel, as expected, sitting down on a small wooden chair in the middle of the room, his arms tied to the chair rests, his calves to its legs. The room was small, just a few feet square, the chair with Wankel upon it the only item in the space. There were no windows, simply a slide viewer carved into the thick door. The ingrained cold seeped from its walls. A dull light bulb screwed into the ceiling provided the only light – but no cord in sight. After all, they didn't want their guests hanging themselves.

'Herr Wankel, we meet again.'

Felix, hands behind his back, paced up and down in front of Wankel. Wankel, breathing heavily, his chin on his chest, viewed him with a sullen expression. The man had already been battered, his left eye blue and swollen, his forehead bruised, and his lips bloodied. Dark stains of blood coloured his shirt and jacket. He wouldn't have been asked any questions yet, just softened up a bit. Nothing too severe, just a statement of intent. Wankel, his face filthy with dirt and dried sweat, was shivering.

It was certainly chilly within these damp, thick walls, but Felix suspected it was more than the cold that was causing Wankel to tremble. The place stunk of the sweat of the many men and women who had found themselves within these four walls. They may not have known it, but those found here could count themselves lucky – this small room was merely for preliminary questioning. If things went well, then this room need be their only experience of the SS's hospitality. For those not so forthcoming, a further room waited, one much bigger, one furnished with a workman's bench laden with all the tools of the trade – pliers, hammers, knuckle dusters and suchlike, plus a set of electrodes, a large water butt and other such joyful things.

Felix reached to the scabbard under his jacket tails and produced a knife. Wankel raised his head, a flash of fear in his eyes. 'An Imperial Army dagger from the war,' said Felix. 'A rather fine specimen. Look,' he said, waving it in front of Wankel's eyes. 'It has the Imperial eagle on it. A fine piece of craftsmanship, I always think. No doubt it belonged to someone who fought in the war, died a hero's death perhaps, a man who gave his blood for this country. And that is why I particularly despise scum like you. Men who want to undermine the efforts of heroes who knew the meaning of sacrifice, men who undermine the work of the Führer and us, his loyal servants.' Prodding the tip of the dagger against the end of Wankel's nose, Felix quietly asked, 'Where are you hiding your Jews?'

'I don't know what you're talking about.'

'What?'

Wankel cleared his throat. 'I said –'

'I heard what you said but somehow I don't believe you.'

Felix began pacing again, hands behind his back, still gripping the dagger. 'So, let's recap. It's been a month now since the law required all Jews above the age of six to display a yellow star prominently on their left breast. No more anonymity. Now we can see clearly the enemy on our streets. Exposed. Fine if they're allowed to work in the factories for our benefit but not fine for those marked down for deportation. They're running to ground. They need places to hide. They can't afford to stay in one place for more than a few nights. So, this is where you come in. For a fee, you can find them a safe place.' He leaned in, their noses almost touching. 'How much do you charge, out of interest?'

'That's not my sort of racket.'

Felix recoiled from the man's breath. Straightening up, he continued. 'No? Easy money, surely.'

Wankel shook his head. 'Not me,' he said.

'Listen, Wankel, it's an easy choice. You either tell me now and save yourself a lot of trouble, or we beat the shit out of you and you tell us anyway.' Wankel's head flew to the side as the back of Felix's hand thwacked him against the side of the face. 'So, save yourself the beating and just tell me. I'll untie you, and you can walk right out of here. And who knows, even a devious little runt like you might feel some satisfaction that you've helped the nation at this most difficult time.'

'I really don't know. It's not…'

'Yes?'

Wankel swallowed. 'I told you; it's not the sort of thing I get involved in.'

'What? Fleecing Jews?'

'I leave that sort of thing to you.'

He hit him again, breaking the man's nose: the snap of gristle and bone, the spurt of blood. 'Right, listen here, scum. I'm giving you one hour to come up with names and places.'

'Sod off, I'm not doing your dirty work for you.'

The blade ripped through the flesh with surprising ease, only coming to a halt on hitting the wood of the chair rest on the other side. Wankel screamed as the blood spurted from his hand, his eyes bulging from his head, his legs, pinned to the chair, shaking violently. Felix removed the knife from the man's hand, the shirtsleeve already soaked in blood. Wankel carried on screaming, his whole body convulsing. Felix wiped the blood from the blade and replaced the dagger back in its scabbard.

'I'll be back in one hour,' he said, rapping on the door.

Chapter 29

It didn't take long for Otto Wankel to succumb. After all, he'd already collected the money from the Jews he hid. And they were hardly in the position to ask for a refund. He left the offices on Prinz Albert Strasse limping and cursing, with his hand heavily bandaged.

On Colonel Friesler's orders, Felix formed an 'aktion' squad. He and his men had borrowed a couple of trucks from their SA colleagues. He had a list of names and addresses. It was simply a matter of finding the names and packing them onto the truck and taking them to the transit camp recently set up at the former synagogue at Levetzowstrasse in the district of Moabit. From there, they'd be taken to the train station and shipped off east to be resettled in the General Government Area of what had been Poland.

It was five in the morning. Nine men stood before him shivering in the darkened courtyard behind the offices. 'Right, pay attention; these are Colonel Friesler's instructions. We are not to cause any distress to members of the general public. If any Jew tries to resist, we are to deal with it...' Here, he read from the sheet of instructions passed to him the previous evening. 'We are to deal with it efficiently, effectively and with the minimum of fuss and the minimum of resources. Understood?'

'So, are we allowed to kick the shit out of them, sir?' asked Leo Höch, a nasty little man with a gammy leg, a legacy of the previous war.

'No, Höch, you may not. We're to cause minimum damage to property. This is not to be a repeat of Kristallnacht. Nice and quiet. OK, let's go.'

Two hours later, the morning aktion was going according to plan. Otto Wankel had done well; every name on his list had proved fruitful. The raids had netted some twenty Jews who were now on their way to the synagogue. Felix's men looked pleased with themselves. This was easy work. There were just the two addresses to go, both within the same block.

It was approaching seven o'clock by the time they turned into Himmlerstrasse, a cobbled street that had been badly hit in a bombing raid. Ominous clouds pressed down on the city. Several of the houses had been badly damaged, roofs caved in, masonry piled high. Uprooted trees lay across the street, forcing the men to park up their truck a couple blocks away. 'Bloody, cowardly English,' said Felix. 'Right, it's down there: number forty-six. Sixth floor, then the fourth. Höch, you want to join me on this one?'

'I would, sir, but I don't fancy those stairs,' he said, slapping his gammy leg.

'Private Thalbach, what about you?'

Together, Felix and Thalbach walked the last stretch to number forty-six. They tipped their hats to various people making their way to work, and a man pushing an elderly gentleman in a wheelchair.

'This is it,' said Felix. 'We'll go to apartment twenty-two on

190

the sixth floor first. Belongs to a Frau Reuter.' They flashed their ID cards at the block warden, and climbed the stone stairs up to the sixth floor, Thalbach huffing behind him. 'Keep up, Thalbach.'

'Sorry, sir. Lungs ain't been right since the war.'

'Gee. What with your lungs and Höch's leg...'

'Hey, Lieutenant, can I ask you a question?'

'If you must.'

'Well, don't get me wrong or nothing but do you know what happens to the Jews? You know, once we've shipped them out?'

'Yeah. They'll be housed in camps out in Poland and put to labour to help the Reich's war effort.'

'Oh, they don't shoot them, then?'

'No. Why would they when they can provide all that free labour? It's invaluable.'

'It's just that I heard –'

'You heard wrong, Thalbach. Now shut up.'

Felix strode along the walkway overlooking the quadrant below. He'd got to number twenty-two while Thalbach was still climbing up the last stairs, his laboured breathing announcing his arrival. Felix knocked on the door. 'Open up. SS.' All the neighbours would have heard but, again, not a single one would dare show their face. He imagined them listening behind their doors, either quivering with fear or silently rejoicing that another Jew was about to have their comeuppance. It opened almost immediately. The woman smiled as if she were expecting someone. The smile froze on her lips. 'My God, Felix.'

His mouth gaped open. 'You? What are you...?'

'I live here. Is that what you wanted to ask?'

She smiled at him, a smile tinged with uncertainty, a smile

that tugged at his insides. He wasn't sure how to proceed, what to do. 'Wait a moment. I'll be straight back' He rushed back down the walkway to the stairway. 'Thalbach, you stay here a minute, catch your breath.'

'Why?' said Thalbach between breaths.

'I think this one needs a delicate touch; know what I mean?'

'Guess so.' He clearly didn't, but, thankful for the rest, plonked himself down on the top step.

Felix marched back to the apartment, letting himself in, buzzing with excitement and apprehension at the same time. He closed the door behind him. He found her standing next to the window, gazing out over the city. 'What brings you here, Felix?' she asked without looking at him.

'I'm looking for a Frau Reuter.'

Now she turned to face him. 'Well, you've found her.'

'You?'

'My married name.'

'Oh. Come to think of it, you said you were married.' This was going to be difficult. 'You know why I'm here.'

'No.'

'Ingrid, please.'

He could see the torment in Ingrid's mind, weighing up the options, the realisation she had none. 'You know Herr Wankel?' he asked.

He saw her deflate, her complexion paling.

He continued. 'He, er… He gave us some names.'

She shook her head, swallowing the betrayal. 'What do you want me to do, Felix?'

'To tell me the truth.'

'You don't have to do this, Felix.'

'I'm sorry, Ingrid. If I don't, my colleague will.'

She went to a bedroom, quietly called out two names. Two

children appeared, their heads bowed, a girl of about ten, a boy half her size, his eyes dark behind round, metal-rimmed glasses.

'You've come to take them away, haven't you?'

'To be resettled.' He saw the girl take the boy's hand.

She stepped behind them, placing a hand on their shoulders. 'Just like your colleagues took their parents.'

'Ingrid...'

'Yes?'

'I thought... You used to be a maiden.'

'We all take different paths, Felix. You've taken yours, I see.'

The words stung. He looked at them, the two kids with their pitiable eyes, the sorrow emanating from them like an odour, leaning into Ingrid, expecting her to save them.

The sharp knock on the door made them all jump. 'Lieutenant?' It was Thalbach. 'You OK in there, Lieutenant?'

Felix froze.

'Aren't you going to let him in, Felix?'

'Lieutenant?'

'Yeah, it's all right, Private; give me a minute.'

He made to leave, pausing at the door. 'It was nice to see you again, Ingrid. Sorry to have missed your husband.'

A ghost of a smile crossed Ingrid's lips but it was in her eyes he saw the gratitude.

'Felix?'

'Yes?'

'There is no husband.'

*

Two floors down, Felix thumped on the door of number 12. He could hear the shuffle of feet on the other side of the door.

193

'Coming,' came a woman's voice, the tremor in her voice audible. He heard the bolts being drawn back. The door opened to reveal a stooped, silver-haired woman. In her hands was a hairbrush, her fingers trembling. 'Frau Hildebrandt?' He showed her his ID. 'We've received information that you're hiding four Jews here.'

She peered up at him. 'No, but I have a circus troupe sleeping in the kitchen.'

Thalbach behind him laughed out loud. He had to give it to the old hag, she had guts. He pushed past her, Thalbach following. He found himself in a living room resembling an antique shop, full of knick knacks, statuettes, figurines, a boar's head on the wall, several paintings of women in bodices and men in wigs. He went through to the bedroom on the left, as Otto Wankel had advised. There, to the right side of the bed, stood a large, heavy-looking wardrobe. Between them, Felix and Thalbach manoeuvred it out of the way. It wasn't easy. There had to be a man in the house, thought Felix; there was no way the old woman could budge this by herself. She stood behind them. Her confidence had disappeared like water through a sieve. She must have known she'd been betrayed and was no doubt trying to work out who had squealed.

They pushed the wardrobe aside to reveal a door. 'So the clowns are to be found here, is that right, Frau Hildebrandt?' asked Felix. Thalbach laughed again. The door was locked. Felix clicked his fingers at her. 'Key.'

'M-my s-son has it.'

'What time's he due back, Frau Hildebrandt?'

'He's gone out to work. He won't be back till this evening.'

'How convenient.' He turned to Thalbach and nodded.

Thalbach produced his revolver and simply shot at the lock. The old woman screamed. Two shots and a hefty push was all it took to weaken it. Thalbach kicked open the door, splinters of wood flying. Everything happened so quickly. A ghostlike figure in white charged out, her arm raised, screeching. The arm came down, with a flash of metal. A spurt of blood shot across the room. Thalbach staggered back, yelling in pain. Felix reached for his revolver. The old woman maintained her screaming. Thalbach fell to his knees, his hands on his face covered in blood gushing from between his fingers, a knife in his eye. The ghost figure, fleet of foot, ran.

Felix gave chase. He could see her hurtling down the circular staircase, her white dress billowing out over the bannister, her sandals slapping on the stone steps. He could still hear Thalbach's screams. He shouted at her to stop, hoping the block warden would hear and come to his aid. He reached the courtyard and saw her charging across, surprisingly nimble, the dress flapping behind her. He leveled his revolver. 'Halt! Halt or I fire,' he shouted. He'd never fired his gun in anger and he knew he had but the one chance. She didn't stop. He fired, the sound bouncing back off the walls. The ghost gave out a little cry and collapsed in a heap. The block warden appeared. 'Jesus, what's going on?'

Felix kept hold of his revolver and slowly walked towards the figure lying face-down prostrate on the cobbled courtyard, her legs at awkward angles. The image of Ingrid with her hands on the shoulders of the two children flashed across his mind.

The block warden reached her at the same time. A circle of red formed on her back, spoiling her white dress. Using his foot, the block warden turned her over.

'Oh, shit,' said Felix, shaking his head.

'What's up? You know her?'

'Yeah, unfortunately. The madwoman from my block, Frau Pappenheimer.' *Our very own prophet of doom*, he thought, *our very own witch who saved me from a braying mob.* He had wondered what had happened to her.

'And now you've shot her.'

'Yes.' His hands trembled. 'Now I've shot her.'

He'd killed the witch and somehow he knew it to be a bad omen for things to come.

Chapter 30

Stella Hoffmann stared at the letter, her fingers trembling, re-reading it over and again. The letter was from the main office of the Reich security services. It informed Frau Hoffmann and her 15-year-old daughter that they were to be resettled in the General Government Area, formerly known as Poland. At precisely noon on New Year's Day, two officers of the Gestapo would pick them up for transportation to the transit camp at the former synagogue on Levetzowstrasse. Attached was a leaflet that provided a precise list of items that they, as evacuees, were allowed to take. They were to pack warm clothing and underwear, medicines and toothbrushes and soap. They were to label their packages with their name and address, and ensure that the yellow star was clearly visible on all coats, jackets or other outer garments. They were to take their passports, but all cash, jewellery, savings books and other financial items had to be surrendered to the Reich authorities.

Charlotte came in, a towel wrapped around her midriff and another around her head. She'd been having a morning bath. 'Mum, have you seen my hairbrush? Is there something wrong? What's the matter?'

Stella passed her the letter. Charlotte gasped on reading it. 'What shall we do? We'll have to go.' Her voice shook.

'Go? Don't be ridiculous, girl. We can't go.'

Charlotte sat down at the table, the letter still in her hand, casting her eyes over all her mother's painting materials. 'So what do we do instead, Mum? Go into hiding? We can't do that.' She spoke quickly, nervously. 'Where would we go? We don't know people, we don't have anyone we can trust.'

'Charlotte, darling, you've heard the rumours.'

'They're just rumours, aren't they? Doesn't mean to say they're true.'

'Oh, and you'd be prepared to take that risk, would you? Prepare to be murdered?'

'No, of course not.'

Charlotte looked close to tears. Stella swallowed; she couldn't cry, not now, not in front of her daughter. She was hard, always had been, and now was not the time to crumble. 'I'll think of something,' she said. 'Go on, you get dressed. You've got school today. It's cold out. You'll need your coat.'

Both of them glanced over at the coat stand next to the front door. Their coats were there, Stella's bright red one, and Charlotte's dark blue one. And clearly visible on both of them was the five-pointed yellow star with the letter J emblazoned in the middle.

Charlotte attended a Jewish school, a school that saw its numbers diminish on almost a daily basis. Charlotte had told Stella that on any given day, one or more of the kids simply didn't turn up, occasionally one of the teachers. No one asked any questions. They didn't need to; they all knew.

Charlotte went to her bedroom. At her door, she paused. 'I'm frightened, Mum.'

'I know, darling. So am I.'

She had to think. Back before the war, Stella had hatched a plan: to lure a Nazi into loving her to the point of offering his protection when things got tough. It hadn't worked out. She wanted to use them. Instead, they used her. They slept with her then pushed her out. She realised that being a man's fantasy was great for kicks but not for longevity. She'd drifted back to her husband. But the stupid sod shot a soldier. Didn't kill him and the man survived, only to be returned to the Eastern Front. But it meant Albert had to go into hiding and she hadn't had word from him since.

But there was one Nazi she almost captured. Felix Stoltenberg. Perhaps the most decent of the lot. He wasn't a natural Nazi, not like the others. She always thought he'd gone along with it out of the folly of youth, because, without thinking about it too much, it seemed like the right thing to do. She could still remember where he lived. Chances were, of course, he'd been sent into action and was probably lying dead and forgotten in some Godforsaken place in Russia. Or maybe he was living the high life in Paris, sleeping with dozens of fancy French women. At the time, Charlotte was living with Albert. Felix never knew she had a daughter, and somehow, she never got round to telling him.

Charlotte re-appeared, fully dressed, ready for school. She put on her coat, glancing at the star as she fumbled with the buttons. 'So I guess today will be my last day of school.'

'Yes.'

'Should… should I tell them?'

'Probably not.'

'I can't bear this. I can't stop shaking.'

'Listen, darling, I think I know what we can do. I can't promise it'll work, but it might.'

Charlotte took a step forward, perhaps to embrace her

mother, to kiss her. But she stopped. Their relationship had never been a tactile one. So why start now? Instead, blinking away the tears, she turned and left.

Stella reached for her cigarettes. She realised her hand was shaking as she tried to light one. She felt so hungry. But she'd used up all her meagre rations. She looked at all her paintings decorating the walls, years' worth of work. It'd be hard to leave all this behind, but she knew the day would come; she'd already resigned herself to it. It didn't matter. Not in the scheme of things.

Yet the bile rose in her throat, the burning hatred of the Nazis. Her breath came in short bursts as she considered all the things on the table: the paint brushes, paint boxes, scraps of paper with doodles and ideas, the tubes of oil paints, white spirit. What had been the point of it all, all that emotional investment in her art, the hours spent perfecting her craft? With a swoop of her arm, she sent the whole lot crashing to the floor.

The last time she saw Felix was *Kristallnacht*, the day those murderers killed her father. He was on the verge of proposing to her. At the time she thought him a silly boy. Not any more. Not now that she needed him. The question was, could she work her charms on him again? Was Felix Stoltenberg foolish enough to fall for her all over again?

Chapter 31

'Silent Night, Holy Night,
All is calm, all is bright.
Only the Chancellor stays on guard,
Germany's future to watch and to ward,
Guiding our nation aright.'

Snow fell as people gathered in the square round a Yuletide tree decorated with candles and twinkling swastika stars. Felix's mother held a Yuletide candle in her gloved hand, lovingly produced by the inmates at Dachau. A band from a SS regiment played the music. Klara smiled at Felix. Felix winked back at her. Things were going well; life was looking up. He took no notice of the piles of masonry stacked up in the corners of the square, more evidence of the English bombs. He smiled at a little girl leaning against her mother's legs, sucking her thumb, staring at the tree. Next to her sat her father in a wheelchair, wearing a balaclava and an army greatcoat, a blanket over his legs. He reached for his wife's hand but she whipped her hand away.

German forces were advancing further and further into Russia. Brest Litovsk had already fallen, as had Smolensk. The city of Leningrad had been totally encircled by German forces and it would only be a matter of time before the city fell. And, most exciting of all, Moscow would soon be within reach. Felix buzzed with the excitement, could see it too in the faces of his comrades, on the faces of the people as they held their candles and sang their Yuletide carols. *'Silent Night, Holy Night; all is calm, all is bright. Adolf Hitler is Germany's star, showing us greatness and glory afar, bringing us Germans the might.'* The man in the wheelchair sang lustily but tunelessly. His wife glanced down at him, looking embarrassed by his exaggerated singing. The little girl, still sucking her thumb, took a step away.

Hitler had proved himself the best military leader the world had ever seen. Under his stewardship, Germany had conquered Poland, Denmark, Norway, Luxembourg, the Netherlands, Belgium and, most spectacularly of all, France. Further south, Germany had defeated Yugoslavia, Crete and Greece. After so many years of deprivation and humiliation, Germany was again master of Europe. Only Great Britain remained undefeated. But that didn't matter now; Germany had its eyes set on the bigger goal – the defeat of the Soviet Union and the rightful subjugation of its people. The Russians were collapsing wherever German forces fought them. *Long live Germany; long live the Führer! Heil Hitler.*

'Happy Christmas,' said Klara.

'Yuletide, Mum. Not Christmas.'

The man in the wheelchair patted his thighs, inviting his daughter to sit on his lap. She hid behind her mother's legs. The woman spoke to him, her voice harsh and abrupt.

The only blot on the horizon, the only slight cause for apprehension was the news that the Japanese had attacked Pearl Harbor and hence had brought the might of the USA into the war. It didn't matter, people said. America was a country of immigrants, blacks and weaklings. But behind the bravado lay the first seeds of doubt.

The woman and her daughter had walked away. The man in the wheelchair whipped off his balaclava. Felix caught his breath. The man's face was unrecognisable as human, a mass of burnt flesh. But he could still sing, lustily belting out the words. '*Silent Night, Holy Night; all is calm, all is bright.*' For some reason, Felix thought he recognised the voice.

*

The day after Yuletide, Felix was at his SS HQ, preparing for the next aktion, checking off addresses against a map of the district. He still worked as a teacher, but the state schools were closed until the New Year. So he had lots of time to devote to his voluntary SS work. The day he was accepted into the SS as a second lieutenant was a day of celebration. The men here were more of his ilk, educated and refined, and all ruthlessly loyal to the Führer. They accepted him into the fold and he felt immediately at home. Stella Hoffmann had been right.

There was a knock on the door, a Waffen SS captain who introduced himself as Hauptsturmführer Reyman of the SS Recruitment Office.

Felix snapped to attention. 'Heil Hitler.'

The man returned his salute. He was, Felix, guessed, about thirty, with strong blue eyes and thin lips. The Waffen SS was the combat arm of the SS. 'I wondered, Lieutenant, whether you'd thought about signing on as a reservist for the Waffen SS. Your Colonel Friesler thinks you're the right kind of man for it.'

Felix had and had dismissed it. He knew his limitations. The idea of being sent to fight in Russia was not something anyone relished, however dedicated to the cause. But he couldn't say so. 'Yes, sir. But I have so much I can do here that is vital to our work. Our aim, as you well know, is to make Berlin Jew-free. Why, at this moment –'

'Of course, I am well aware of the tremendous job you are doing here, and we wouldn't want anything to come in the way of it. It's too important a task for that.'

Felix could hear the "but" in his voice.

'Now, we are fine for manpower as it stands but should the nation find itself in a situation of peril, for whatever reason, then it will need to call upon every man of military age to present himself for duty. The Waffen SS is always on the lookout for able men and I've heard good reports about you, Lieutenant. Now, the Wehrmacht is doing a fine job. Their job is to conquer land. Our job in the Waffen SS is perhaps even more demanding, it is to Nazify that land, to root out resisters and ensure that the population accept our authority. It can be ruthless work and not for the weak minded. I'm sure you understand.'

Felix shuddered. No, he didn't understand. Not fully.

Reyman continued. 'So this is what I propose… You sign on as a reservist, that is all. That means you'll only be called upon if the situation demands it. And frankly, the way things are going, I doubt if you need ever see me again. Meanwhile, you can carry on with your sterling work here. What do you say?'

No. Felix wanted to scream the word 'no'. The man stood, waiting for his reply, his head tilted to the side. He knew, thought Felix. He had him exactly where he wanted him. There was no way he could refuse without looking suspect. Felix bowed. 'I'd be honoured, sir.'

*

It was New Year's Eve and Felix was preparing to go out. He

was meeting a number of his comrades and they were going to paint the town red. He put on his uniform and slipped on the Waffen SS armband which, as a reservist, he was now entitled to wear. He stood at the mirror in the living room, straightening his red tie. 'You look very handsome, Felix,' said Klara. 'You look more like your father every day. Try not to get too drunk.'

He laughed. 'Why not? I've got every excuse to.' *Yes*, he thought, he looked the part. *Mothers of Berlin, lock up your daughters, here comes Felix Stoltenberg, Waffen SS reservist.* 'Don't wait up for me.' His mother had taken on a job working a few hours a week in a munitions factory. She hadn't wanted to but it was expected of her. Anyway, the money would come in handy. Her widow's pension didn't stretch as far as it used to.

'Don't catch a chill.'

He laughed again. 'Mum, we've got soldiers fighting in Russia with the temperature down in the minus forties. I'm sure I'll be all right for one night in the bars of Berlin. Right, then.' He patted his pockets. Money, cigarettes, matches, condom. Yep, he had everything. He took his coat from the coat stand. He gave his mother a hug. 'Happy 1942, Mother.'

'And you, my son. May the year finally bring peace.'

'And victory.'

She smiled a sad smile. 'And victory,' she echoed.

He opened the apartment door to leave. There were two figures there, an adult and a child, standing in the darkened corridor. He jumped back. 'Jesus,' he shouted. 'What the... who are you?'

'Hello, Felix,' said the familiar voice.

She took a step forward into the light of the living room.

Felix's legs gave way. It was her; it was Stella Hoffmann.

Chapter 32

Felix was shocked by her appearance. She looked so much older, her skin had turned grey, her face lined. Her hair too was back to its normal colour, almost black, but streaked with grey and still a hint of the peroxide blonde at the tips.

He made to close the door on her. 'Get out of here.'

'Please, Felix, a minute of your time,' she said in a hollow voice.

'You heard my son,' said Klara behind him.

It was only then he looked at the child biting her lip. 'Oh my god, I know you.'

'Hello, sir.'

It was the little Jewish girl from his class, not so little now, much taller, almost a woman in her own right. She'd be fifteen now. Charlotte. That was her name. Charlotte Wolff.

'My daughter,' said Stella.

'Your... You never said.'

He allowed them in, closing the apartment door behind them. After all, he didn't want the neighbours seeing that he had two Jews on his doorstep. Both had the yellow star stitched to their coats. Stella was wearing that red coat she

206

always used to wear. Little Red Riding Hood. They all remained standing in the living room, the four of them, two sides, eyeing each other, verbally circling one another.

'I told you she was a Jew,' said Klara. 'Remember? That time –'

'Shut up, Mum,' he snapped back, his eyes still on Stella, still not believing it was her standing in front of him. 'Why did you never tell me?'

'I didn't see much of her in those days. She lived with her father, the florist's son. We were separated. Still are.' Her voice had lost its swagger, tinged now with a constant timbre of uncertainty.

'I meant why didn't you tell me you were Jewish.'

'Because... because you would have judged me.'

'Rightly so,' said Klara.

'Because I'm German. Being a Jew didn't define me. Being a woman did.'

'You're well and truly defined now, though, aren't you?' he said, pointing at her yellow star. 'What happened to your husband?'

'My ex-husband, Albert. He's... he's in hiding. Don't ask me where.'

'But you know?'

'Yes, I know.'

She held his gaze and for a moment the years swept back, the time he spent in her apartment... he could see all her paintings on the wall, the smell of oil paint and turpentine, could feel her body against his. He'd had girlfriends since, but none like her. They were all so dull in comparison, so insipid and bland, so uniform in their faith and loyalty to the Führer and the party. Outside, he heard the jubilant voices of young men already out celebrating the New Year.

'You look well, Felix.'

'Leave him alone,' hissed Klara.

'What is it you want?' he asked.

'I need your help.'

'My help?' He laughed. 'Look, do you see what this is?' He pointed at his armband. 'Waffen SS. And you have the nerve to come here and ask me for help.'

'We don't have anywhere else to go.' It was Charlotte who spoke.

'Hardly my problem, is it?' he barked at her. He could see her mother in Charlotte's eyes now. A steely determination behind the veil of fear.

Klara tried pulling him away. 'We can't feed you,' she said over her shoulder. 'We don't have enough rations, not that I would if we did.' Turning to Felix, she whispered, 'We should report them.'

'I've received our deportation letter,' said Stella. She fished a piece of paper from her coat pocket and offered it to him.

'I don't need to see it. When?'

'Tomorrow,' said Charlotte.

'They're coming to get us at noon.'

'Where they taking you?'

'The old synagogue at Levetzowstrasse in Moabit.'

'We're allowed one suitcase each,' said Charlotte.

'Fine. Be ready on time. Those chaps don't like to be kept waiting.'

'They're going to give our home to some other family,' said Charlotte.

'Help us, Felix.'

'You'll have a new home in Poland somewhere and made to work for once. It'll do you good.'

'Do we really believe that?'

'Don't talk to my son like that, you –'

'Shut up, Mum. Of course I do.'

'They'll murder us.'

'No. No, they don't. They –'

'Felix, please.'

'Get out. Go on, get out of my home. How dare you come with yet more lies.'

Klara had slipped round them and opened the apartment door and now stood there as if bidding a polite farewell to her guests.

'Don't send us away, Felix.'

He wanted to push her against the wall. He stepped up to her. She didn't flinch. 'That night, that last night, I had a ring in my pocket. I was going to ask you to be my wife. And then I found out I didn't even know you. That the life you presented me was a lie.'

'And I would have said yes.'

'What?'

'I would have said yes. I would have been your wife.' She placed her hand on his sleeve.

He shook it off. 'Don't touch me.' He glared at her, his breathing coming hard, his head reeling. He fucking hated her; he wanted to throttle her, to smash her pretty face in. Her face blurred in front of him as the tears came. He so wanted to hurt her, to cause her pain. He so wanted to kiss her.

*

Felix did go out that night and, along with his comrades, celebrated. They toasted in the New Year; they toasted the Führer. They toasted each other. 1942 would see another round of glorious victories for the Führer and the Fatherland. Russia would be defeated. Stalin would be hauled away in a cattle truck. Bolshevism would be dead. National Socialism would rule. The future awaited. It was theirs to take. And Felix did get drunk, drunker than he'd ever been in his life. It had just gone two in the morning. He found himself in another bar, singing with his friends, raising his tankard.

A girl dressed traditionally in a dirndl approached him. Her name, she said, was Helga. 'A good German name,' said Felix. A pretty girl she was: blonde hair, perky nose. They danced. She talked, and though he couldn't concentrate nor hear a word she said, he said 'Really?' several times and nodded his head. Within the hour, she'd taken him back to her apartment, stomping through the snow, although he had no idea where it was nor had any recollection of how he'd got there. She slammed the door shut behind them, then shushed herself, giggling in the dark. He couldn't see a thing. Then, without warning, her lips were on his. She took his hand and pulled him through the dark apartment.

He clattered into something and tripped over. She shushed him again, still laughing. He found himself pushed down onto a bed. He heard her shuffling round. She pulled his trousers off, yanking them down as far as his ankles. Yet he felt no arousal. He heard a voice, not Helga's but hers. *Help us, Felix. Help us.* A light came on, a pleasingly soft light. Sitting astride him on the double bed, Helga had stripped down to her bra and pants. She leant down and kissed him hard on the mouth, her hand running up and down his chest. *They'll murder us.* She noticed his lack of arousal, asked him what the matter was. 'Maybe this will help,' she said. With a deft movement of her hand, Helga unhitched her bra. *Don't send us away, Felix.*

She kissed him again, her fingers inching closer to the waistband of his pants, her breasts flattened against his chest. Her fingers crept further down, half an inch away from his cock. *I would have said yes.* Helga touched his flaccid penis and, as if electrocuted, sat bolt upright. 'What the fuck is wrong with you? Are you a man or what?' The bile rose in his throat, and the alcohol swirled in his stomach. *I would have said yes. I would have been your wife.* He pushed Helga off, caught the frightened expression on her pretty face. He stumbled out of the bedroom, pulling his trousers up, retching, tripping over something again in the living room, and made it out into the corridor. He staggered down the stairway, through a courtyard and out into the street. He breathed in the cold air, his head pounding.

A man in a long coat and a Trilby passed, walking his dog, his boots crunching on the snow. 'Heil Hitler,' said the man. 'Happy New Year.'

'She would have been my wife,' he said. 'My wife. She would have said yes.'

The man, clearly alarmed at having bumped into a madman, scuttled away.

'She would have been my wife,' he called after him. 'My fucking wife.'

Chapter 33

New Year's Day. Klara brought Felix a cup of sugary tea. It was gone ten. He opened his eyes and a shot of pain exploded in his head. 'What happened last night, Felix? You came in at about four, cursing and stomping round. You seemed awfully upset.'

His mouth was too dry to answer. He sipped his tea. His mother handed him a couple of headache tablets.

'It was her, wasn't it? That blessed woman, she upset you.' She stroked his arm. It irritated him greatly but he lacked the strength to object. 'Forget about her, son. You did the right thing. She had no right to blackmail you like that. You know, I don't even reckon that girl was hers. I think she borrowed her to make you feel bad. Anyway, she's gone now. It's just you and me, like it's always been.' She smiled a sickly smile. Felix sipped his tea. 'You know, I don't think you should go out drinking like that again. It's not becoming to your uniform. You're in the Waffen SS now. Even if it's just the reserve, you have to maintain certain standards. Think what your colonel would say. What's his name?'

'Friesler.'

She patted his arm. 'I'll leave you to wake up. Lucky you don't have any work today. Happy New Year.'

Half an hour later, he dragged himself out of bed and plonked himself in an armchair in the living room. His mother wouldn't stop talking. She droned on about what a fine man he was, with frequent references to his father, the saint he'd become. He wanted to tell her to shut up. She heated up some soup for him, horribly thin soup with just one small chunk of meat in it. Still, it wasn't her fault. There was a war on.

He returned to his room, got changed and, feeling a little better, told his mother he was going out, that he needed some air to help clear his head.

More snow had fallen during the day and it was mightily cold. Few people were about. He walked with no particular destination in mind. He simply needed to get away from his mother and the claustrophobia of home. It was certainly good to breathe in the cold air. He passed a group of children having a snowball fight. They tried to tempt him to join in but he was too fragile for anything that energetic. He tried not to think of her. At noon today, she would be collected by the Gestapo and taken to the synagogue they now used as a holding camp before shipping them off east. Part of his job now was to find Jews who had had failed to obey their deportation orders. They went into hiding. They never lasted long. The SS intelligence and the Gestapo were aided in their work by a city full of informants, people like Otto Wankel, more than happy to expose the Jews in their hiding places.

After half an hour, chilled to the bone, he decided to head home. He passed Café Flamingo and, lured by the thought of coffee and warmth, went in. They still had the 'No Jews' notice on the door. Not that any Jew would dare these days. The cafe could only offer ersatz coffee now, a sort of chicory substitute.

And no cake, not with the war on. Still, it was nice and warm inside. He sat down and placed his order.

'Hey, Stoltenberg, is that you?'

He turned to see someone in a wheelchair and realised it was the man he saw with his wife and daughter at the Yuletide carol service. He squinted. Under the scarred, burnt skin, he recognised those eyes. 'Oh my god, it's you. Gluck.'

'I know. I look a bit different these days. Can I join you?'

Ernst Gluck wheeled his chair next to Felix's, bringing his cup of coffee with him, the cup shaking slightly on its saucer. 'You remember that time we were last here?'

Of course he did. It was one of their boycott days.

'As you can see, I've got rid of me scar,' he said, placing his finger against his cheek. 'Much better, don't you think?'

'I'm sorry to see you like this.'

'Ah, don't be. At least my war's over. I see you're in the Waffen SS now,' he said, motioning to Felix's armband.

'Only as a reservist. I haven't been called up yet.'

'Huh, you will, mark my words, mate. Especially...' He glanced around then, lowering his voice, added, 'The way things are going.'

The waiter brought Felix his coffee.

They chatted about the boycotts they held outside the Jewish shops. It was, to be frank, their only shared experience, the only thing they had in common. If truth be told, he and Gluck had never been friends. Felix knew that the man had considered him a sissy, and Felix thought of the man as being rather uncouth. But he felt sorry for him now. He remembered how his wife and daughter had spurned him at the carol concert. Still, once they'd exhausted their boycotting reminiscences, they had little else to say.

'Seems like such a long time ago,' said Gluck, lighting a

214

cigarette.

'Yes.' Felix realised that both the first two times he'd met Stella Hoffmann, he'd been on duty with Gluck. *Help us, Felix. They'll murder us. Don't send us away.* Felix leant forward. 'Can I ask you something, Gluck? In confidence?'

The man caught his tone. 'Sure,' he replied quietly.

'What happens to the Jews once they're sent east? They're made to work, aren't they?'

'Yeah, sure. If that's what you want to believe.'

Felix's heartbeat quickened. 'What... what do you mean?'

'There's a nice park over the road. Fancy a walk?' He stubbed out his cigarette. 'You'll have to push me a bit. My arms get tired.'

Gluck pulled his gloves on and wheeled himself as far as the cafe door. Felix noticed he'd dropped his balaclava. He picked it up and was about to give it back to him when he bumped into Höch from the office, the ex-soldier with a gammy leg. Apparently, Thalbach was doing well in hospital. He'd lost his eye, thanks to that maniac woman, but he'd be OK. Indeed, Höch was just about to go and visit the 'old sod'. 'Do wish him well from me, Höch.'

'Will do, sir. Thanks.'

Pushing a wheelchair through snow was hard work. But Felix persevered. He didn't want to come across as a sissy. They entered the park and followed the path round. They stopped at a bench covered in snow. Felix brushed the worst off, tucked in the tails of his greatcoat and sat down. It was obvious to him now that Gluck had a story to tell.

The man exhaled. 'You know, on days like this, when it was really cold, my scar used to hurt. Doesn't any more. How lucky am I. You say one word of this, and –'

'I won't say a word. I promise you that. I just want to know the truth.'

'OK, I'll give you truth. And then I shall swear until I'm blue in my burnt-out face that I never said a word of it.'

'Of course.'

He didn't say anything for a while. They both sat, Felix on the snowy bench, Gluck in his wheelchair, simply staring out over the park and its frozen lake, to a little clump of trees beyond, their branches hanging heavy with snow. A robin landed nearby, pecked at the snow, then flew away. The air was heavy with cold and anticipation. A man passed pulling a child on a sledge, breaking their trance. They exchanged cheery hellos and Happy New Years. 'I worked as a truck driver for a Waffen SS regiment, like the sort you will join soon. And you will, mark my words. We were in Kiev, in Ukraine, last September. One morning, me and this Ukrainian bloke was ordered to drive a truck out of town. Along the way, we passed all these Jews, whole families of them, marching in columns heading the same way we was heading. They were carrying their stuff in suitcases and bags and in wheelbarrows. There were thousands of them. So, me and my Ukrainian workmate drove on into this field.

'In the field, there were these other Ukrainians ordering the Jews about, telling them to heap all their cases and things in one big pile. Then they were told to take their clothes off. I mean everything, shoes, shirts, the lot, even their underwear. If anyone hesitated, the Ukrainians kicked them. So, they were standing there, men, women, kids and even the very old, all naked, shivering, trying to cover themselves. My job was to chuck their clothes and stuff onto the truck and drive it back to this warehouse where these blokes were sorting it all, keeping the good stuff and burning the rest. I thought if it was me standing naked in that field, I'd run away, at least try. But you know, not a single one of them did. Not one.

'So these Jews, all naked, were led to this ravine. It must have been some twenty-five metres wide and maybe fifteen metres deep and went on for ages. The ravine was already half full of bodies. I knew then I'd found hell. They made the Jews stand on the edge of the ravine. Then, the German soldiers and policemen forced them to lie down on top of the corpses. You can't imagine. They were weeping, fainting, pissing themselves, you name it.

'So the Jews lay on top of the other bodies and a soldier came along and shot them in the back of the head. The soldiers didn't care who it was. I saw them shoot kids and even babies.

'There was one girl I remember, standing near the truck. She was about four. She, too, was naked, but even at that age she knew enough to cover her modesty with her hands. She looked at me straight in the eye. The thing is… Christ. The thing is, she reminded me of my daughter. I won't forget her eyes until my dying day.

'I didn't stop for long. But I saw all these naked bodies covered in blood, twitching. It's seared here, on my brain. I can't get it out of my head, not ever.

'The ravine was about two hundred metres away from where the Jews were taking off their clothes, and a strong wind was blowing, so, really, you couldn't hear the shooting coming from the ravine. I guess they didn't know what was going to happen until the last moments. So, there you have it, now you know. We tell them they're being resettled. Cos it's easier that way.'

Felix put his head in his hands, tried to control the dizziness. A thread of cold ran through him. Gluck couldn't look at him. A couple of starlings skipped across the snow leaving tiny imprints before taking flight. The man and his

217

child were now throwing snowballs at each other, their laughter floating through the freezing air. So it was all true. He hadn't wanted to believe it but he had devoted his life to the Devil. He had served Satan, had done so willingly. Gluck wiped at his eyes with his bear-like gloved hands. Frau Pappenheimer's prophetic words came back to him as she stroked Stella's cheek. 'She's all right this one, but it won't save her.'

His shame was complete.

Chapter 34

Felix looked at his watch. 11.40 a.m. Twenty minutes.

He should have stayed and helped Gluck get out of the park, pushed him back to the café at least. But he did not. He ran away, leaving Gluck to his own devices. 'Hey, where you going? You can't leave me. I need your help, for Christ's sake. Stoltenberg, please...'

He caught a tram to Charlottenburg. He kept checking his watch. Not a minute to lose. He urged the tram to go faster. He looked out at the streets, the people trudging through the snow, everyday Berliners – on this, the first day of the New Year – and it all looked different. He looked at the people on the tram, all sitting in utter silence, hands in pockets, scarfs pulled up, hats pulled down. He saw now that ordinary people looked frightened. How is it he'd never seen that before?

Now that he could see it, it was so obvious. He thought Hitler had won the nation over but, now, for the first time, he realised he was wrong. These people were frightened. They were frightened of the enemy, the British, dropping their bombs on them. They were frightened of the regime that ruled in their name; they were frightened of each other.

He caught sight of his reflection in the tram window. How monstrous he looked with his greatcoat and the uniform beneath. Then he realised – they were frightened of *him*, of his uniform and his SS armband. He was a man to be feared. He sat down, put his hands in his pocket and remembered he still had Gluck's balaclava. He'd been about to give it back to him when he had been interrupted by Höch.

The tram stopped. A couple boarded, an elegantly dressed middle-aged man and woman. *Hurry up*, thought Felix, *just get on*. They'd been out somewhere nice, perhaps lunch with friends. The woman wore a long green coat with big buttons and a large hat with a wide brim decorated with a couple of feathers. A younger, scruffily dressed man, sitting down, had noticed them too. 'Here,' he said, getting to his feet, tipping his hat. 'Would you like a seat?'

The woman glared at him, noticing, as did Felix, the yellow star pinned to his coat. 'Do you really think I want to put my arse where a Yid's been sitting? Bugger off, Yid.'

A few people laughed. Someone clapped. The young man glanced nervously round. The tram stopped and the man, pushing his way through, got off as the applause gained momentum. Felix doubted it was his stop. The woman with the feathery hat shrugged and sat down anyway in the vacated seat. The man next to Felix winked at him.

Two men in long coats boarded. 'Please have your IDs at the ready,' one said. *Gestapo*. Felix could feel the temperature rise. One by one, they checked people's identity cards, their expressions hard. They didn't check his ID. His uniform showing under his coat was enough. Instead, they both acknowledged him with a curt nod of the head. The comradeship of tyranny.

The tram reached his stop. Felix jumped off before the

tram had stopped, slipping on a patch of ice. He ran. He ran down streets he hadn't seen since the winter of 1938, passed shops now boarded up, down dismal streets briefly prettified by snow. It was 11.55. Five minutes. The Gestapo were never late. Three years since he'd been here, but he knew every step. He found Stella's block of apartments, spotted a tarpaulin-covered truck waiting outside, the driver smoking a cigarette, cleaning out his ear with his finger. As soon as Felix stepped into the block, a door opened. It was the block warden. 'Does Fraulein Hoffmann still live here?'

'Funny that, two other blokes just asked the same question. Gestapo, I reckon.'

He sprinted across the courtyard, up the stairway, two steps at a time. Her apartment was at the end of the corridor on the fourth floor; you could see her door from the top of the stairway. The door was ajar, emitting a shaft of light. Someone had already painted a large red Star of David on it. He slowed down, trying to catch his breath. Didn't want to appear flustered. For some reason, he pulled on Gluck's balaclava, placing his cap on top. It smelt of sweat and cigarette smoke.

He heard a man's guttural voice from inside. 'Hurry up. You should've packed already. You've got two minutes. Essentials only. Warm clothing.'

He had no plan, had no idea how to play this. He knocked gently on the door and stepped inside. He was disoriented by being back here, back in this familiar apartment with paintings adorning every wall. It still smelt the same and the olfactory memory left him momentarily dizzy.

He stepped into the living room. 'Who are you?' said a small, sinewy man with a wide-brimmed Trilby.

He flashed the man his ID card, quickly returning it to his pocket, not wanting the man to see his name. 'I've got orders

221

to collect a Fraulein Hoffmann and her daughter for resettlement,' he said, patting his breast pocket to indicate a list. He could hear Stella and Charlotte in the bedroom, whispering to each other, packing their meagre suitcases.

The second man appeared, this one as tall as the first one was short. 'You joking, right? This is our job. Here,' he produced a sheet of paper with a long list of names.

'Well, let me save you the bother of this one.' He made sure they could see his armband.

The short one narrowed his eyes. 'You by yourself?'

'Schmidt's sick. Too much partying last night,' he added with a roll of the eyes although he doubted they would notice, his eyes obscured by Gluck's balaclava. 'I need to get on, so if you don't mind.'

'No, hang on a minute,' said the shorter one. 'We've got our orders.'

'And so have I,' he said, talking quickly. 'And I think you'll find...' Stella appeared wearing her red coat, the yellow star clearly visible, a small, bulging cardboard suitcase in her hand. 'Frau Hoffmann?' he asked.

He could see the puzzled expression on her face. She dropped her suitcase. 'Fräulein, please.'

'Of course. If you and your daughter are ready –'

Charlotte appeared, taking her place next to her mother, her star equally visible on the breast pocket of her coat. He noticed Stella place her foot firmly on her daughter's.

'No, no. Something's not right here,' said the taller one. 'I can't allow you to take this Jew and her sprog away from us. If we get this wrong, we're in the shit.'

'Rest assured, this has been totally authorised. If you're so worried, ring it through to your office. I'm sure one of the neighbours has a phone.'

'You can use my phone if you like,' said Stella. 'In the bedroom. I think it still works.'

'You have a phone?' barked Felix. 'Yids aren't allowed phones.'

'I never use it. Who am I going to call?'

Fair point, thought Felix. The two men looked at each other. They were not happy. The taller one said he'd make the call. 'Don't let them out of your sight,' he said to his colleague.

'Your keys, Fräulein,' said Felix, clicking his fingers. 'Hand them over.'

He knew he was being scrutinised by the shorter man. 'Wait a minute, it's against regulations to operate on your own.'

'Told you, Schmidt, my partner, is off sick.'

'Why you wearing that thing round your face? Can't see who you are. It's cold but it ain't exactly the Eastern Front.'

Stella went to give him her keys, her eyes fixed on him, ready to obey. He didn't take them. 'Come here, child,' he said, clicking his fingers at Charlotte. 'Let me see you.'

'Show me your ID again,' said the shorter man.

'Are you questioning my authority?' He clenched his fist.

'Just fucking show it to me.'

He swung his fist, punched the man hard in the stomach. The man doubled over. Stella dragged Charlotte's hand and pulled her out of the apartment. Felix pushed the man over, slamming the front door shut behind him. He held tight on to the doorknob. He heard the men shouting inside. Stella, not needing to be told, her fingers fumbling, tried to lock the door. He could feel the pull on the door. 'Hurry up,' he urged.

He heard the satisfying clunk as the lock engaged.

'Leave your coats here,' he said. 'Better cold than have the star showing.'

For a moment, they stood there, the three of them, looking

at each other. A flicker of a smile on all their faces, a sharp pang of love in Felix's heart.

And then they ran.

Chapter 35

'You can't hide them here.' Klara was almost hysterical.

'Mother, keep your voice down, for god's sake. You want the neighbours to hear?'

'It's suicidal. You're mad. Keeping them here, it's... it's as good as a death sentence.'

'It'd only be for a night or two, Frau Stoltenberg,' said Stella.

'A night or two too long.'

'Frau Stoltenberg...'

'Don't talk to me, I don't want to hear it.'

'Mother, calm down, please, just...'

'You bring two wanted Jews into our apartment and you ask me to calm down? What would your father say? I can hear him –'

'Stop harking back to my father. It's of no relevance; it doesn't interest me.'

Klara stopped short, as if absorbing her son's heresy. He saw her deflate. He gripped his hands on her arms. 'Mother...' She shook his hands off. 'Mum, I have a plan. Don't laugh at me, it's serious. I know what to do. Look at her, Mum, look at

225

Charlotte. She's so young still, she's got her whole life ahead of her. Do you really want to see her delivered into the hands of the Gestapo, to see her deported to her death?'

They all looked at Charlotte, standing without her coat in Klara's living room, both hands holding on to her little suitcase, her eyes dark as night. She may have been fifteen, thought Felix, but she looked so much younger. Stella placed her hand on her daughter's shoulder.

Klara shook her head. 'They don't die –'

'Mother, stop. I know what goes on there. I've always known, I just didn't admit to it. And you know too. We all know.'

'No, no I don't. I don't know what you're talking about.'

'Mum.'

'I haven't got enough food. Where will they sleep, what –'

'Stop, Mum. Just stop. Look, I have to go to work tomorrow.' He looked at Stella. 'Gotta find some more Jews who haven't obeyed their deportation orders. But when I get back, about six, then I'll get them out of here.'

'Where to?'

'To…' He almost told her. But stopped himself in time. The less she knew, the better. 'Like I said, I have a plan.'

'You promise? One night only. I won't sleep a wink tonight.'

'I promise. I promise on my father's grave.'

*

As soon as he got to work the following morning, Felix asked reception for the home address of one Otto Wankel. The SS offices on Prinz Albrecht Strasse were awash with excitement. Firstly, Colonel Friesler was leaving; he was being transferred out east, a certain death sentence. He was to be replaced but no one knew the new man's name.

Then, the second bit of excitement. A fellow called Bosch, an ex-soldier with several missing fingers, told Felix the story. Apparently, at about noon the day before, two Gestapo officers were about to arrest two Jews, a mother and daughter, when some guy posing as a Waffen SS reservist saved them. Apparently, he punched their lights out and locked them in the Jew's apartment before making off with the Jews. 'Would you credit it?' said the wide-eyed Bosch. 'Apparently, they're looking for a man of about five foot ten, nicely spoken who wears a Waffen SS armband and...'

'What is it, Bosch?' Though he knew full well what was coming next.

'Hey, you're about five foot ten, sir, and you speak nice and...'

'No, Bosch. No. I was at my mother's all day yesterday, most of it spent in bed nursing a hangover. You ask her. I've got my alibi.' *Stop*, he thought, *just stop. I protest too much.*

Bosch laughed. 'Out on the town for New Year's, then, sir? Wouldn't have thought you'd be the kind to...'

'I'm not just a uniform, Bosch. In fact, if I remember rightly, a rather attractive woman by the name of Helga – or was it Greta? – anyway, whatever her name, took me back to hers. You know that situation, when one thing leads to another and neither of you have a rubber and...'

'No, sir. I do not. I've been married 25 years.'

He limped away. The man looked genuinely shocked. Hopefully so shocked, it would be the latter part of conversation he remembered and not the former...

Chapter 36

Felix stood at the end of the darkened alleyway, checked the address on the slip of paper handed to him by the receptionist at work. He'd come straight here from work, almost an hour's trek across town. Removing his armband, he wore his longest coat and wrapped a scarf around his neck, trying to hide his uniform. Number eighteen. Six months ago he'd been here, arresting Otto Wankel, stuck in the bathroom window. Back then, Felix knew who he was, sure of his place in the world. No longer. That man had gone. He was still trying to work out what had replaced him.

He knocked on the door. Otto Wankel's wife answered, her hair obscuring her face, holding a baby to her chest. 'Yeah?'

'Where is he?'

'What?'

'Your husband.'

A child, maybe four, peered round her skirt. 'Hang on, I know you. You've been here before.'

'I'm by myself this time. I'm not on official business. I need a favour of your husband.'

The woman peered up and down the street behind him. '*You* want a favour? Get out of here.'

She went to close the door. He placed his boot against the door jamb. 'Tell me.'

She hesitated.

'Please.'

'He's where he always is, of course,' she said, hoisting up the baby. 'At the beer hall.'

'Which one?'

'Fritz's. On Bülowstrasse.'

'Thank you.'

He made to leave.

'Oi,' she shouted after him. 'If you see him, kick his arse back here, will you?'

Felix entered the beer hall and was hit by the heat, the veil of smoke and the thunder of boisterous voices. The place was rowdy, but he didn't expect anything different. A few women and numerous men filled the place: young and old, many in their lederhosen, several soldiers on leave. They were sitting on long benches, their elbows on the tables, slurping at their tankards. Many were devouring plates of beef stew served by young girls in red dresses and blue pinafores. Poor girls, he thought, they had so much to contend with, trying to dodge the unwelcome advances of these drunken louts. Uncouth – that's what they were. And they made so much noise. Their shouts and laughter reached the curved ceilings, drowning out a three-piece band aloft on a small raised platform in the far corner. And how they smoked. It got into one's eyes. Still, it was all very German. He cast his eyes about, trying to find Wankel. 'Hello, handsome,' said a voice.

He turned to see a woman dressed in a waistcoat, its front held together by bootlaces. 'You look stuffy hot. Why don't

229

you take that coat off and buy me a drink, hey?'

'I'm sorry? It's very loud in here.'

'Clear your ears out, love. I said, why don't you buy me a drink?'

He tried to sidestep her. 'I'm sorry, no.'

'Go on, handsome. One drink won't do any harm. Good looking boy like you. What you doing all on your own? Wouldn't you fancy a bit of company?'

'No. Look, I'm looking for a friend. Otto Wankel? Know him?'

'Course I do. Every blighter knows Otto.' He followed her painted eyes and, sure enough, there he was, sitting at a bench, talking loudly, surrounded, the centre of attention, waving his arms about.

'Thank you.'

'Hang on, dearie, how about that drink?'

Felix pushed on, bumping into people, zigzagging his way through the melee. He stood the other side of the bench from Wankel and looked down, waiting. The man looked up, laughing, a tankard of beer in his hand. The laugh died on his crooked lips. 'Oh, god.'

'Hello, Otto.'

'What you want? I ain't done nothing.' The woman to his right laughed.

All eyes were on him, this fish out of water. 'I've come to ask for a favour.'

Wankel placed his tankard on the bench and guffawed. 'I've heard it all now. Well?'

Felix motioned with his head that he wanted to speak to Wankel alone. Wankel took the hint without fuss, rising to his feet and pushing past his companions. 'Anyone touches that drink, they're dead. Get out of the way, will you.' He came right up to Felix. 'What you want? Or should I say, to what do I owe the pleasure?'

'Let's go outside? It's too loud in here. And hot.'

Wankel, perhaps fearing it was a trap, said nothing for a few moments, then: 'As you wish.'

Wankel led the way, limping, winding his way through the mass of warm bodies. They passed the woman with the waistcoat. 'Found Otto, then?' she asked loudly, holding up a glass of wine. 'Don't forget you owe me a drink, pretty boy.'

Ignoring her, he pushed on, following Wankel.

It was a relief to step outside, to feel the cold air on his face. Wankel fished his hat out of his jacket pocket and carried on walking. After a couple of minutes, they reached a canal, its still, murky waters stretching around a gentle bend and beyond. He stopped. 'So, what's up? Must be something for you to come all this way to find me.'

'Yeah.' His eyes darted around, taking in the dismal surroundings, the empty street, the canal, the litter, graffiti. He was very much alone here, alone and vulnerable without his uniform on show, without back-up, miles away from anywhere. There were no shops, no houses, just high warehouses made of solid red bricks with large, arched doorways. The soupy air made it harder to breathe. 'I need your help.' The words came fast as if he was trying to deny them.

'You need my help,' Wankel repeated, one slow word at a time.

Felix took a breath. 'It's like this. I need to get two friends out of the city. Out of the country, in fact.'

'Whoah.'

'Yes, I know. Switzerland.'

'Well, I didn't think you meant Russia. Two people, you

231

say?'

'Yes.'

Wankel faced the canal. He kicked a pebble over. They heard its splash. 'So, I tell you what to do and try to help you, and next thing, you're saying "gotcha!" And the next thing I know I'm experiencing the delights of Gestapo hospitality. Again. Come on, I weren't born yesterday, you know.'

'You really think I've come all this way, by myself, to trap you. You don't think I'm busy enough already? Anyway, I don't need an excuse. You know how it works.'

Wankel seemed to consider this. He removed his hat, flattened down his hair, and then replaced the hat. 'All right,' he said with a sniff. 'If you say. So, what's in it for me?'

'I'm prepared to pay.' Felix coughed. 'Within reason.'

'Surely that depends on how desperate you are. And looking at you, you kind of look desperate enough to me.'

'Can you help? If not, I've wasted your time and mine.' He pulled down his coat sleeves and made to leave.

'All right, all right. Not so hasty, man. I'm just thinking.' He produced a pack of cigarettes from his inside jacket pocket, offered one to Felix, who shook his head, and, taking one himself, lit it. Nearby, two cats got into a brief but intense fight, their piercing cries loud in the surrounding silence. Felix tapped his foot in an oily slick of a puddle. Wankel blew out a plume of smoke. 'You'll need money, someone who can do the job, false papers and a lot of luck. It's a lot to ask.'

'I know.'

'And no guarantee. Not with people like you about. You know that. But...' He took a drag of his cigarette. 'I reckon I know a man who could help for the right price. He don't come cheap though.'

Felix nodded, unsure how to proceed.

'I'll sound him out. See what I can do. Come back day after tomorrow. This same time. Alone.' Wankel threw his half-smoked cigarette into the canal, turned heel, and made to leave.

'Hey, before you go,' said Felix. 'Your wife wants you home.'

'My wife? You were at my house?'

'Yeah, Wankel, I was at your house.'

The man absorbed this piece of information. Then, with a raised eyebrow, he muttered, 'She ain't my wife, stupid bitch.'

Felix watched him leave, his shadowy figure disappearing around a corner, his limping footsteps loud in the murky silence. It was only then he was able to breathe.

Chapter 37

'Why, Felix, is that you? What brings you here?'

'Hello, Granddad.' For a seventy-five-year-old, Gottfried still looked mightily strong, a stocky man with massive, square shoulders, a square head with a good sweep of silver-white hair and a large, walrus moustache.

'I say,' he said on seeing Stella and Charlotte. 'Who are these pretty ladies?'

'I wonder if we could come in.'

'Of course, come in, do. This way. Mind your head.' The three of them stamped the snow off their boots and entered.

Felix, Stella and Charlotte followed Felix's grandfather into his living room. He lived in a thatched bungalow in the small village of Bad Bernsdorf, some thirty miles west of Berlin. A welcoming fire roared in the hearth. A bearskin rug lay on the floor, another pinned up on the wooden wall. Everywhere there were shelves stacked with numerous earthenware pots and jugs. A large crucifix hung above the mantelpiece; half an upturned beer barrel made do as a side table. The place smelt of woodsmoke and wood polish.

Felix introduced Stella and Charlotte. 'I haven't been here

for years,' he said, taking in his surroundings.

'Well, welcome back. Take a seat. I'll make the coffee, at least that disgusting stuff we call coffee. Help you warm up a bit.'

Apart from the one armchair, the only place to sit was a pew. The three of them sat there, their hands on their laps, looking as if they were in a waiting room. The walls were decorated with a number of painted plates showing hunting scenes and a rack with a display of a dozen identical-looking penny whistles, all no doubt whittled by Gottfried himself. A large wireless took pride of place on the sideboard.

Grandfather brought in a couple of hardback chairs with cushions attached and invited the two women to make themselves more comfortable. Felix's grandfather asked after Klara, his daughter, how life was in Berlin and whether they'd been affected by the air raids, predicting the situation could only get worse. He told them about the village mayor who had a farmer arrested for calling one of his cows Hitler. 'You see, the beast was white but it had this black strip of hair between her lip and her nose, so of course…' He laughed loudly. 'So, how old are you, sweetheart?' he said, slapping Charlotte's knee.

'Fifteen, mein Herr.'

'Fifteen, eh? What a great age. Now, young lady, I insist you call me Gottfried. And you,' he said, turning to Stella, 'I presume you're Charlotte's older sister.'

Stella forced a smile. 'Her mother.'

'No, that can't be. You look far too young. So, Felix, tell me, what brings you here with these two lovely ladies.'

'It's a bit delicate, Granddad. You see, they're in hiding and —'

'Hiding? Not from the Gestapo, I hope,' he said, rubbing

his hands like a man enjoying himself.

'No, not that. No, it's, erm… Stella's husband, her ex-husband.'

'Oh? Say no more, say no more. I understand perfectly,' he added tapping the side of his nose. 'Men can be such beasts to their women. Well, if you need somewhere to hide away, then you're welcome. And you can stay as long as you want. One night, one year, for evermore; I don't mind. I'd be happy for the company. Not that I can spare too much in the way of food, not on my rations.'

'I can help there,' said Felix. 'I have some savings. Always useful on the black market.'

'Excellent. I hope you don't mind sharing a room, the two of you?'

'Not at all,' said Stella.

'But, Charlotte,' he said, shaking her knee with his calloused hand. 'If you ever get frightened, you can always climb in with me.' He laughed raucously. 'Now, we need to concoct a story for why you're here. You know what village gossip's like. I know; we'll say you're Felix's wife and daughter, and you've been bombed out of your home. Felix is worried for your safety. As simple as that.'

'Perfect,' said Felix.

Stella smiled.

'I'd give you a guided tour but I can simply point at everything from here. My bedroom there, your bedroom next to it, the kitchen there, and there, behind that door, the bathroom. No key so you'll have to sing loudly when you're using it. You can take as many baths as you want, young lady,' he said, addressing Charlotte. Turning to Stella, he said, 'I say; you don't cook, do you? Anything to help eke out the rations.'

'Not really.'

'Pity.'

'I can try, I suppose.'

And so it was settled.

Felix stayed the night, sleeping in the living room on a filthy couch Gottfried dragged in from one of his sheds. The following morning, he slipped his grandfather a few Reichsmarks for food, etc., kissed Stella goodbye and returned to Berlin greatly relieved that his plan had worked out.

*

Felix stood within the shelter of a doorway, the brim of his hat pulled down, his collar turned up against the steady drizzle. He kept his eyes peeled for Wankel. A couple of soldiers passed, leaning into each other, unsteady on their feet. One asked Felix for a cigarette. Felix shook his head, apologising. Laughter came from farther down the street: a couple leaning against a warehouse wall, kissing. Ten minutes passed. The rain intensified. Another ten. He began to despair. Wankel had to turn up; he was utterly dependent on him now. And then he heard the familiar footsteps, limping through the puddles.

Wankel approached, his hands in pockets. With a nod of his head, he motioned Felix to follow him. Wankel made his way to one of the warehouses, checking left and right before pushing open the arched door and stepping into the darkened interior. Felix followed. He heard a scuffle behind him. Before he had chance to turn around, someone pushed him. 'Hold still,' said a voice. Something tightened around his waist, his arms manhandled behind him.

'Secure?' said a high-pitched voice.

'Sure, boss.'

A light flicked on. Felix blinked. Standing before him were Wankel and three others. The warehouse was empty, a huge cavernous space and wooden beams high up, piles of empty wooden crates, gas bottles and, in the corner, a forklift truck. Two of the men searched his pockets, the lining of his coat and jacket, ran their hands down his legs. One of them tightened the rope, pinning his arms behind his back. Satisfied, they stepped back. A rotund man in a long mac, trilby and thick, black-rimmed glasses, sneezed. Stepping forward, he said, 'Your name is Felix Stoltenberg?'

'Yes,' said Felix, wondering how such a large man could have such a high voice.

'You're SS.' He had narrow, dark eyes behind his glasses that seemed to pierce into one.

'Yes. Waffen-SS reservist.'

'Are you indeed? How noble. So you could be chasing down Soviet partisans at any time?' He shook his head. 'If there was ever a guarantee of an early grave.'

One of the men behind him laughed.

The man continued. 'My name is Herr Metzelder, divisional criminal police inspector.'

Felix shivered. He'd walked straight into a trap. Bloody Wankel.

'I apologise for this inconvenience,' said Metzelder, waving his hand about. Felix noticed the number of rings on his fingers. 'I'm sure you understand. We must be careful.' He clicked his fingers. His men untied the rope. 'So, Herr Wankel here says you need to get two friends of yours out of the city and even out of the country?'

Perhaps it wasn't a trap after all. 'Y-yes. Can you help?'

'Maybe, maybe. It won't be easy.'

'I...'

'Yes?'

'I appreciate that, Herr Metzelder.'

'They've tightened security all along the Swiss border. Anyone caught trying to illegally cross will find themselves in a camp, pronto. You have to tell me, these friends of yours, are they Jewish?'

Felix heaved a sigh. 'Yes.'

'Shit,' said Wankel. 'You didn't tell me that.' One of the others shook his head.

Metzelder rubbed his eyes. 'It's OK, Otto, it's OK. But it makes it even more interesting. And more dangerous. You know, Herr Stoltenberg, the Swiss aren't that keen on accepting Jews, however desperate their situation. What is it they say? The lifeboat is full. They could easily get across, only for the Swiss to send them straight back into the hands of the Gestapo. You know that?'

He didn't. 'Yes.'

The man sneezed again. 'This bloody dust. Gets everywhere.' He wiped his nose with the back of his hand. 'But... it's not a given. Sometimes they do, sometimes they don't. We have the means to get them across the border but, whatever happens to them in Switzerland is beyond my control. Now, I hardly need ask how urgent this is but you and your friends have to be patient. Otto, here, can arrange false papers. You shouldn't need them because I'll be escorting them. They'll have my protection, so need not fear police checks. I *am* the police. But I like to take the belt and braces approach, you understand? Do you work for Colonel Friesler?'

'Yes, but he's leaving soon. He's going east.'

'Is he, poor man? Who's he being replaced with?'

'We don't know yet.'

'Hmm. Interesting. Back to the matter at hand, are they a couple, your friends?'

'No, mother and daughter.'

'OK. You're not going with them?'

The thought appealed. But no, he thought of his mother. 'No.'

'Fair enough. OK, now let's discuss the fee. Twenty thousand Reichsmarks.'

Felix sputtered. 'How much?'

'Per person.'

'P-per per-person? Forty thousand?'

'In advance.'

'Sounds reasonable to me,' said Wankel from behind. One of the others laughed again.

'It's a little excessive, Herr Metzelder.'

Metzelder narrowed his eyes. 'So we have wasted our time, is that what you're telling me? I have other matters I could be attending to, so tell me straight, Herr Stoltenberg, what's it to be?'

'Could we not –'

'No, the price is not for negotiation.' He smiled a slippery smile. 'Now, let me tell you, there was a fellow, like you, who thought he could get one over on me. Thought a bit of blackmail could persuade me to waive the fee. After all, this little sideline of mine could get me the guillotine. I know that. Said gentleman is now lying in the bottom of that canal with a block of concrete for company. Would you like a minute to think it through?'

'Yes. Thank you.' Forty thousand Reichsmarks. He clenched his eyes shut. He had that much in his savings earmarked for a new apartment, a future free of his mother. The thought of handing it all over made him quite ill. He paced away from Metzelder, kicking an old bottle across the dusty concrete floor. He noticed the rust building up on the forklift truck. He could keep her hidden, both of them, but for how long? They faced betrayal at every turn, the consequences of which were unthinkable. He was putting his grandfather at risk too. Every day would be a torment. He loved her, she was his future, and the war couldn't last forever. One day, they'd be reunited. There'd be plenty of time to save that sort of money again. He had no choice, he knew that. He turned to face Metzelder's expectant face. He had to give it to the man; he knew what he was doing. But could he be trusted? Who else was there? He was an inspector, after all. It had to be someone like Metzelder, with power, with knowledge. Someone on the inside. It'd be impossible without. 'How… how would it work?' he finally asked.

'It's a fair question. We'd take a night train from here to Lobenstein. Then a drive through the woods. Then a boat across the Rhine and into Switzerland. I know a man with a boat. We've worked together many times and he's utterly reliable. My man will deliver them into the hands of a man on the other side who can accommodate them. We don't know this man; we don't have any contacts with the Swiss. But my boatman can vouch for him. From there, they'll be resettled within a network of sympathetic households. And there're many to choose from. The Swiss people are essentially decent people. It's a trusted and well-oiled process. Nothing is guaranteed, as I've already said, but it's a hundredfold better than any alternative that I know of.'

'Can I come with them? Right up to the river?'

Herr Metzelder shrugged. 'Don't see why not. You'll have to make your own way back. Wear your uniform.'

'When?'

Metzelder turned to Wankel. 'I can get the papers within the week.'

'So, I suggest, Herr Stoltenberg, you come back tomorrow

with passport photos of this woman and her child. Give them to Otto here. Then, meet Otto here this same time in exactly a week. He'll give you your papers and exact instructions and times. Your friends will meet me at the fixed time and place with the money. And then the journey can begin. A week will also give you enough time to have the money ready in cash.'

'Cash?'

'I'm hardly likely to want a cheque, am I?' The man offered Felix his hand. 'So, Herr Stoltenberg, we have a deal?'

Felix hesitated. Again, the words floated through his mind – what choice did he have? He exhaled. Eventually, he took Herr Metzelder's hand. 'Yes, Herr Metzelder. We have a deal.'

Metzelder tightened his grip on Felix's hand and stepped right up to him. 'You try double crossing me, Stoltenberg, your Jewish friends will find themselves shipped off East, and you, young man, will be joining the chap in the canal. Got it?'

Felix nodded. He knew full well the man wasn't joking; he had just made a bargain with the devil and it was too late to turn back.

PART FOUR

Chapter 38

Berlin, September 1942

The key turns in the cell door. Felix sits up. Is it now? Is it his turn? Has Death come for him? His body quakes. But no, it's just the hunched orderly bringing them their food with Corporal Bulbous in attendance. The old man deposits the metal trays on the bench. Felix knows what to expect. Sure enough, the food is gloopy and grey; it looks revolting. It probably is, but Felix eagerly takes his tray and the little wooden spoon. Not a fork, never a fork; a man could do damage with a fork. He sits on the edge of his bunk bed and starts eating. For a moment, he fears he might be sick. This usually happens but he swallows it down. He can't afford to lose any sustenance, even something as thin as this. There's a beaker of water. He gulps its contents down in one.

Rudolph asks the orderly for the time. The man simply shrugs as if knowing the time is something he never bothers about. They're not allowed to say; Rudolph knows that. It could be midday; it could be midnight. The orderly shuffles out. Corporal Bulbous closes the door behind him. They eat in silence. The process doesn't take long. Felix licks the plate clean. There's nothing left. His stomach is just as hollow. It craves more; it aches with emptiness.

Rudolph finishes also and wipes his mouth with the back of his hand. He rubs his belly. 'That's better,' he says. 'A tad overdone, maybe.'

Felix smiles. *Silly man.*

They fall silent again, each lost in their thoughts. Felix thinks of his mother. She knew he'd been arrested and taken away. First her husband, then her son, nine years apart. He knows she'll be trying to find out whether he's OK, whether he's still alive. *Yes, Mama, I am still here, not much longer but they haven't put a bullet through my brain yet.* He just hopes that when the time comes it is just a bullet. He knows they're partial to the guillotine. They lay the condemned on his back and force his eyes open so he can see the blade looming above him, waiting for the rope to be slashed. He shudders at the thought.

Will his mother survive on her meagre factory wages, without his teacher's pay? And without his savings, forty thousand Reichsmarks in Metzelder's pocket. Will she be shunned again? A woman with both a husband and a son as traitors. She had no friends, no support. What hope did she have now?

There are footsteps out in the corridor again. And those aren't the footsteps of the orderly; this is different. Rudolph has sensed it too. They both stand. They glance at each other as the key turns in the lock. Felix holds his breath; his hands shake. This is it, he thinks. The door opens. But for a moment, no one comes in. And then someone almost falls through the door, as if pushed from behind.

Rudolph yells, his hands on his cheeks. His knees buckle as he screams out the name.

The man has been beaten, his face red with his own blood, his nose buckled to one side, his moustache caked in blood, his left eye obscured by swelling. He holds one bloodied hand against his chest, clasping it with the other. He looks confused, lost.

Rudolph is crying. 'Anton, Anton. My God, what have they done to you? What have...' The tears swallow his words.

Corporal Bulbous now appears. 'Is this him?' he asks.

Anton opens his mouth but cannot speak. His teeth are tinged red.

'Is it him?'

Anton nods, incomprehension clouding his eyes.

Corporal Bulbous spins Anton around and pushes him back out of the cell.

'Anton. No, wait, please, let me speak to him. Please...'

But the door closes; the key turns in its lock. Anton is gone.

Rudolph staggers to the bench. His knees give way and he almost falls onto it. He puts his head in his hands and sobs.

Felix sits on his bed, not knowing what to say, mute with pity. He says nothing; there is nothing he can say. He lies down and after a while closes his eyes. He tries to block out the sounds of the captain's distress. He is embarrassed somehow. He can understand the torment he is suffering but, still, something about an officer displaying so much emotion... But he worries for his new friend. He's been identified by the man he loved so much. It does not bode well. Anton, the poor man, the poor sap, will undoubtedly be on his way to a camp by the end of the day, made to wear a pink triangle, ass fucker. And Rudolph? It's all too frightening to take in.

He hums, trying to distract his thoughts. The tune is significant for some reason, yet he has trouble naming it. It takes a while but then he has it: it's Schubert's *Winterreise*. He remembers his father playing it on the piano back home. Just before they came for him that second time. Such a long time ago. Rudolph finally calms down. He blows his nose and he too lies down, stretching out on the bench. The silence is heavy now after all that commotion, just the occasional sniff.

Time passes. How much time, again, it's impossible to tell. Both men drift into sleep. The piano sonata continues to play in Felix's mind, joyfully singing in the hinterland between wakefulness and sleep. Felix dreams of his father, his father in a car, Gestapo officers either side of him, driving through the countryside, fields stretching, a woodland on the horizon. The car stops, his father forces his way out, runs across the fields. A gunshot rings out, a second, His father falls. Crows caw in the trees, taking flight, circling round the heaped figure in the field still wearing his coat. Shot while trying to escape. Such a long time ago.

A voice penetrates his brain. 'Felix?' It's his father speaking.

'Dad? Daddy? Is that you?'

'Felix, are you awake?'

Felix's subconscious snaps into wakefulness. His heart hollows. 'What? Rudolph?' He shakes his cheeks. 'Yes, I'm awake.'

'Listen, my friend, if they come for me first, will you do me a favour?'

'Go on.'

'Will you... I know I've been disgraced and stripped of rank, but when I leave, will you call me "sir"? Despite everything, I was still proud to be a soldier and I'd like to die believing I am still an officer.'

'Of course.'

Rudolph smiles to himself. 'What happened next? Felix, tell

250

me.'

'What?'

'What happened next, Felix? After you made your pact with the devil, Herr Metzelder?'

Felix sits up. Rudolph is already sitting up. Felix rubs his eyes. 'You don't want to know, not now.'

'I do, Felix. I can't bear the thoughts going round my head right now. So I do. You have to tell me.'

'If you're sure?'

'Yes. I'm sure. Please. Please tell me.'

Chapter 39

Nine months earlier: Berlin, January 1942

Felix had wanted to return to his grandfather's as soon as possible, but work got in the way. School opened for the new term and, when he wasn't teaching, marking homework or lesson planning, his hands were full with his SS work. Over the coming week, the snow melted away, while his mother had finally calmed down. The whole affair with Stella and Charlotte had played havoc on her nerves. Felix had never realised until now what a jumpy, nervy woman his mother was. Berlin had suffered a few more air raids but nothing too drastic. The work of deporting Jews carried on. Finally, a Sunday came when Felix had the day to himself. He told his mother he was going out for the day. She didn't question it or ask him where he was going.

Thus, Felix caught the train from the Anhalter Bahnhof to Bad Bernsdorf. From there, it was a mile-long walk to the village. It was a damp, cold day, the sky blanketed in grey. Nonetheless, he walked with a spring in his step, excited by the prospect of seeing Stella again. A couple of dogs came to greet him as he entered the village. The village had been built either side of a large river banked by solidly-made stone walls. The timber-framed, whitewashed buildings with steep roofs were certainly attractive.

The church bells rang the half hour. Felix checked the time on his watch. Walking down the main street, virtually every balcony sported a swastika flag. Swastika bunting stretched across the street. At least this was one place the English bombs had thus far spared.

His grandfather's bungalow lay a few hundred yards beyond the main part of the village. The door to the bungalow flung open. It was Stella, wearing a new red coat he hadn't seen before, a hessian bag in her hand. She trotted down the street to greet him. She stopped short, as if unsure what to do. Then, ridding her inhibitions, she flung her arms round him. 'You look so much better,' he said. 'Country air is doing you good.'

'Oh, Felix, yes. Beats sitting in a flat too scared to go out.'

'How is it?'

'It's OK, I guess. Your grandfather's so loud; he likes his radio, always listening to music. He bought Charlotte and me new coats.'

'Still red, I see. Little Red Riding Hood.'

She lowered her voice. 'It is nice not to have to wear a coat with that star on it. But I couldn't live in a place like this forever. I'm so bored. I've started painting again. I walk out into the woods with my brushes and breathe in the fresh air and paint.'

'That's great. How's Charlotte finding it?'

'She's bored too. Even more because she doesn't paint. Next time you come, could you bring some books to read. Nothing too difficult. Felix, I'm worried about her. She's gone all quiet. She's not eating well. I think she's finding it hard adjusting to rural life. She misses the excitement of Berlin, well, old Berlin that is. At least her education isn't suffering. Gottfried tells me he was a teacher and now he's teaching Charlotte all sorts.'

'Poor girl.'

She laughed. 'Yes, but it's good for her.'

'Where you going?' he asked, motioning to the hessian bag.

'Shopping. You go in, say hello to Gottfried. Charlotte's having a bath, I think. I won't be long. It's my price for freedom – being your grandfather's skivvy.' She kissed him on the cheek and left. Felix smiled.

He pushed open the front door, calling out. Sure enough, the radio was on, playing loud music. He recognised it as a Brahms symphony. 'Hello,' he called out again. He entered the living room. The fire had been lit, producing a lot of black smoke. He saw his grandfather bending down, something odd about what he was doing.

'Granddad?'

His grandfather shot up. 'Lord, where did you come from?'

'Sorry, I didn't mean to make you jump.'

'I thought I'd dropped something. Let me turn that radio off.'

The day went well. Stella cooked them all an omelette. Felix enthused; eggs were in short supply in the capital. Gottfried talked about the village's Nazi mayor, Felix talked about his teaching, Stella about village shopping while Charlotte said nothing. She did look pale, thought Felix, and she barely touched her omelette.

After lunch, Gottfried tried to teach his grandson how to play *Für Elise* on the penny whistle. He soon gave up. 'Ah, you're as useless as your mother. Could never teach her to play either. How is your mother? Haven't seen her in years. She never visits. Strange that, don't you think? After all, as you know, it's only half an hour away. Here, keep the whistle. Practice at home. I have plenty more, as you can see.'

While Felix was talking to his grandfather, Stella sat nearby, a small wooden canvas on her lap, painting. Felix had never seen her at work before. She hummed continually, a habit he could tell Gottfried found irritating. When Felix made to move, Stella instructed him to keep still. 'Are you painting me?' he asked.

'Uh-huh.'

He remained still. Gottfried disappeared. Another half an hour passed before she declared herself finished. Felix was astonished. It was simply a head and shoulders portrait, slightly in profile, his eyes looking at the viewer with a contented expression. The painting was dominated by various shades of subtle blues and greys, his skin streaked with yellow and pale reds, yet she'd caught him somehow. 'It's marvellous, Stella. It's so good.'

'You can have it.'

'Are you sure?'

'Yes. Something to remember me by.'

'Stella, that night you came to me, you said your husband was in hiding. Are you…?'

'Albert. Ex-husband. No.' She placed her hand on his. 'He killed an officer. Someone informed on him. So, they're desperate to find him. So I don't know exactly where he is now. He moves from place to place. All I know, he never stays in the same place for more than two nights. Until he shot that man, we kept in contact. He is Charlotte's dad, after all, and yes, I'm fond of him. But I don't love him any more.'

He smiled, more than he meant to.

A couple of hours later, Felix was sitting on the train,

returning to Berlin, his grandfather's penny whistle in his jacket pocket. He looked at the painting, still slightly wet, and wondered how she'd managed to capture him so well with so few brushstrokes. He wondered how she felt about having lost all of her previous work, whether the Gestapo had binned it or, whether, recognising Stella's talent, they had purloined it for their own profit. He didn't know which was worse. He gazed out of the window, at the passing countryside.

He felt sorry for Charlotte, having to readjust, to pretend to be someone she wasn't, always worried in case someone found out her true identity. It was at that moment, thinking of Charlotte, that a thought, a realisation, hit him. He cried out. His grandfather, bending over when he walked into the living room... he hadn't dropped anything; he was... Surely not; he couldn't have been. But yes, it was the bathroom door. He was. Felix had caught his grandfather peering through the keyhole while Charlotte was inside having her bath. But it didn't matter now. If things went according to plan, Stella and Charlotte would be safely in Switzerland within forty-eight hours.

Chapter 40

Eleven o'clock at night. Berlin's Anhalter Bahnhof railway station was almost deserted. Stella, holding Charlotte's hand, looked up at the huge dome roof between the dozens of swastika banners hanging down, fluttering in the gentlest of breezes. She took in the huge, church-like windows. A porter, whistling, ambled by, pushing a trolley laden with suitcases. Felix, next to her, looked tense enough to snap at any moment. She listened to the murmur of people, passengers and staff, the echo of many quiet conversations under this cathedral of a railway station. The whistle of an idling train shot through the air. She shivered; it was cold here on the platform. A tearful woman leant into her man, her head on his chest. He kissed the top of her head.

God, she wished it was over, that they were somewhere safe over the border. Her breath, she realised, was coming in short bursts, her stomach muscles clenched. She was tired, exhausted even, yet the adventure had barely started. She eyed every passing person. Did that man with his arm in a sling give them a second look; was that woman in the headscarf suspicious of them? Everyone around them seemed to be whispering to each other, eyeing them from afar, gazing in their direction: a swirling mass of echoing whispers gaining momentum and volume, increasing in intensity. She shook her head, trying to chase away the cries and whispers from her mind. She was glad Felix was wearing his uniform, glad of the protection it afforded her and Charlotte. But she could tell that the sight of another uniform, whatever its colour, made him stiffen. It was like looking in a mirror and being frightened of one's own reflection.

Stella tried to comfort her daughter. Charlotte seemed on the edge of breaking down any moment, her eyes wide with fear.

Felix noticed too. 'Charlotte, try not to look so worried,' he said.

'I can't help it, sir.'

'You don't have to call me sir now. We're not at school any more.'

Stella squeezed her daughter's hand. She knew they were even more vulnerable without their yellow stars pinned to their coats. A Jew caught without their star faced immediate execution. Stella carried the smallest of suitcases, Charlotte, a small haversack slung over her shoulder. Not much with which to start a new life, but apparently those were Metzelder's strict instructions, relayed to Felix. Lots of luggage would cause suspicion.

As promised, Wankel had obtained two false IDs. Stella was now one Annelise Schiller, travelling with her daughter, Greta. Their story, if asked, was a sudden call to look after her sick father in Lobenstein, hence the late train. Stella wore bright lipstick with a bit of colour on her cheeks. Another instruction – to look nice, to look confident. She'd re-dyed her hair an even more intense shade of blonde. She knew she looked stunning and she knew Felix wished she didn't – it made her stick out too much. Now, at the train station, they huddled in a corner near platform three, again as instructed. And now they had to wait for Wankel.

'You've got the money?' asked Felix.

'Yes,' she snapped. 'For the twentieth time, I've got the money.' Stella smiled, aware of her abruptness. 'Thank you, Felix.'

He was putting on a brave face, she could see that, for the sake of both of them, but she could see the lines of worry, the strained look in his eyes. He seemed in a faraway place, as if clutching on to a memory, a safer place in his mind. Divorcing himself from the here and now, from this place, this time, the tension, the fear. How did he think she felt? Ahead of both of them, mother and daughter, lay a journey into the unknown, a journey whose outcome was dependent on too many people they knew nothing about: a corrupt inspector, a man with a boat, a man on the other side, a sympathetic family. And the constant risk of being found out, caught out, betrayed.

But the alternative was too awful to contemplate. They had no idea where their final destination lay, or with whom. It was like walking down a long corridor in the pitch black, not knowing what lay at the end, seeing only the spot directly in front of them. What creatures lay behind those closed doors left and right; how long was this corridor?

A train arrived, a metallic shriek heralding its arrival. They watched it as it drew in, coming to a screeching halt, billowing dark grey smoke. Doors flung open, people were jumping off before the train had fully come to a stop. So intent was her concentration on the train, Stella didn't see the man approach.

'Come, the inspector's expecting you,' said the man.

Charlotte jumped, her eyes wide with fright.

'It's OK,' said Felix. 'This man is a friend.' This, she guessed, was Herr Wankel.

Wankel took Stella's suitcase. The three of them followed as Wankel walked quickly along the concourse, turning onto platform five and the awaiting train. Wankel walked fast for a man with a limp. They walked almost its entire length before Wankel stopped and opened a carriage door. He motioned for Stella and Charlotte to get on. Felix was about to follow when Wankel blocked his way. 'Has she got the money?' she heard him ask, looking behind him.

Felix nodded. Satisfied, Wankel stepped aside, allowing Felix to climb aboard. Inside, Stella passed a uniformed police officer standing guard, who eyed her suspiciously. A rather fat man with several rings on his fingers stood, obviously waiting their arrival. 'Well, hello,' the man said, offering his hand. 'You must be Annelise. Delighted, I'm sure. My name is Inspector Metzelder. Your hair, it's so... Is it naturally that colour?'

Stella opened her mouth but couldn't speak.

'And this must be your daughter, Greta. How lovely,' he said, also offering her his hand.

Charlotte stared at him wide-eyed and Stella had to nudge her to take his hand.

'Ah, Stoltenberg,' said Metzelder on seeing Felix. 'Come in, come in. Shall we take a seat and make ourselves comfortable? We have a long night ahead of us.' He checked his watch. 'We should be leaving in a few minutes but, of course the service is so damn unreliable now, what with the bombs, etcetera. Still, mustn't grumble; these things are sent to try us. Come, sit, sit. This is Schmidt, by the way,' he said, referring to the guard. 'He'll be escorting us tonight.'

Stella could almost laugh. It was as if she'd walked on the set of a light-hearted drawing-room play, Metzelder playing the part of the genial host.

The man called Schmidt asked Felix to raise his hands. He ran his hands down Felix's back, checking his pockets while Stella and Charlotte removed their coats, whispering to each other. She saw Metzelder slap Wankel on the shoulder. 'Herr Wankel, thank you for your services.' Stella watched as Metzelder took Wankel to one side. 'You spoken to the other side?' he asked quietly.

'Yeah.'

'They're ready?'

Wankel nodded.

She glanced at Felix. He too had heard the exchange. Then, more loudly, Metzelder said, 'Excellent. Well, I think that's it for tonight, Wankel. You go home and get yourself a good night's sleep.'

Wankel nodded, shot a parting look at Felix and left, slamming the carriage door behind him.

Stella and Charlotte sat together, side by side, on one side of the table. Felix slid across and took a window seat, opposite Stella. Metzelder took his place beside him. 'Trust me, you're under my protection now.' He smiled and seemed momentarily put out by the lack of appreciation or comment. 'Now, Frau Schiller, shall we get the unpleasantries over and done with?'

Stella nodded and produced from her pocket two stuffed envelopes.

Metzelder thanked her. She watched as he slipped Felix's money out and quickly and expertly counted it. She saw the expression on Felix's face. *Poor man, so much money.*

'Excellent, thank you, that's all good.' He slipped the envelopes into his inside pocket and rubbed his hands together. 'Is it me or is it getting colder?' He talked at length about the weather, about his love of snow as a boy.

Stella heard the sound of the train guard blowing his whistle. Eventually, the train inched forward. It slipped through the darkened city and slowly out through the suburbs, the sprawling mass of the capital. Stella peered through the dirty window, gazing at the pockets of destruction, skeletal buildings and spireless churches. The bombs had always been the least of her worries. She feared her own countrymen far more than the English. But soon, she thought, she and Charlotte would be free of this, free to live again, breathe again. Hopefully, she'd never see Berlin again. She wouldn't be sorry; she'd come to hate the place. She longed to be a person again, to be seen as what she truly was – a woman, a mother, an artist: not a Jewess identified and identifiable by a stupid star.

*

The five-hour train journey proceeded without incident. Schmidt kept his guard at the carriage door. Stations came and went. Metzelder talked incessantly at first before declaring he'd better catch up on his paperwork. Felix winked at Charlotte and smiled at Stella. They smiled back, tired, weary smiles. Stella closed her eyes.

At one point, she awoke. How long she'd been asleep, she didn't know. Felix and Charlotte were asleep. Metzelder was not. The train hurtled through the dark countryside. Metzelder, on seeing Stella awake, smiled. He was working on something, a clutch of papers and a pen. After a while, he leant over the table and whispered, 'Frau Schiller, listen, I've been thinking about your fee…' He hesitated. 'Look, I can see you're a smart woman. Now, how about I refund you ten per cent?'

She paused before answering. 'I don't understand. What for?'

'Ten minutes of your time.'

Stella didn't answer.

'Think about it, Frau Schiller. When have you ever earned four thousand Reichsmarks for ten minutes' work, hey? Our secret. Think of what you could buy with that money.'

Felix's money, she thought. Still, Stella didn't answer. Eventually she said quietly, 'No, thank you.'

'Fifteen per cent. Six thousand. Here and now. Well? What about it, Frau Schiller?'

'No, Herr Metzelder. I cannot.'

Metzelder heaved a sigh. 'Your choice.'

'I'm sorry.'

'It's fine. I understand. I won't hold it against you. Still, if you change your mind, I'm not going anywhere.'

I'd rather kill you first, she thought. And she would; if push came to shove, she knew she would not hesitate. She had become that strong. Strong enough to deceive Felix, adept at wrapping him around her finger, persuasive enough that he was willing to risk everything for her, risk his money. Poor Felix; she felt sorry for him, she really did, but if he insisted on playing the gallant hero, so be it. She had to do what she had to do.

Chapter 41

The slowing-down motion of the train woke Felix up. He opened his eyes and was immediately conscious of his unease. Something was bothering him but he couldn't work out what. Often, during the preceding week, he'd reflected on what he was doing. But it was only now – now that he was committed – did the precariousness of the situation hit him. He was a teacher with a decent salary, he was serving the Führer and prepared, if necessary, to fight for the survival of the nation. And here he was, sitting on a train in the middle of the night, having parted with all his savings, and prepared to risk his life for a woman whose affections he wasn't even sure of. For he knew, if caught, he'd be dead.

He realised his fingers were digging into his calf. Was he doing it for love? Perhaps it went even deeper than that. He was saving a life, two lives. Did that mean he no longer believed in the Führer, in the nation, in the righteousness of the cause? His faith had been shaken; Gluck had given him pause for thought but he still believed; he knew he did, had to. So, why? Why? Because he sensed an injustice? He didn't know. All he did know, was he and Stella and Charlotte were dependent on a series of interactions to link up at the right moment. The potential for it to fall apart was enormous. Despite his sleep, he felt so tired. Drained.

They were coming into the station. He saw the sign – Lobenstein. They had arrived. The others were awake too. Charlotte, her eyes rimmed red, had been crying. Her mother stroked her arm. The station clock showed half three in the morning.

'Here we are,' said Metzelder, stating the obvious. He gathered his paperwork, stuffing it haphazardly into his briefcase, muttering to himself. And it was that muttering that brought it back to Felix… why had Metzelder asked Wankel about the people on the 'other side'? 'Are they ready?' he'd asked in a whisper. They? Who were 'they'? Time would tell.

Metzelder squeezed out of his seat, grabbed his coat and case and slapped his hat upon his head. The others followed suit. 'Ready?' asked Metzelder.

Stella nodded.

Schmidt, the guard, returned to his place and opened the carriage door. Metzelder stepped down first.

They gathered on the platform. Felix noticed Charlotte blanch. Following her eyes, he could see why. The Germans had set up a checkpoint at the end of the platform. Two soldiers stood guard, rifles slung over their shoulders. A queue of passengers had already formed, their papers being checked. 'Don't worry,' said Metzelder. 'Just stick with me. Have your papers ready, just in case.'

Metzelder skirted round the outside of the queuing passengers; he didn't need to join the hoi polloi.

Felix took Stella's suitcase. 'Are you OK?' he asked.

'Just about,' she whispered. 'Stay calm, sweetheart,' she said, turning to Charlotte. 'Charlotte?'

Charlotte had stopped. She was visibly trembling, her face ghostly white. 'I… I can't do this,' she muttered.

'Don't stop,' barked Schmidt, bringing up the rear.

'Yes, you can, sweetheart,' said Stella. 'Come on now.' Taking her daughter's elbow, she tried to push her forward.

'I can't, Mama. I just can't.' Her eyes were fixed on the soldiers checking everyone's papers.

'You must, sweetheart. We've no choice.'

'Herr Metzelder will look after us,' said Felix.

Metzelder, on hearing his name, turned round. 'For God's sake, don't slow down,' he said between his teeth. 'You're making yourself look more conspicuous.'

Felix realised Metzelder himself was nervous. This didn't bode well, he thought.

'Please, Charlotte,' said Felix.

Metzelder slowed down. Charlotte put one foot in front of the other and, with her mother's help, edged forward. But she couldn't stop shaking. She looked on the verge of tears.

Felix could hear the soldiers. 'Papers!' he heard one snap. 'Where are you going? How long for? What is the purpose of your visit?'

The queue had stopped moving. Metzelder led his group forward.

'This photo – it looks nothing like you.'

The guard had stopped an elderly man with a long grey beard and a long, scruffy coat 'It is, I assure you.'

The guard showed his colleague the photo.

'I was younger, that's all.'

Metzelder, his left hand behind his back, motioned by clicking his fingers for the others to hurry up.

'It's OK, Charlotte,' said Felix in a whisper. The girl was trying to swallow down her tears.

266

'What d'you think?' asked the soldier.

'Looks nothing like him.' The queue scrunched up behind the old man. 'Stop pushing,' shouted the second soldier.

Metzelder pulled on his coat lapel. 'Heil Hitler,' he called out, passing the checkpoint. 'Good morning.'

'It *is* me. Can't you tell by the eyes? Look.' The man pointed at his eyes as if the soldier wouldn't know where to look.

'Heil Hitler,' said the second soldier, not looking up.

'They're with me,' said Metzelder. Felix noticed the tremor in his voice.

'What's your date of birth then?'

'Quick, quick,' said Felix, almost pushing Charlotte. Charlotte, realising she was almost there, picked up speed.

The old man hesitated, as if he'd forgotten his date of birth. Felix passed as the first soldier pushed the old man against the train. 'Right, you stay there. We'll deal with you in a minute.'

The old man started to protest but, by now, Felix, Charlotte and Stella had joined Metzelder out on the concourse, Schmidt joining them.

'We did it,' said Stella. 'Come on, sweetheart, don't cry. We've done it.' Metzelder had marched on. Charlotte's legs seemed to give way.

Felix hoisted her up. 'Come on, Charlotte, you're doing well but we've got to keep going.'

They followed Metzelder out of the railway station onto the street outside. The cold morning air bit into them. Metzelder approached a car, a dark-green Maybach. The driver reached across and opened the passenger door. 'Hurry up, folks, get in,' he said. 'Not you, Stoltenberg. This is far as I can take you.'

Stella seized Felix's hand.

'I'm not leaving them. You said I could go as far as the river,' said Felix. 'We can sit on each other's laps if need be.'

Metzelder checked his watch. 'Your funeral,' he said, climbing in. 'Schmidt, put their cases in the boot.'

Charlotte sat on her mother's lap. Felix, with his heavy coat, sidled up to the middle, and Schmidt squeezed himself in last.

The driver started up the car and drove through the dark, ghostly streets of Lobenstein. Even a town this small hadn't been spared by the bombs, evidence of destruction at every other turn. Even at this time, four in the morning, there were people on the streets, shadowy figures shuffling along beneath their umbrellas, factory workers off to work their early shifts, others on the way home from their late shifts. Germany's industrial output was a twenty-four hour process, no respite from the production of war. Felix shivered with the cold. They drove in silence, Metzelder and the driver's silhouettes in the front. They drove out of the town and into the pitch-black countryside, illuminated only by the glare of the car's dimmed headlamps. Felix looked up at the sky, a black canvas devoid of stars or moon. He felt Stella's hand looking for his. He took it, cold to the touch.

After about forty-five minutes, the driver took a sharp right onto a narrower, bumpier road. Still, no one talked. Metzelder lit a cigarette, its smell soon pervading the back. Charlotte coughed.

'Almost there,' whispered Stella.

'I'm so cold,' said Charlotte.

'I know, sweetheart. We all are.'

After another ten minutes, the driver turned onto a yet smaller road, barely a track. The car bumped along. Metzelder wound down his window and threw his cigarette butt out, the cold blast of air hitting those in the back.

'Here we are,' said Metzelder after another few minutes. The car drew to a halt. Metzelder got out, the others likewise. Schmidt got the suitcases while Stella hugged Charlotte. Felix blew into his hands. They were surrounded by trees. The darkness behind the car seemed so thick, almost impenetrable. Felix could hear the faint sloshing of water. 'That's the Rhine,' said Metzelder, as if reading his mind. 'And over there,' he added, pointing into the darkness, 'is Switzerland.'

'Did you hear that, sweetheart?' said Stella to Charlotte. 'Switzerland.'

'Freedom,' added Felix.

He noticed a light coming towards him, its beam swinging left to right.

'Aha, here's Kretschmann,' said Metzelder. 'Bang on time.'

A figure emerged from the darkness. 'Right,' said the man, his features invisible in the dark.

'Kretschmann, we meet again,' said Metzelder. 'The others are here?'

Kretschmann grunted something by way of affirmation.

'Others?' asked Felix. 'What others?'

'You will have company but nothing for you to worry about.'

Kretschmann flashed his torch at Felix, Stella and Charlotte by turn. 'You said two of them.'

'Yes,' said Metzelder. 'This gentleman is their escort. He'll be there to see the Jews get away safely.'

'You didn't say nothing about an escort.' Kretschmann considered Felix. 'I don't like it.'

'You've done it before, Kretschmann.'

'It'll cost you extra.'

'As you wish. Well…' he said, addressing Stella. 'It's time

for me and Schmidt to get back. I'll leave you in the capable hands of Kretschmann here. Just keep him in sight and you can't go wrong. He knows what to do. I wish you both well, ladies. Once you're safely tucked up in Switzerland, don't forget to raise a glass in my name.'

'Thank you, Herr Metzelder,' said Stella.

'Yes, well. Pleasure.' He pulled on his coat lapels again. 'Right; ready, Schmidt?'

The question that had dogged him since waking up remained on Felix's lips – *Are they ready?* Surely now, it was just Kretschmann. He still couldn't work out who Metzelder meant by 'they'. He wanted to ask but something wouldn't let him.

Chapter 42

Kretschmann swung his torch round. 'Follow me,' he said.

Felix took Stella's case again. Mother and daughter held hands, Felix brought up the rear. But as they followed Kretschmann, the path became too narrow. Stella went in front. Felix could hear the car drive away, and the sense of unease intensified. Kretschmann's torch hardly lit his path, restricting him to see only an arm's reach in front of himself. But the man seemed to know where he was going. Felix shivered; the cold cut into his clothes, the icy wind tugged at his coat. The world seemed so quiet: just the crunching of their feet on the forest floor, the occasional flutter of a bat, the whispering of the branches in the faint breeze.

And still, his mind swirled with anxiety. Something felt wrong but, apart from the identity of these mysterious 'they', he had no reason to doubt Metzelder. Or Kretschmann. So why, he wondered, this knot at the base of his stomach?

Eventually they came to a small, wooden hut, a hint of light glowing through its solitary window. 'It's like Hansel and Gretel,' said Charlotte.

Kretschmann marched up to it and unbolted the door,

motioning for them to enter. Felix went first. 'Oh?' There were four people in there already, a family. The children were so heavily dressed and, with hats and scarves obscuring their faces, he couldn't determine their sex but he guessed them to be both under ten.

'Hello,' said the man, lifting his hat as Stella and Charlotte entered. 'The name's Weichmann.' Despite the cold, his brow glistened with sweat.

'No talking,' said Kretschmann, closing the door behind him. 'Ten minutes.'

It was no warmer inside than out. Felix dearly wanted to sit down, but there was only the one chair, occupied by the man's wife who sat there jiggling her leg, her husband's hand on her shoulder. A small lantern hung down from the beam, its glow illuminating the dust and cobwebs. No one spoke, all eyes on Kretschmann who kept checking his watch. It seemed strange, thought Felix, that they'd already come so far. Now it was simply a matter of rowing across the river. The branches of a tree brushed against the window pane, producing an eerie sound.

Weichmann cleared his throat. 'What are we waiting for?'

'I said no talking, didn't I?' said Kretschmann.

'It is safe, isn't it?'

'As safe as it can be.'

Weichmann and his wife exchanged glances. They weren't reassured by the man's answer. Nor was Felix. Are these the people Metzelder meant when he referred to 'they'? He hoped so. They seemed more frightened than Stella and Charlotte.

Finally, after another few minutes, Kretschmann declared it was time to go. Stella and Charlotte looked at each other, their eyes wide with apprehension. Kretschmann produced a revolver from his coat pocket and, spinning the barrel, checked the cartridges. 'Right; listen,' he said. 'Follow me. No talking. It's three minutes' walk to the river. Boatman's not turned up though. You'll have to row yourself,' he added, addressing Weichmann.

'Me? I don't –'

'Ain't difficult. It's only a half kilometre across.'

'Look here, we paid –'

'So what you gonna do? Ask for a refund?' He sneered and made sure Weichmann could see his revolver.

One of the children started crying. 'Eduard, don't cry, it'll be OK. Hey, mister,' said Weichmann, addressing Felix. 'Can you row?'

'He ain't on the boat,' said Kretschmann.

'It's OK, Eduard. So what's he –'

'No more questions. Let's go.' He waved his gun round, motioning everyone out of the hut.

Felix stepped out. A hint of dawn was approaching. The birds were singing, their shrill voices a strange accompaniment to the terror seizing his heart. Still so cold. Eduard's mother knelt down and whispered words of encouragement to her son. Weichmann eyed Felix with suspicion. Stella and Charlotte stayed together.

Kretschmann locked the hut. 'This way,' he said, heading off slowly with his torch lighting the way.

The Weichmann family followed first, so heavily laden with coats, they walked like penguins, the father carrying their two small suitcases. Stella and Charlotte followed, glancing back frequently at Felix, reassured, perhaps, by his presence. They followed Kretschmann and his torch, picking their way along the stony path, the trees either side leering down at them.

Metzelder's words came back to him: *Are the people on the other side ready?* Are they ready? It wasn't these people; it wasn't the Weichmanns. They weren't on the other side. It had to be Metzelder's Swiss contact. But he didn't know anyone on the Swiss side, he'd said. Nor did Wankel. *We don't have any contacts with the Swiss.* So, why had Metzelder asked Wankel if the people on the 'other side' were ready? Wankel wouldn't know. Felix's heart seemed to stop. He almost screamed. What had started as a suspicion had manifested itself into a certainty – they were walking into a trap.

He could hear the lapping of water just ahead. Another few steps down an incline, turning a sharp bend in the path, passing a large boulder, they came to a clearing, the silhouette of the rowing boat on the edge of the river. Kretschmann had his revolver but Felix would have the advantage of surprise. But what if Kretschmann had men waiting for him near the boat?

He reached forward and seized Stella's hand, pulling her back. Stella made to speak. He hushed her and reached out for Charlotte's hand. Ignoring their confusion, he jerked his head, telling them to follow him. Pushing them ahead of him, he walked briskly back down the path. Neither stopped to ask why. He knew they trusted him enough not to question him. He spotted a small path veering off to the left. They took it. It soon ran out and they found themselves assaulted by bushes and shrubbery. They pushed on.

They heard Kretschmann's voice, calling out for them. They knelt down. Felix put his fingers to his lips. 'You bastards, where are you?' Felix could hear Kretschmann's footsteps pounding along the path, saw the torch beam through the bushes. 'Fucking Jews, I'll get you for this.' The footsteps stopped, then started again.

'He's going back,' said Stella, her voice coming through the dark.

'What's happening?' said Charlotte.

'It's a trap.'

'How do you know?' asked Stella.

'I don't know, but something's not right.'

'What about the Weichmanns, Felix? You have to save them.'

Felix's heart hollowed. She was right. 'OK, you two hide further in. Keep your heads down. I'll come find you later.'

'We need a code word,' said Charlotte. 'We won't show ourselves unless you say…'

'Turner,' said Stella. 'As in the artist.'

'Turner.'

Stella kissed him. 'Go.'

Felix scrambled back through the bushes, finding himself back on the main path to the river. Daylight still seemed an age away under the canopy of trees. He ran on tiptoe, his ears straining for the slightest sound. All he could hear was his own frantic breathing. He reached the incline and the sharp bend. He ducked behind the boulder, his shoe kicking at a loose rock. He was too late; the Weichmanns had already cast off in the little boat, Herr Weichmann rowing. Kretschmann stood at the river's edge, a silhouette, watching them, his torch switched off. All seemed quiet. Only the rhythmic flap of the oars hitting the water breaking the silence and the constant twitter of the birds.

Everything seemed to be going according to plan. The Weichmanns were on their way to Switzerland and safety. He almost wept. He'd fucked up. Stella and Charlotte should have been on that boat with the Weichmanns a third of the way now across the river, the haven they'd been seeking just a stretch away. He had no money left and he knew there was no way Kretschmann would help him. Not now. The boat was making good progress. The river, placid and still, was being kind to them. He felt like smashing his head against the boulder.

And then there was a flash of light. Felix looked up. Kretschmann was waving his torch and flashing it on and off, up and down, on and off. It all happened so quickly. The little boat was suddenly bathed in a bright white light. He heard Frau Weichmann's frantic screams. The light was coming from a second boat, not more than thirty yards away. Herr Weichmann, in his panic, dropped an oar. Frau Weichmann stood up, her arms around her children. The burst of machine-gun fire shattered the silence. Frau Weichmann fell, as did the girl. Herr Weichmann slumped. One of the children, Eduard, jumped into the water. A line of bullets followed him, the spray of water caught within the piercing light. Felix heard the *thud, thud* as they made contact. And then it all stopped as abruptly as it had started. The morning air was filled with the screeching of hundreds of birds. Then, as the birds drifted away, the *putt-putt* of the German boat's engine starting up. A voice shouted across the river. 'Same time next week.'

Kretschmann waved back. The boat chugged its way to the rowing boat. They wouldn't want to leave them there in case they washed up on the Swiss side.

Kretschmann turned and started walking back up towards the path, his revolver in one hand, the torch in the other. Felix knelt down behind the boulder, twitching at every sound. He picked up the fist-sized rock he'd kicked, weighed it up and down in the palm of his hand, and waited.

Chapter 43

The sound of the German boat's engine was still sounding in the distance as Kretschmann traipsed back along the path. He reached the boulder on the bend and stopped. Felix grunted as he smashed the rock down on the back of Kretschmann's head. Kretschmann collapsed without a sound. Felix, holding the rock still, peered down at him. Kretschmann, prostrate on the stony path, his skull caved in, breathed his last. Felix puked up.

Then, having caught his breath, Felix switched off Kretschmann's torch and then dragged the man as far as he could into the bushes, surprised at how difficult that was. He snapped off a few branches and covered the corpse. He was too exhausted to do more. It was a feeble effort but it might buy him some time. Hopefully enough to get back to Lobenstein, onto a train and back to Berlin. He glanced back over the river. Through the branches, he could see the outlines of men hauling the bodies of the Weichmanns onto their boat. He shook his head at the pity of it all.

*

It felt as if they'd been walking for days. They'd used up the last of their food and water. Felix's logic dictated they walk upwards, away from the river and hopefully back towards Lobenstein. After an hour or so, the day had finally dawned. They made it out of the woods but there was no way of telling on which side. They came across a farm. An ox lowed as if welcoming them or alerting the farmer of their arrival. Stella and Charlotte held back, hiding behind a clump of trees, while Felix, his uniform on show, went to ask for directions, scattering a brood of hens as he approached the cottage. The farmer's wife, clearly intimidated by the uniform, gladly offered Felix half a loaf of bread and a bottle of water. Lobenstein, she told him, was a good five kilometres away, due north. Felix thanked her.

And so they carried on walking, Stella coaxing Charlotte almost every step of the way. The bottoms of their coats were streaked with mud; it had begun raining. Soon Stella's blonde hair hung limply, exposing her roots. They stopped after another half an hour and shared the bread and water. 'Eat this in remembrance of me,' said Felix under his breath.

Stella laid her hand on Felix's. 'Thank you, Felix. We owe you our lives.'

Not knowing what to say, he smiled weakly.

Five kilometres didn't sound so far away. But by god it was. They walked in silence, one tired step after another. They passed more farms, the occasional hamlet, passed fields and woods. They kept to the road but darted out of sight at the sound of a vehicle. But as they reached closer, the traffic became heavier and they were forced to find a side road. Felix thought of his mother. She'd be up and at work by now. She worked six hours a day in a munitions factory. It was exhausting work, on her feet all day, forty minutes commute

278

each way, continually under the watchful and bullying eyes of her supervisors. She may have been fifty years old, but that didn't excuse her. Everyone up to the age of sixty had to be doing something. The individual didn't matter; only the nation mattered. *For our Führer and our nation, the work goes on. We work today for victory tomorrow.*

And what of Stella and Charlotte now? They couldn't buy themselves out of trouble, Metzelder had seen to that, so what else was there? He'd have to return them to his grandfather's again and hope the old man was OK with it. But Gottfried's patience, he knew, would soon start to wear thin and he had no idea of what to do with them long-term. The thought of it all made him quite sick. He tried not to think of the forty thousand Reichsmarks.

They came across a village. Felix left Stella and Charlotte resting on the trunk of a fallen tree while he went to buy some food. It was, under any other circumstance, a quaint place, made up of white-timbered buildings, thatched roofs and tall chimneys. But he was too exhausted and on edge to appreciate its architectural delights. He passed a large wooden notice board pinned with various posters and notices. But the one that stuck out, read, *We are proud to announce this village is now Jew-free.* He entered the only bakery and took his place behind a couple of women in headscarves. He bought a loaf of cinnamon bread and six cakes which the baker wrapped in waxed paper. 'Is it far from here to Lobenstein?' he asked as nonchalantly as possible.

'Aye, a good three kilometres. I'd get a bus if I was you.' The woman checked her watch. 'There's one leaving in fifteen minutes from the square. Catch that, you'd be there in no time.'

The three of them approached the square and found a long

279

queue already waiting for the bus within the shadow of a clock tower. A mechanical rooster crowed the hour atop the town hall. Conversations paused while every one of them clocked Stella with her distinctive hair. One of the women sniffed the air. She had a live hen in her bag, its head poking out. Talking over her shoulder, she carried on her conversation. 'They say his head was battered in.'

'Dead?'

'What d'you think, deary? Of course. They say the place is swarming with Kripos.' The hen clucked. 'Shut up, you stupid bird. They've even got a description from some old farmer's wife up in the hills.'

Stella and Felix exchanged shifty glances. Felix fixed his concentration on a large statue of Martin Luther seated on a chair, his chin resting on his fist. Someone had tied a swastika banner around the back. The bus came rumbling round the corner, into the square, coming to a halt at the bus stop. At the same moment, the first woman said, 'Look, Kripos. Another police check.' She rummaged in her handbag and had her papers at the ready.

The two policemen approached the front of the queue. 'Papers,' shouted one.

'Just get on the bus, get yourself back to Berlin and to my mother's apartment,' said Felix quietly. 'Wait for me there.' He edged back slowly, while the two policemen checked papers. Satisfied he hadn't been noticed, he darted behind the statue plinth. He could hear the policemen making their way down the queue, the bus idling. He remembered the old man and his forged papers at the railway station. Stella and Charlotte's papers hadn't been checked yet. He just hoped they fared better. He could see them in the reflection of a glass shopfront.

'Why, hello,' said one of the policemen on seeing Stella as

she and Charlotte approached the bus. 'Can I ask for your papers, please?'

'Certainly, officer,' said Stella in a playful voice, handing over her and Charlotte's papers. 'What a fine job you're doing.'

'Why, thank you, madam.'

It did the trick; the man was so busy admiring Stella, he barely glanced at her identification. 'Thank you, madam. Have a good day.'

'And you. Thank you, officer.'

Felix almost laughed. He watched as the policemen sauntered away. He heard the second one say, 'She was all right, weren't she?'

'Bloody right.'

The bus doors snapped shut. Felix ran up to the bus and rapped gently on the doors just as the bus began pulling away. He glanced behind, hoping the Kripos hadn't heard or seen him. The bus stopped, the doors opened, and Felix hopped on, thanking the driver. The bus pulled away. Felix made the mistake of looking at the Kripos again. This time they saw him. He locked eyes with the first one. It took him a second to register that he was looking at a man that, by all accounts, matched the description of the man they were looking for. Then, on realising it, they both started to run. Felix, holding on to a bar, started talking loudly to the driver, trying to block out the Kripos' shouting. 'My, it's cold, don't you think? I swear I feel the cold more with every passing year. I've heard it may start snowing later...' He carried on as the driver eased the bus away.

'You need to sit down,' said the driver, interrupting him.

Instead Felix stepped closer to him, hoping to divert the driver's attention away from his mirrors. 'Sorry, say that again, I'm a bit deaf.'

'I said…'

Felix gripped the bar as the bus turned the corner. Oh, the relief. With a satisfied sigh, he took his place in the seat in front of Stella and Charlotte.

'You OK?' she whispered.

'Never better,' he said. And just for a fleeting moment, he meant it.

Chapter 44

'Heil Hitler.' The silent rows of expectant eyes were upon him. Felix turned his back on them to face the blackboard. He needed a moment to compose himself. He had something unpleasant to do, an order from the headmaster. The head had spotted his hesitation.

'What's the matter, Stoltenberg? It's important. Shows the other kids what's important and that there's honour in death when one's life is given for the greater cause.'

The 'greater cause'. It was always about the greater cause. That and honour. 'Yes, sir.'

'We live in difficult times, Stoltenberg. So let's not get all sentimental over this.'

Felix wrote the day's date on the blackboard. He supposed the headmaster was right in a way. At least the man had died fighting, his honour intact. Unlike his own father, 'shot while trying to escape', dead with his name besmirched, the family honour ruined, their home requisitioned. Such a long time ago.

Someone coughed. Another giggled. He turned round, ready to face the class. 'Hannah, stand up, please.'

Hannah, the girl who had beaten Charlotte in the 100

283

metres, stood up, her face bright red.

'Tell us about your father, Hannah.'

The girl looked around at her classmates, her face deepening in colour. No one looked at her in return.

'Your father, Hannah.'

'Sir. My… my mother got a telegram yesterday.' Her voice quivered. 'My father was killed fighting the enemy in North Africa.'

'My condolences. Well?'

'We're…' He could see her clenching her fists, trying her damnedest not to cry.

'Yes?'

'We're very proud that he gave his life for the Führer.'

'An honour.'

'Yes, sir.'

'Thank you, Hannah. You may sit down now.'

She didn't at first. She glared at him, gathering strength from somewhere within her. Felix looked away, out of the window, saw a flock of starlings hurtling across the lead sky. He could feel her hate, was happy to absorb it for he knew he deserved it.

*

Afternoon. Felix had been teaching his class about the role of mothers in Hitler's Germany. He hated teaching now. Every time he talked of the Führer and his wondrous deeds, Ernst Gluck's words came back to him, haunting him. 'The German maiden has to be beautiful and strong, athletic and supple. It is their duty to remain fit and healthy; it is not a private concern, but their civic duty. German women should bear at least four children, no less. Women who remain childless are *traitors* to the Fatherland.' *So, these Jews, all naked, were led to this ravine.* 'And remember; mothers with four children or more will have the honour of receiving the Mother's Cross of Honour on the twelfth of August, the birthday of Hitler's mother. And what should you do if you are to meet a bearer of the Cross?'

'To greet her honourably, sir,' said one of the boys.

'Good lad.' *The ravine was already half full of bodies.*

One of the girls raised her hand. 'Sir, if children are so important to the Führer, why is it he doesn't have any?'

'Young woman – what a question. The Führer runs the country. He has said it many times: he is wedded to the nation.' *I saw them shoot kids and even babies.* 'It is the most demanding job of all. Even more demanding than being a teacher.'

'Sir?' Another of the girls had put her hand up. 'Is it true that our Führer was a really good artist and he did lots of lovely paintings and, erm, he wanted to be a proper artist so he wanted to go to college? And he applied to some art school in Venice –'

A round of laughter stopped her short. Felix shook his head, trying not to laugh. 'Venice? Really?'

'No, not Venice, sir –'

One of the boys shouted out, 'Hey, imagine our Führer in Venice. Maybe he worked as a gondolier.'

Another, giggling, added, 'Yeah while singing Italian opera–'

'OK, OK, stop this,' shouted Felix. 'How... how dare you mock the Führer?' The mirth stopped in an instant. *All these naked bodies covered in blood, twitching.* 'I will not tolerate such irreverence.' Although, he had to admit, the image was rather amusing. 'You should wash your filthy mouths out with soap. I expect better. Our Führer did not and would not find himself in Italy. As much as we admire Benito Mussolini, it is still a country of Mediterraneans and hardly worthy of being home to our Führer.'

'Sorry, sir. I meant to say Vienna, I got my –'

'Yes, Vienna, Jew-infested Vienna. It doesn't matter now.'

I guess they didn't know what was going to happen until the last moments.

'Are you OK, sir?'

'Hmm? What? Yes. I just need to sit down for a moment. Do excuse me.' *We tell them they're being resettled because it's easier that way.* 'I'll be fine in a minute.'

*

Late that evening, Felix sat at home reading a book. He'd hidden Stella's painting of him in the chest of drawers in his bedroom. Somehow, he didn't think his mother would like it. He thought about Stella's ex-husband, wondered what he was like, what he looked like. She'd said he'd killed a soldier. Well, they had that in common now. But the man was mad to think he'd get away with it. He'd be caught sooner than later and, once they had him, well, it didn't bear thinking about. He'd popped into work after school. Colonel Friesler had gone; Felix had missed the leaving do. He wasn't particularly sorry. The new man was due to start within a matter of days.

His mother was in the bath. Her work at the factory always tired her out. He thought of the incident in the bungalow. He tried to explain it away; maybe his grandfather really had dropped something. But no, however much he wanted to believe that, he knew now it was a lie. His grandfather really had been looking through the bathroom door keyhole while Charlotte was inside. Did it mean anything, apart from being simply wrong? He would have asked his mother for advice, but he hadn't wanted her to know Stella was staying with her father. He should warn Stella. Perhaps find them somewhere else to hide. But where. Where?

His mother came out of the bathroom wearing her dressing gown, drying her hair with a towel. She went through to the kitchen. He could hear her clattering around, putting away plates and dishes.

Idly, he found his grandfather's penny whistle in his jacket pocket. He sat back down and decided to give it a go. He managed the first couple of bars of *Für Elise* as Gottfried had taught him, before faltering. He tried another couple of times, getting no further.

His mother emerged from the kitchen, a tea towel in her hand and the bath towel wrapped around her head like a turban. 'Felix, stop that. Do you have to play that thing?' she asked.

'I've just taken it up. I –'

'Don't, please. Just… just don't.'

He rose slowly from his chair. 'What's the matter, Mum? Why does it upset you so much? It's just a silly little whistle.'

She toyed with the tea towel. 'I don't like it. It…'

'What?'

'Reminds me of things, that's all.' She shook her head as if trying to dislodge a memory. 'It's nothing. A long time ago. I'm going to bed. I've got another long day tomorrow.'

'What is it, Mother? Tell me, what does it remind you of?'

'Nothing. Nothing at all.' She shot a look at the photograph on the wall, the one of his grandfather as a young man. 'Your grandfather likes those things.'

'I know, he…' He screwed up his face; the words had come out before he could stop them.

Klara blanched. 'You're not telling me he gave you that thing?'

He looked at the photograph, trying to bide time, trying to

287

think of an answer.

'Felix, answer me. Oh no. Oh my god, no.' She almost fell into the armchair.

'Mum? Mum, what's the matter?' He leapt over to her, fell at her knees. 'Mum, are you OK?'

'That's where you took them, isn't it?'

'What?'

She sat forward abruptly. 'Don't lie to me, Felix. You took that woman of yours to stay with my father.'

He couldn't lie, not now, there was something in his mother's eyes that he'd never seen before, a fear almost, a dread of something. He nodded.

'Tell me, you took the girl as well.'

'Yes. Why?'

'She's fifteen, isn't she? Yes, I remember. That's just about young enough. Preferably younger, but fifteen's OK.'

'Mum, what on earth are you... Oh no, I don't believe this.' The sound of laughter drifted up from the courtyard, the sound of glass smashing on the cobblestones. He spoke slowly. 'Are you telling me... What did he do to you?'

She fought for air, her eyes skywards, her mouth gaping open. 'Nothing. He never touched me. But there were others... many of them. He used to be a teacher...'

'That was years ago. It'd be OK now.'

'No, Felix. The man's a monster. All those pupils over the years. That girl. That p-poor girl. She's in danger, Felix. You have to take her away from that man. Now. Before it's too late.'

Chapter 45

Stella had been painting out in the woods behind the village, trying to capture the last hints of snow melting on the forest floor. The day was cold, the clouds dark, and the painting had not gone well. She trudged back to the bungalow, wearing the red coat Gottfried had bought her, her easel and painting paraphernalia tucked under her arm.

She hated it here, in this remote, soulless village, with its suspicious inhabitants and their sullen expressions. Charlotte disliked it too. She had no one to talk to, nothing to do. They couldn't stand Gottfried, with his loud voice, his stupid opinions and his Nazi sympathies. The two of them had become the old man's skivvies, his cook, cleaner, shopper and his talking post. And he was always *there*, never went out. Without asking, he'd become Charlotte's teacher, haranguing her for her lack of historical knowledge and her failure to grasp basic algebra. There had to be an alternative to this. Her husband had friends; surely one of them could help. There were still plenty of Jews legally living in Berlin, made to work in the factories for the Reich's war effort. Surely, somewhere, she could find a sympathetic soul.

She returned to the bungalow. As always, Gottfried had the radio blaring out, playing that bland light music that he always liked. She sighed. She called out for him. No answer. She went to her bedroom. What was he doing there? He jumped on hearing the door open.

'Oh, it's you,' he said, his hand on his chest.

Her handbag was open on her bed. He'd been rummaging through her things, the bastard. 'What are you doing?'

'Looking for something.'

'In my handbag? You were looking through my things. You have no right.'

He rounded on her, flashing her passport in his hand. 'You're a Jew.'

She took a step back. 'So what?'

'So what? You ask me "so what" as if it didn't matter. You've duped me into thinking you were hiding from your husband, but it's not that at all, is it? You're a Yid, a filthy Jewess. And that daughter of yours.' He flipped open her passport, pointing out the large red 'J' as if she wasn't aware it was there.

'Where's Charlotte?' she asked. 'Where is she?'

'Don't fret. I sent her out shopping for eggs and milk. I fancy another of your delicious omelettes for lunch. I can't believe you're Jewish.'

She had to think, had to find a way out of this. 'I'm sorry it upsets you so, Gottfried. I'll pack my bags. We'll be gone by nightfall.' She stepped closer to him, trying to smile. 'You don't have to tell anyone. You'll never have to see us again.'

'That's not the point, though, is it? It's my duty, my duty,' he said, jabbing his thumb against his chest, 'to report you.'

She took another step closer to him, reaching out, stroking his arm. 'Just because it's your duty, doesn't mean to say you

290

have to do it.' She spoke softly, as if trying to calm a rabid dog. 'Surely we can come to an arrangement, Gottfried.' She smiled, trying to hide the venom in her heart.

He looked down at her hand traversing the length of his arm. 'What… what are you saying?'

He was softening, she could tell. 'Well, Gottfried, the moment I met you I could see you were a man of principle. It's something I like in a man. My, what strong arms you have, Gottfried.'

'I like to keep myself fit.'

'I can tell. Tell me, how long have you been alone, Gottfried?'

'Long enough.'

'Too long, I'm sure.' She moved her hand up to his shoulder, her fingers creeping over his flesh like the legs of a spider.

He narrowed his eyes. 'You think I'm stupid, don't you?'

She sprung back.

'I wasn't born yesterday. What is this? Little Red Riding Hood? You in your red coat, and me as the wolf dressed up as a kindly old grandfather. *My, what strong arms you have, Gottfried.* What you take me for, you silly bitch?'

'You can call me a bitch as much as you like, Gottfried, but I know you want to. I can see it in your eyes.'

He turned and went to the window, flicking the curtain back. With his back to her, he said, 'Maybe you're right. It has been a long time. So you want to buy my silence and this is what you propose?'

She shut her eyes as she said yes.

'It sounds so easy, doesn't it? But you make assumptions, Stella. How old are you?'

'Thirty-one.'

'Exactly. You're old. I don't like old women. I like them young and untainted. I like them fresh.' He turned and glared at her. 'I like them virginal.'

'No. No. You… you can't.'

'No? Why not? It's a small sacrifice, all things considered.'

'No.'

'A very small sacrifice. Think of the alternative. Do you really want your daughter to fall into the hands of the Gestapo? I give you to nightfall tomorrow. That should give you enough time to persuade your daughter.'

Chapter 46

First thing the following morning, Felix was ready to leave. It was a Tuesday; he should have been at school. He called in, said he had urgent SS business to attend to. They accepted it readily enough; most of the male teachers worked part time for one of the security services. What he hadn't expected, was to see his mother with her coat and shoes on, looking ready to go out. 'Off to work?' he asked. But he knew she wasn't dressed for work; she'd put on her finest dress, her best shoes and smartest coat. He even detected a hint of lipstick. She looked like she was going out for the evening.

'No, I'm not going to work. I'm coming with you.'

He started to protest but he could tell her mind was made up. 'This is my father we're talking about here, Felix. That man has blighted too many lives and I want it to end now, today. I am coming with you, like it or not.'

He did persuade her to change into a more practical pair of shoes. After all, it was almost a mile to walk from the train station to her father's village.

They didn't speak on the train, too many people. Felix ended up playing peekaboo with a little boy. But as they walked the mile to the village, his mother spoke. A sharp wind cut through their coats. The road leading to the village was awash with sludge, the last hints of the week's earlier snowstorms. 'You were right about the shoes,' she said. 'He never touched me, your grandfather. But he did others. He was always known as a caring teacher and a devoted headmaster. I was one of his pupils. I used to wonder why so many parents took their children away from the school.'

'You don't have to tell me this, Mum.'

'You need to know. And do you remember that lovely girl next door but one?'

'Ingrid. Of course I do.' The image of her hiding the two Jewish children flashed through his mind. He always flushed on thinking of Ingrid. It still baffled him why, as kids, he'd treated her so badly when she deserved better.

'Well…'

Felix let out a groan.

His mother shook her head at the memory of it all. 'Whatever happens today, I need you to realise we're not dealing with a gentle old man here, a kindly grandfather – but a beast of a man. One day, when I was about sixteen, a friend of mine told me. Ursula was her name. Same age as me. She told me how my father used to order her into his office when she was about twelve to fourteen. He made her sit on his lap. I'd heard rumours before but I never believed them. How could I? I hit this girl, Ursula. She responded by bringing more girls who told me their stories.'

'Please, Mum.'

'No. You will listen to me. He used to go into the girls' changing rooms. He was the head; no one complained, no one said anything. But he was forced into retirement at a young age. I remember people couldn't understand. Your father was one of them. "But he loves his job; he'd stay till he was a hundred if he could." But I knew why he loved his job so much. The governors had finally cottoned onto what was going on under their noses. They forced him out. But he left with a golden handshake and a good pension.'

'I want to tell you something too.' Felix told his mother about catching Gottfried spying on Charlotte through the bathroom door keyhole.

She shook her head. 'It doesn't surprise me. Why didn't you tell me, Felix? I would have told you it wouldn't have been safe for them there. You've led them straight into the lions' den.'

Felix tightened his scarf. It struck him that while his mother was keen to protect this young girl from the clutches of a lecherous old man, she'd shown no concern when they risked being taken by the Gestapo and sent to their deaths. You can fight a single man but you can't fight sixty million of them.

They'd come to the bungalow. As usual, the front door was not locked. Felix went in first. He heard an unfamiliar voice coming from his grandfather's bedroom. He went in to find an elderly doctor attending his groaning and stricken-looking grandfather, sprawled across the settee, his skin a strange shade of blue. 'What's happened?' asked Klara, behind him.

'Who are you?' He wore half-moon glasses, topped with caterpillar-like black eyebrows.

'I'm his daughter. This is my son. Is my father ill?'

'Very much so, I'm afraid.'

Gottfried, with wet flannels on his forehead and across his chest, opened his eyes, catching sight of his daughter. 'Klara?' he wheezed. 'Is that really you? Come to me, my girl.' She took his hand. The man was poorly; he wouldn't have noticed how tense his daughter was, the look of apprehension and disdain in her eyes. He was having difficulty breathing, he was bathed in sweat. 'I knew you'd come back one day. That wicked woman poisoned me.'

Klara asked the doctor what was wrong while Felix checked the spare bedroom for Stella and Charlotte. They'd gone. The wardrobe and drawers were empty of clothes, no sign of their suitcases. And in the bedroom lay a sick man. What had happened here?

He heard the doctor explaining. 'No, you don't need a prescription for Veronal, a type of barbiturate. Just a sleeping potion; you can get it over the counter. That's why he's cyanotic.

'Cyanotic?'

'His skin is discoloured blue.'

'Will he be OK?'

The doctor led her to one side. 'I have to tell you, I came late. His neighbour heard him crying out. By time I arrived, the poison had done its work. His pulse is dangerously weak. I have to tell you, madam, he won't survive this. Whoever did this, is a murderer. I know your father, he's not the suicidal type. God knows how much Veronal he's had. Fine in small doses, but he must have had a hundred grams or more to be in this state. I've tried flushing him out with warm water. It hasn't worked. His temperature is shockingly high. I need to call an ambulance. Look, can I leave you with him? I'll only be ten minutes. The quicker the better. Even then, Frau, I fear we'll be too late.' He placed his hand on hers. 'I'm so sorry.' He picked up his medical bag. 'I'll be quick as I can. Meanwhile, try and keep him cool. Fresh flannels every few minutes.'

Felix watched the doctor leave. 'Where are Stella and Charlotte?' he barked at his grandfather.

'She poisoned me, Felix. That terrible woman, she put that poison in my omelettes.'

'And why would she do that?' he asked.

He groaned loudly, clasping both hands to his belly. 'Because... oh, it hurts. Because I found out she's a Yid. I found her ID card with the "J" on it. I told the Gestapo. I had to. My duty. Ah, my stomach. Klara, my sweet daughter. Thank you for coming. I think I'm dying.'

Klara looked up at her son.

'She poisoned him because she found out about Charlotte,' whispered Felix. 'Mum, I need to get back to Berlin. I need to find her.' His mother nodded. 'Will you be OK?'

'Oh yes,' she said, patting her father's hand. 'We'll be just fine, won't we, Dad?'

'Mum, don't do anything stupid.' He bent down and kissed her on the head.

'I don't need to, do I? He doesn't have long.' He made to leave while his mother sat next to her father still holding his hand. 'Dad, do you remember a girl called Ursula at your school? Pretty girl, glasses, spoke with a lisp. Or Lisl, or Hilda. Or Claire, perhaps? The one who liked algebra. You liked Claire very much, didn't you? You liked them all.'

He saw it in his grandfather's frightened eyes – yes, he remembered; he remembered it all. 'Oh, Klara, I can't breathe. Help me.'

'And what about Sophie? Good at the high jump. Do you remember her? This Jewish girl, Charlotte? Was she one of them, Dad? Was she another?'

'Klara, I'm in such pain. Please, not now, have mercy on me...'

Felix closed the door behind him.

PART FIVE

Chapter 47

Berlin, September 1942

The disgraced captain sits on the bench, his arms wrapped around himself. 'God, it's cold.'

'You should complain.'

Rudolph laughs. 'Ha, you're beginning to sound like me. You're learning.'

Felix is unsure what it is he's been learning; maybe it's that irony in an irony-free world is a form of self-defence. But he's right: it's bloody cold in the cell.

'So,' says Rudolph, drawing the word out. 'I guess you've not seen her since.'

'No.'

'She and her daughter could be anywhere. Let's hope they're safe, although…'

'I know.'

'And you? How did you end up here?'

Felix focuses on the bucket. Someone had come and emptied it a second time. He assumes it still stinks but he can't smell it any more. 'I came into work the following day. I knew

I had to keep up appearances but, as soon as I walked in, the receptionist called me back, saying that the new colonel had asked to see me. I admit my world stopped for a moment. Friesler had rarely asked me to see him, so why would his replacement want to straightaway? She asked me to wait in the waiting area, you know, a place where the hoi polloi sit: usually half-petrified wives fretting about their husbands, mothers like my own wrung out with worry, asking about their sons. I remember sitting opposite this shabbily-dressed woman, wearing a headscarf, twisting a handkerchief around her fingers. It was uncomfortable for both of us. She was probably wondering why one of the men she feared so much should be reduced to a status no better than hers. We didn't talk; no one talks in eight Prinz Albert Strasse unless you work there. I was already an outsider.

'Then, after about forty minutes, a couple of privates and a corporal appeared. I knew something was wrong by the way they talked to me, the way they addressed me by my surname. They brought me to here, this cell, and this is where I've been ever since. God knows how long now.'

'Hmm.'

'And that's it; that's the end of my story.'

Rudolph sighs. 'Well, well, well. So, you've not met Colonel Friesler's replacement?'

'No. I hope not to. Have you?'

'Me? No, no, I haven't.'

He's lying, thinks Felix. *Why is he lying?*

They fall into silence. The minutes tick by. Rudolph groans. *He's thinking of Anton*, thinks Felix. He thinks of his mother, his father, little meek Hans, Heinrich Richter, all the people who had featured in his life. He wonders what happened to Hans and Heinrich. He dreads to think. There is no joy in his

302

memories, just a dull ache in the pit of his stomach – a sense of longing, but for what, he doesn't know. He remembers the boating trip on Lake Tegel with Stella, the sound of the geese, the family of ducks, the mother duck calling out for her young to follow. He'd sleep but it's too cold. Time passes slowly as it always does within these four, bare walls.

They hear those footsteps approaching outside in the corridor once more. Again, they can tell it's not the orderly coming with their food. Both men stand, a nervous glance exchanged.

The key turns; the door opens. It's the corporal with the bulbous nose and Hitler moustache, a pistol in his hand. A second guard waits in the corridor. 'You,' says Corporal Bulbous, pointing his pistol at Rudolph. 'You need to follow me.'

Rudolph blanches; his jawline twitches.

'Now,' says Corporal Bulbous. Then, after a moment, he adds the word, please.

Rudolph turns to Felix, pulls the creases out of his tunic. Felix can see the terror in his eyes, but his voice, when he speaks, does not betray his fear. 'I think this is it,' he says, trying to maintain calm, flattening his hair with the palm of his hand. 'It's my turn.'

Felix nods, his heart pounding from within.

Rudolph attempts a smile but it doesn't quite materialise. 'It's been nice knowing you, Lieutenant Stoltenberg.' He offers his hand.

Felix takes it. 'And you, Captain Karstadt.'

'I shall remember you for the rest of my life.' He winks. 'All five minutes of it. I'd wish you luck but...'

'I know.'

The former captain places his hand on Felix's shoulder.

303

Felix feels the warmth of his flesh and is somehow reassured by his touch. 'You're a good lad. Your heart was in the right place, I know that. Goodbye, my son.'

Felix stands to attention, his back straight, and gives an old-fashioned salute. 'Goodbye, sir.'

Captain Karstadt stiffens and returns the salute. He turns to face the open door. 'I'm ready. Shall we go, Corporal?'

'After you, sir.'

'Thank you, Corporal.'

The door slams shut. He is gone and Felix realises he is still saluting.

He sits down on his bed, puts his head in his hands. His heart pounds in his ears. He stands again, paces up, down, up, down. He runs his fingers through his matted hair. He leans against the door. Rudolph said he was forty-three years old, the same age as his father when they took him. He has an urge to scream. Instead, he turns and thumps the door with the sides of his fists. In an instant, he loses the strength. His hands slide down the rough surface of the door. He wants to cry but he can't even do that. Then, as if summoned by his thumping, he hears the key turning. He steps back, his stomach knotted with fear. The captain has only been gone two minutes; why have they come back so soon? Sure enough, it's Corporal Bulbous again. He quivers.

'Come,' says the man. 'Follow me.'

'M-my turn already?'

'No, not for you, not yet.'

'Wh-what then?'

'The new colonel wants to see you.'

Chapter 48

Corporal Bulbous leads Felix up the stairs. It is like coming up for air. With each step, the atmosphere feels different, lighter and cleaner somehow. Reaching the ground floor, they pass the reception desk. A clock on the wall shows eleven o'clock. Felix's body clock clunks back into place. He follows the corporal down the corridor, although he knows perfectly well where to go. Portraits of Germans, great and good, follow him with their eyes, a far cry from the paintings adorning the walls in Stella's apartment.

Reaching the colonel's office, Corporal Bulbous knocks on the huge double door. The nameplate still has Colonel Friesler's name on it. The corporal stands aside on hearing the word 'enter' from within.

Felix steps into the office. The new colonel is on his feet, behind his desk. But Felix is blinded by the sunlight streaming through the window behind him. 'Heil Hitler,' he says, throwing his arm out and straightening his back.

'Well, well, well. Felix Stoltenberg. Who would have thought, after all these years?'

He knew that voice, deeper now, but unmistakably his…

but no, it couldn't be; it simply couldn't…

'Please, take a seat.' The colonel sits down himself and the light shifts.

'Thank you, s–' The words die on his lips, the blood in his veins chills. The jet-black hair, the high cheekbones, the Roman nose… Felix stares at him. Is it really *him*? After all these years? Is it really Klaus Beck in a SS colonel's uniform sitting before him?

Klaus laughs. 'Your face, Felix. You should see it. Oh, what a picture! Sit down, do sit down.'

Felix sits. 'Klaus, what…' He finds himself bereft of speech.

'I often thought about you over the years. I'd say to myself, I wonder what happened to my old friend Felix Stoltenberg. And then I saw your name on the staff list and I thought, ha! What a small world; and here you are. I was delighted. Tell me, how are you?'

'I'm… I'm great. Thanks.'

'All things considered. You look well. A bit thin perhaps. Your mother, how is she?'

'She's… she's well. Working in a factory, you know.'

'Of course. Good for her. And are you married, Felix? Kids?'

'No, not…'

He laughs again. 'Too busy with all your work. I see you're a teacher now and, what with your commitments here, I guess you don't have time for the gentler sex.'

'No.'

'Same here. Same here.'

The spacious room, with its dark red velvet wallpaper, its plush blue carpet, its chandelier and art deco lamps, resembles more a ballroom than an office. Two full-length windows overlook the city, a huge portrait of Hitler in between, his hard eyes fixed on the young lieutenant now sitting in the office, trying his best not to show his fear. Klaus's black hair seems to glisten under the chandelier.

'I'm so sorry you had to be detained. That was Friesler's doing. This is only my second day. A step up for me. A lot of responsibility as you might imagine. It's good to see you again, Felix. We must go out for a drink sometime, catch up on old times. What do you say?'

'Yeah, of course.'

'I often think back to our time together as kids. Such happy days. Blood brothers. Life seemed so simple then, don't you think? Remember that time those commie scum tried to jump us? Ha! What idiots. We'd been to see that film. Remember – the flag means more than death?'

'Yes.'

'Funny thing is, that still applies, don't you think?' He lowers his voice. 'In fact, if anything, it means even more now. The flag really does mean more than death.'

Felix stares at him, his old friend, and realises he is frightened of him, has always been frightened of him.

'Do you still play chess? Of course not, who has time for chess these days?' Klaus smiles. 'Still got the stamps?'

'Oh, yes, in a cupboard somewhere.'

'Yes, me too.' He smiles again and a shiver runs down Felix's spine.

'Yeah, blood brothers, you and me. Oh well, I'd love to talk about the old times all day but alas…' He opened up his palms. 'To business. After all, there's a war on.'

Felix tries to laugh appropriately. He notices Klaus is wearing the Death's Head Ring, a silver ring decorated with a skull, bestowed personally by Heinrich Himmler himself as a gift to his most loyal servants.

Felix holds his breath as he asks, 'How's your father?'

Klaus' eyes narrow. 'Died in the camp at Oranienburg. Just like your father, Felix. We always did have so much in common.' He pauses.

Felix remembers the one time he met the man with his huge belly straining under a stained white shirt and braces, chewing on a toothpick. *A useless piece of shit*; that's what he called his son. And now that useless piece of shit sits in front of him, dangling his life from his fingers.

Klaus looks at his watch. 'Oh, it's time.' He gets up abruptly from his desk and walks around it towards the door. 'Felix, follow me, will you?'

Felix follows Klaus out of the office, down the corridor, past more grand paintings, and into another office.

This office is deserted, small and dark, the curtains drawn. The smell of mothballs pervades the space. Felix waits by the door while Klaus goes to the window and pulls back the curtains. An infusion of light floods the room, dust motes dancing. The room is almost bare, just a Führer portrait on the wall and a small table with a blotter and a globe on it. Klaus looks down out of the window. 'Ah, we're ready, I see. Come here, Felix. I want you to see this.'

Felix does as told and joins Klaus at the window.

He lets out a little cry, unable to prevent it. Down below is a small courtyard, a few bushes, paved ground, a small fountain at its centre. And there, his hands tied behind his back, his back to a brick wall at the far end, is Rudolph Karstadt. In front of him, four soldiers, their rifles at their sides, and to their side with a relaxed Alsatian on a leash, Corporal Bulbous.

'I suppose after spending some time together, you and this

man got to know each other.'

Felix tries to speak.

'Did he mention he's a pervert, one who contravenes everything that is natural in this world? Probably not. Too ashamed, and rightly so. Disgusting creature. An insult to the Führer.'

Felix braves a glance at his old friend. *Blood brothers, that's what we are.*

Klaus' focus remains on the scene below. 'Brave, though, I give him that. Impeccable service in battle; got an Iron Cross. And I see he's forgone the blindfold. I respect that, even if he is a pervert.'

Corporal Bulbous looks up at the window. Felix sees Klaus nod. The corporal clicks his heels. The dog stands, his tail gently wagging. The men straighten. It is time.

Felix swallows. He wants to look away but knows he can't. Klaus is enjoying himself too much.

Corporal Bulbous puts his hand in the air. 'Rifles at the ready.'

The men lift their rifles to their shoulders. The dog barks. Rudolph breathes in and holds his head high.

'Take aim.'

Rudolph looks up, locks eyes with Felix. Felix steps back, almost as if he's been hit. There is no fear in those eyes, no nervousness, just a calm, defiant acceptance. Is this how his father died, he wonders.

'Fire!'

The sound of four gunshots echoes through the air, gently fading away. An array of birds take flight, squawking. The former captain, brave to the last, lies in a heap at the foot of the wall. Felix sways on his feet, battling his nauseousness.

Klaus leads the way back to his office. Felix follows,

summoning the strength to put one foot ahead of the other, his stomach hollowed out.

Klaus orders Felix to sit. 'Now that we've got that over with, there's something I think you may be able to help with. It was virtually the first thing to land on my desk. Colonel Friesler didn't have time to deal with it so he left it to me. More's the pity.'

Felix feels obliged to say something but manages only a feeble 'OK.'

'So, let me summarise…' He picks up a sheet of paper from his desk. 'Apparently, on New Year's Day, two officers of the Gestapo were assigned the task of arresting a Jewish woman and her daughter ahead of deportation and resettlement. The name of this Jewess was Stella Hoffmann.' He stops and looks up at Felix. 'Her daughter, Charlotte Wolff, aged fifteen. Mean anything to you?'

Felix shakes his head, conscious of the colour draining from his face.

Klaus continues. 'The officers were prevented from completing their task by the illegal and immoral actions of a man dressed in the uniform and coat of the SS Security. The man wore an armband indicating he was a Waffen SS reservist, an armband identical to the one you used to wear.' He pauses, as if allowing time for this information to absorb. 'What do you know of this incident, Lieutenant Stoltenberg? But before you say anything, I advise you to think carefully about how you answer.'

Felix clears his throat. 'I am aware of the incident.'

'Is that all?'

'Yes, Klaus.'

Klaus leans forward, his elbows on his desk. 'Listen, Felix, I know we're old friends but I think while we're at work, you

310

should call me "sir". Is that all right? Do you mind awfully?'

Felix nods. 'Sir.'

Klaus flashes a smile. He picks up the telephone on his desk, presses a button and speaks. 'Show them in.'

Felix hears a knock on the door behind him, the door opening and the sound of footsteps on the carpet. He doesn't dare turn round. Klaus and his visitors exchange a round of Heil Hitlers. The two men stand to his side. It is them, the two Gestapo officers.

Klaus is speaking. 'Gentleman, thank you for your time this morning and I am sorry to have kept you waiting. Could I ask you to look carefully at the lieutenant before you and tell me whether you think this is the man who attacked you on New Year's Day? Take your time.'

Felix concentrates on the Führer's portrait, trying to keep control of his breathing. When he was a boy of about seven or eight, years before Adolf Hitler came to prominence, there was a boy who lived in his grandfather's village, a fat little boy who had the same Hitler haircut, shiny black hair swept to one side. Max was his name. Quiet boy, hardly ever spoke. Occasionally, they went fishing together at the river. Never caught anything, but it didn't seem to matter. Strange, he'd seen Hitler's image thousands of times over the years but it is only now, this moment, that he makes the connection between the Führer and Max.

The two men look at Felix, look at each other, and back at Felix. The shorter one breaks the silence. 'It's hard to say, Colonel. He was wearing a balaclava –'

'Pulled down over his eyes,' adds the taller one.

'And it all happened so quickly.'

'He's about the same size though.'

'Can we hear him talk?'

Klaus clicks his fingers. 'How does that rhyme go, Lieutenant? The one about Mary and the little lamb.'

He wondered whatever happened to fat little Max with his Hitler haircut. Perhaps he grew a moustache to match and learnt how to shout.

'The rhyme, Lieutenant?'

Felix clears his throat. 'Mary had a little lamb. Its fleece was white as snow. And everywhere that Mary...'

'That's him,' both men say in unison.

Klaus raises an eyebrow. 'You sure?'

'Yeah,' says the shorter one. 'He spoke kind of nice.'

'Like an officer,' adds the taller one.

'That's him all right, sir.'

'Interesting. OK, gentlemen.' The men click their heels. 'That was most useful. Thank you again for your time. Please feel free to go.'

Another round of Heil Hitlers ensues.

Klaus waits until the door closes. 'Is there anything you'd like to say at this juncture, Lieutenant?'

'No, sir.'

Klaus shakes his head. 'I'm afraid I'm marking that down as a positive identification.'

Felix is sure Klaus is able to hear the pounding of his heart. He tries to think of Max, of fishing together, of sweeping away the years to escape this present, to return to a time when everything in the world was wonderful and exciting and pure.

'But is it?' adds Klaus. Felix wants to be sick. 'Perhaps they were a little too keen to say what they thought I wanted to hear. Perhaps, their memory isn't as good as they think. After all, there are a lot of men who are Waffen SS reservists, of your height and speak nicely.' He picks up a brass-coloured letter opener and taps it on the side of his desk. 'I've read your reports, Felix. Frankly, they read very well. You've impressed everyone. You have a future in front of you. I'd be doing the Führer a disservice if I wrongly condemned a man of such great potential. So, I'm going to leave your fate in your hands. I'm setting you a test, Felix. After all, I know you of old. I know you wouldn't betray us. After all, you put the party ahead of your father, didn't you? What sort of man does that? A very loyal man. So, prove to me that you are a good and still loyal servant of the SS and all will be well.'

He presses the tip of the letter opener against the end of a finger. 'But fail me, Felix, and you'll find yourself in Russia in the blink of an eye, stripped of rank and fighting in a penal battalion. I don't think you'd cope with that. No one does.' He pauses as if to allow the threat to sink in. 'However, I believe in you so I am sure it won't come to that.' Klaus stands abruptly. Felix breathes in. 'There is one person I know for sure who can tell us the identity of this rogue officer that allowed the Jewish woman and her daughter to escape. Follow me,' he says.

Standing in a lift next to a man who has threatened you with a penal battalion, even if you were once the best of friends, is not the easiest of situations. Felix has heard of these battalions. They are reserved for criminals and traitors of the Reich. The men are treated with utmost brutality, and their work consists of various suicide missions, like walking over minefields or defending a position against overwhelming opposition. A death sentence in all but name. He shudders.

The lift comes to a halt in the basement. Standing outside the lift, as if waiting for the colonel, is Leo Höch, the one with the gammy leg. Sure enough, Höch nods at him. Together, Klaus leads the way down the dank, dark corridor. Felix thinks he can hear the dead whistling their sad laments. They come to a halt outside Room 2J. A guard clicks his heels and Heils Hitler. Felix knows the room well. It was here in September he interviewed Otto Wankel. It seems a lifetime ago.

Klaus orders the guard to unlock the door. 'We shall go in together. I'll be present as a witness and to monitor your progress.' He motions for Höch to go in first. 'Remember,' he says, his hand on Felix's sleeve. 'Your life depends on this, Felix. Please, I beg of you, don't let me down. Now, after you.'

Felix pushes open the door. His heart collapses within him. There, in the centre of the cell in front of him, her arms and legs strapped to a chair, is Stella.

Chapter 49

Stella's red-rimmed eyes widen on seeing him. She tries to move, forgetting she is strapped to the chair. He can see a thousand thoughts shoot through her mind: *what is he doing here, what does he want; has he been on their side all along?* He purses his lips, a split second only, hopefully enough to express his sorrow. The last time he was here, with Otto Wankel in front of him, he felt so strong; he had right on his side, or so he thought, he'd felt invincible. Not now. *How cold it is here.* A dull light bulb screwed into the ceiling provides the only light. In the corner is a spare chair and a number of straps.

Klaus beckons him back out into the corridor and gives Felix his instructions. They return to the cell. Felix takes his position directly in front of Stella; Klaus behind him on his left, Höch to the right.

It is all horribly unreal somehow, as if it is not him but someone else standing now facing the woman he thought he loved. He knows what he has to do: to beat the truth out of her, the truth that would confirm it was him that aided her escape from the clutches of the Gestapo. She raises her eyebrows a fraction. He swallows. She is telling him she is ready. Let the charade begin.

Felix begins. 'Stella Hoffmann, on New Year's Day this year, a man dressed in the uniform of the SS helped you evade arrest. What was the name of this man?' She doesn't answer. *Just tell them*, he thinks. *Save yourself the pain, just tell them.* As if reading his doubts, she raises her eyebrows again. 'Frau Hoffmann? An answer please.'

'I'd never seen him before.'

'So, what you're saying is that an unknown man for unknown reasons took it upon himself to rescue you.'

'Yes.'

'Frau Hoffmann—'

'Fräulein, please.'

He almost cries out on hearing their familiar and affectionate exchange of words. 'Fräulein Hoffmann…' He has to stop, has to clear his throat. 'We do not believe you. Please, tell us the name of this man.'

'I can't because I don't know it. He refused to give me his name.'

'What happened after he rescued you?'

'He said he worked for a group of Jews that were resisting Hitler. He took me and my daughter to an apartment somewhere, I don't know where. Then, we were sent to stay with an old man in the village of Bad Bernsdorf. But the pervert tried to seduce my daughter so I poisoned him. When he realised he was dying, he called the police. And a doctor.'

'I can tell you the doctor came too late to save him.' Nonetheless, hearing his grandfather, his own flesh and blood, called a pervert, slices him somehow.

He could hear Klaus's foot tapping against the stone floor. 'So how did your accomplice know to rescue you and at that specific moment?'

'He didn't tell me that.'

'How much did it cost you?'

'He didn't ask for payment.'

Klaus steps forward. 'OK, cut this shit. It's like watching a pantomime. We know full well the name of your accomplice, you stupid bitch. But we want to hear it from your own lips. So, a name. Now.'

'I told you—'

'Stop. I beg you, do not insult my intelligence. What was his name?'

Stella's body sags in the chair. She knows he knows. They all know. But Felix didn't want her to be the one to say it. 'Klaus... Sir, it was me.'

'OK.' He put his hands on his hips. 'OK, that's good. Wasn't too bad, was it? Thank you. Now that we have that out of the way, we shall continue. Lieutenant, if you please.'

Felix knew that the next part was going to prove so much more difficult. 'Stella, your husband is wanted as a suspect in the attempted murder of a Wehrmacht captain on the first December last year. Where is your husband?'

'Ex-husband. We are divorced. I've no idea where he is.'

Felix swallows. 'Before you disappeared on New Year's Day, we had you followed. Officers saw your daughter with a man fitting your husband's description. When they approached, they ran off.'

'I told you, I don't know. I haven't seen him.'

'For Christ's sake, Stella. You cannot play games here. You have to tell me before...'

'Before what, Felix?' She doesn't say any more, but she doesn't take her eyes off him for a second.

'You know damn well.' He is shouting but he knows how brittle his voice sounds. 'Where is he, Stella? Where is your husband?'

'I don't know.'

'Lieutenant,' says Klaus, behind him.

He clenches and unclenches his fist. The moment has come. Hitting Otto Wankel had been so easy, but that was then, this is now, he is a different person now.

'An address,' he shouts. Still no answer. Her head flies to the side as the back of his hand smacks her against the side of the face. Not a sound comes from her. Her head falls back into place, the red mark of his hand clearly visible on her cheek.

Höch, behind him, laughs.

'Try hitting her, Lieutenant,' says Klaus. 'Not patting her.'

He slaps her again, his eyes clouded with tears. He can see her biting her lips, determined not to let the pain show.

'OK, enough,' says Klaus. 'Höch, if you please.' Höch steps forward. 'Watch and learn, Lieutenant.'

Höch piles into her with both fists, punching her repeatedly. She yelps and screeches in pain, her head thrown side to side. Felix grips his hair. There is nothing he can do.

'Stop,' orders Klaus. Höch stops. Stella's face balloons, blood pours from her mouth and nose, her left eye little more than a slit. 'Your turn, Lieutenant.'

His legs give way. 'Stella, I'm begging you, tell me where he is. At least a name of someone who knows.'

'I don't know.' Her voice sounds different, muffled.

He clenches his eyes shut. 'Stella,' he shouts.

'I don't know.'

He raises his hand. Stella stiffens but does not turn away. He spins away, screaming. 'I can't do this.'

Klaus laughs. 'You always were a pathetic creature, Felix. Weak, weak, weak.' He clicks his fingers at Höch. Höch advances on her. Felix lunges at him but Höch, perhaps expecting this, elbows him in the chest, sending him sprawling to the ground. Höch hits her again, the sickening sound of his fists on her face, the cracking of bone.

Klaus orders him to stop.

Stella's bloodied face is already unrecognisable. Felix weeps.

Klaus nods at Höch who clicks his heels in return. He seems to know what he is being asked. Rubbing his knuckles, he leaves the cell.

Klaus paces behind her, his hands behind his back. 'Now, what shall we do? Our next course of action is to use enhanced interrogation. And I'm more than happy to do that. But you're a stubborn and strong woman, Frau Hoffmann–'

Stella spits a tooth out and says something, her words unintelligible, blood drooling from her mouth. And Felix almost laughs. He knows what she said. She'd said, 'Fräulein, please.'

'And I am a man in a hurry. So, I think we'll dispense with the enhanced interrogation and try something different altogether.' With a quick movement, he wraps a handkerchief round Stella's head, across her mouth, tying it at the back of her head. 'And you, *Private* Stoltenberg,' he continues. 'A trip to Russia is in order, I believe.'

He doesn't care. His soul has been crushed. Klaus can do as he pleases; Felix is beyond caring, he doesn't give a damn.

They wait. Stella's head droops, her chin on her chest, her laboured breathing the only sound in this terrible cell. Presently, the door opens. Höch has returned and he has someone with him. Stella looks up. Her eyes seem to pop out of her head before screaming into the handkerchief.

*

319

Höch pushes Charlotte into the cell. Felix's heart plummets. Charlotte sees her mother. For a moment she makes not a sound. It is as if she can't believe her eyes. And then it registers. Her hands go to her head, her mouth gapes open. She screams and sobs. 'Mummy, Mummy…' She makes to reach her mother, her hands reaching out, but Höch catches her round the waist and pulls her back, lifting her off the ground, her legs kicking at the air. Klaus put his hands to his ears. Stella struggles in her chair, her screams muffled by the handkerchief. Klaus takes the spare set of straps and throws them at Felix. 'Tie the girl up,' he orders, shouting above Charlotte's screams.

Felix throws them on the ground.

Stella shakes her head violently from side to side.

Klaus draws his pistol from his holster and aims it at Stella's head. Felix stands his ground while the air reverberates with Charlotte's hysterics. Klaus straightens his arm, pressing the muzzle against Stella's temple. 'Tie her up, Felix.' The pistol, it is an old Luger, circa 1915, the inscription still quite visible: *Für den Gott und Land*. For God and Country.

Höch forcibly carries Charlotte over to the chair in the corner and forces her down. Felix clutches at one of Charlotte's arms but Charlotte wrenches it free. Höch grabs the girl's arm and pulls it down. With trembling hands, Felix fastens it against the back of the chair. Charlotte fights against them, her screams unbearably loud. Höch slaps the girl. It silences her. Quickly, while she absorbs the pain, Felix ties the other straps.

Klaus lowers his gun. 'Right, *Fräulein* Hoffmann, this is easy.' He stands directly behind Charlotte. 'You tell me where your husband is hiding and you tell me now.' He yanks

Charlotte's head back by her hair, pushing the tip of the Luger against her temple. Charlotte turns white, her eyes bulging from her head, her brow wet with sweat. He clicks back the hammer on the pistol. Felix's head spins. He braces himself, but Klaus, as if reading this intention, shouts, 'One move, Stoltenberg, and the girl's dead.'

Klaus nods at Höch. Höch removes the handkerchief from Stella's mouth.

Her head falls forward as she gulps for air. 'Number twenty-three, Wilhelmstrasse, Wannsee.'

'Thank you, Fräulein Hoffmann.' Klaus keeps the Luger, Felix's father's Luger, at Charlotte's head.

He pauses. Felix shakes his head. No, he thinks, you can't... you can't...

EPILOGUE

Berlin, April 1943

She sits at the mirror in her bedroom, dressed in her dressing gown, twisting her head this way and that, her fingers touching various points on her face as if checking everything is still there. She smiles at herself. She can hear children playing outside. Ten o'clock in the morning. After several days of rain and cold, the sun has finally decided to shine. She stands at the bedroom window absorbing the warmth of the April sun. She looks down at the children playing football in the courtyard, boys and girls together. How she envies them. One of the girls sees her. The girl waves up at her. She waves back. A boy of about twelve, following the girl's gaze, sees her too and makes an obscene gesture. She shakes her head. *Be careful, little boy*, she thinks, *I know your father. One word from me and I'll have your whole family in a concentration camp before you can say Jack Robinson.*

She returns to her chaise lounge in front of the mirror. It is lovely to be blonde again. She's always suited blonde. She pouts her lips and applies a layer of lipstick. She blows a kiss at her reflection. That little girl reminds Stella of Charlotte when she was that age. Poor Charlotte; she'll have to tolerate prison for a while longer, perhaps a lot longer. She is sixteen now. She'll be OK. They are keeping her in relative luxury. She's tough, like her mother. She'll cope.

She is expecting Albert, her husband – not her ex-husband as she'd always told poor old Felix – back any moment. She can't wait. She's pleased she looks beautiful for him. He loves her being blonde as well. She squirts some perfume on. Gorgeous. And a little squirt between her legs. She'd made the bed, plumped up the pillows and made sure she had a good supply of condoms. After all this time away from each other, they'd be needing them.

Poor old Felix. He deserved better. He was so gallant, so trusting, and so damn naive. He really had fallen in love with her. That was the problem; men always did. Still, he helped out when she needed a man and served his purpose when she needed help. And he paid the price. He'd be dead now. Sent over a field of landmines or something equally hideous. And she had to admit, it had been a close-run thing. She'd almost got used to her nose now. It wasn't as pretty as before, but still, it gave her character, she supposed. The scars have healed, and with a bit of make-up, no one would know. Her body has recovered too, although sometimes she still awoke a little stiff in the mornings. Occasionally, at night, she'd have a nightmare about it, and wake up shivering. But it could have been worse, she knew that.

And now, she has a second chance. She has to work for them now. She, a Jewess, has been given a job – Jew Catcher. She and Albert are to go out, roam the streets, identify and catch other Jews and hand them in to the SS. And that's fine; in fact, she's looking forward to the challenge. And Charlotte? Well, as long as she does her job OK, Charlotte will be safe enough.

She hears a knock on her door. Is it that time already? She removes her dressing gown and checks herself in the mirror one last time, runs her fingers over her silky peroxide hair. Yep, there was no denying it, she looks bloody fantastic. Albert is not the sort of man to stand on ceremony. It'll be straight to the bedroom and straight to it. And why not. He's been away long enough, he deserves it. She blows herself a kiss. *Let's go get 'im.*

*

The train trundles into Anhalter Bahnhof. It is still early morning. The lazy sun falls upon the glass panels of the station's domed ceiling, through the large church-like windows. Someone opens the carriage door and the carriage is filled with a rush of fresh air, clearing away the stench of so many unwashed bodies crammed in together. Felix staggers out, almost falling onto the platform. 'Bloody good to be back, eh?' says a private with jug ears. The man had spent much of the journey relating his sexual exploits to Felix, unperturbed by Felix's lack of response.

Felix gazes round, his haversack at his feet. A couple of pigeons dive ahead. He almost expects to see Otto Wankel limping up the platform. The train belches billows of black smoke.

Further up, nurses and orderlies are carrying off the wounded and maimed. One of the soldiers, a huge bloodied bandage around his head, urinates against a post. A nurse tries to intervene, telling him off as one might a small child but to no avail. Felix slings his haversack over his shoulder and joins the procession towards the terminus, pausing as the Gestapo checkpoint eyes them all, one by one.

'Well, it's been good talking to you, mate,' says the jug-eared private as they step onto the concourse. 'Cheerio. See you again.'

'I doubt it,' says Felix under his breath. Felix never did learn his name and he doubts whether the scores of women in Russia ever did either.

Felix sits on the U-Bahn. Opposite, a young woman with a red-cheeked toddler wriggling on her lap smiles at him. Another woman, bedecked with a fur collar, has given her seat up for him. He almost refused, but his legs are throbbing, so he thanked her and sat down. He removes his cap and catches his reflection in the window: a shallow man, empty behind the eyes, stares back at him. He flinches. The toddler giggles.

He emerges from the U-Bahn. Dark clouds scud across the sky, blotting out the earlier sun. The streets, full of hurrying people, look almost normal. Yes, many of the shops have closed up, there is litter everywhere, but this area, at least, has been spared the bombs. People still have their lives to lead. Cars pass by, a horse and cart. Two chatty Hitler Youth boys pass, their boots polished, their Sam Browne belts gleaming and hair neatly combed. They both Heil Hitler him. Felix and Klaus.

He turns a corner and sees a number of men pushing a cart piled high with blankets and rugs. One holds aloft a banner asking for civilians to donate their textiles. A string quartet is playing outside the entrance of the Kaiser Wilhelm Memorial Church. He stops, recognising the tune. Of course, it's Schubert's *Winterreise*. He remembers his father sitting at the piano all those years ago. Various people drop coins in the upturned cap on the ground before them. Another collection for the war effort. *Support our brave boys. Give gladly*, says the sign attached to a box in big, bold letters.

Felix pauses and allows the music to soothe him. The viola player winks at him. After all, wasn't he one of their "brave boys"? He had survived this far. He had done what not many do – survived a penal battalion. His officers had praised his bravery in the face of such terrible odds. He had survived the minefield, had fought with great distinction against superior numbers. He had earned the right to be accepted back into the fold. He had done his time and paid his price. He could hold his head up high.

And now he is back. Two weeks' leave. Then off again, but where, he doesn't know. Italy perhaps, North Africa. He doesn't care; as long as it isn't Russia again. No one wants to go to Russia. It's good to feel the tarmac beneath his feet, to feel reconnected to the civilised world. To leave behind the searing cold, the unending Russian forests, the lice, the dead, the maggots feeding on the dead, the rats, the stench of it all. Somewhere, far away in his mind, he could hear the crows flying over the desolate Russian field, cawing and mocking the traitors beneath them. He could hear the poor boy whimpering, crying, still as a statue, his boot on a landmine, the terror in his eyes – the deadly explosion that tore him apart. Walter. He could hear the jeering laughs of the ones watching from the side of the field. He senses Walter's presence. Death is but a step away.

A loud bang rips through the air. Instinctively, Felix throws himself on the ground, covering his head, his breath coming in short, panicked bursts.

'Hey, you, you all right?'

Felix peers up. A man in a tweed suit looms over him. 'Here, give me your hand.' With the man's help, Felix gets to his feet. 'Nothing to worry about, soldier. Just an old banger backfiring,' the man says, wiping his hand on the back of his trousers.

Felix thanks him and walks on, leaving the main thoroughfare behind him, finding his way through familiar streets, past familiar landmarks. He walks down the street where they'd attacked the elderly Jewish couple; he can still see the look in her eyes as she gripped on to the scarf. He passes the block of apartments where he'd killed Frau Pappenheimer and, a bit further on, the block where Stella had lived and worked. Stella. He knew she'd never loved him. He knew it at the time, he just couldn't face admitting it. He'd allowed himself to be used by her. It didn't matter. In trying to save her, and Charlotte, in trying to save two Jews, he was trying to save them all. But in the end, they were too strong even for her. She'd be dead by now. With a dismissive nod of his head, Klaus would have sanctioned her execution. He just hoped that even Klaus would have had a slither of compassion for Charlotte.

And now he is home. It seems OK, untouched by bombs.

He climbs the two storeys up to the flat, breathes in the old smells of boiled vegetables and dirty diapers, hears the crying of a baby, a mother yelling at a child. Some things never change. And here he is. He lifts his arm, hesitates, then knocks on the door.

For a brief moment, she doesn't recognise him. It is only when he says, 'Hello, Mother,' does she stop squinting at him and lets out the most piercing scream.

'Felix, Felix, Felix!' She carries on repeating his name at volume, her arms tight around him, peppering his sodden cheeks with kisses. 'Oh my God, oh my, it's really you.'

'Mama, let me in.'

'Yes, yes, yes.' She steps back and puts her hand to her nose.

'I'm sorry; I know I stink.' His mind slips back; his father returning home from the camp at Oranienburg, stinking, barely able to walk.

'Well, yes, you do! It doesn't matter. Come in. Oh, Felix, the gods are shining on me. I thought, oh God, I didn't know what to think.'

He drops his haversack on the living room floor. God, it was good to be back.

'Oh, Felix, you're alive. You must be so… What can I do for you? What do need most?'

'Food, drink, sleep and a bath. But I don't know in what order.'

She laughs. 'Let me make your bed and run you a bath. We're about to have breakfast. We can always do a bit extra.'

'We?'

'Y-yes…' She stops. 'Yes… we.'

A figure in an apron appears at the kitchen door, her hair in a bun, the little scar still visible on her chin. She looks beautiful; that gentle, reassuring look in her eyes, a look that pulls you in, one that brings warmth and comfort. The years roll back as something lightens in his heart, like a slight unburdening of himself.

'Ingrid?'

She smiles. 'Hello, Felix.' She approaches and hugs him, slightly awkward but warm nonetheless.

'Ingrid lost her home in the bombing, so I invited her to move in with me. I hope you…'

Neither spoke.

'Yes, well,' says Klara, slightly flustered. 'Let me run that bath for you. You must be desperate.'

Felix and Ingrid stand a few feet apart, unsure of themselves. 'It's lovely to see you,' she says eventually.

329

'You too. Listen, Ingrid…'

'Yes?'

'I'm sorry about…'

She shakes her head, a ghost of a smile. 'There's no need. We're different people now. It was…'

'A long time ago?'

She smiles. 'Yes, a long time ago.'

'Yes,' he says. 'Yes, it was.'

'It was as if we couldn't see the truth that was there right in front of us.'

'You saw it.'

'Yes, but it still took a while.'

'It was like a fog before us obscuring the truth, a mist.'

She smiles. 'Yes.'

'The mist before our eyes.'

The End

Novels by R.P.G. Colley:

The Love and War Series
Song of Sorrow
The Lost Daughter
The Woman on the Train
The White Venus
The Black Maria
My Brother the Enemy
Anastasia
The Darkness We Leave Behind
The Mist Before Our Eyes

The Searight Saga
This Time Tomorrow
The Unforgiving Sea
The Red Oak

Rupertcolley.com